THE FUTURE IS NOT OURS

EDITED BY DIEGO TRELLES PAZ

TRANSLATED BY JANET HENDRICKSON

THE FUTURE IS NOT OURS

NEW LATIN AMERICAN FICTION

First edition, 2012

Library of Congress Cataloging-in-Publication Data: Available upon request.
ISBN-13: 978-1-934824-64-1 / ISBN-10: 1-934824-64-X

Printed on acid-free paper in the United States of America.

Text set in Minion, a serif typeface designed by Robert Slimbach in 1990 and inspired by late Renaissance-era type

Design by N. J. Furl

Open Letter is the University of Rochester's nonprofit, literary translation press:
Lattimore Hall 411, Box 270082, Rochester, NY 14627

www.openletterbooks.org

CONTENTS

BRIEF INTRODUCTORY NOTE TO THE U.S. EDITION

The Future Is Not Ours is an entirely Latin American literary project. It began in 2007 with a free electronic anthology published in the Colombian magazine *Pie de página* that featured the work of sixty-three authors from sixteen countries. In 2009, an Argentine publishing house, Eterna Cadencia, took a risk and published a print anthology that included stories (different from those in the digital edition) by twenty authors from fourteen countries. Its success was immediate, and the book has since been published in Bolivia (La Hoguera), Chile (UQBAR), Hungary (L'Harmattan), Panama (Fuga libros), Mexico (SurPlus), and Peru (Madriguera).

As *The Future Is Not Ours* took shape and gained readers and supporters, I imagined that the project might have some significance, and I felt proud to have forged a multinational team of writers who valued literature above all else. What I didn't predict was the rising success we would achieve working little by little, with excitement and enthusiasm, and with honesty as our shield. One of my greatest aspirations was to present this generation of writers to which I belong in an orderly way, laying out small rules that would grant the book autonomy and a unique personality. The anthology didn't seek canonical rigidity, nor did it seek to establish a sacred and impregnable list of writers. It set out to be an anthology made by writers in search of readers. We had no interest in the sometimes blurred relationship between literature and publicity. We had no slogan. No pompous critics sponsored the anthology's birth. We didn't need to declare the book at customs. Nor did we need an all-powerful publisher to turn our noble gesture into a mere commercial transaction. It worked, and here we are.

The table of contents in this edition contains small changes. First, it adds three authors who were already included in the electronic version of the project: Alejandro Zambra (Chile), Federico Falco (Argentina), and Inés Bortagaray (Uruguay). Second, one of the stories, "The Curious," by Juan Gabriel Vásquez (Colombia), had already been translated into English and published in the English magazine *The Drawbridge* in 2009, and so I replaced it with another story of his titled "The Last Corrido." Because of these changes, I made a few small revisions to the content of my prologue.

Diego Trelles Paz
Binghamton, New York
December 2011

PROLOGUE

1.

Novelty and the present. The literary instant captured and framed to document the violence of change. The possibility of transcendence, the possible future, and the anthologist stands at the center of this random machinery, acting like a demiurge, asking himself in secret, in the words the Uruguayan critic Angel Rama (1926–1983), "Who will remain in history?"[1]

Rama's question isn't indiscreet, nor is it impertinent in its attempt to unravel the laws and motives behind the genre of generational anthologies. In fact, it rather accurately illustrates the secret aspirations of every anthologist. His criteria, his values, the way he draws hierarchies, how he separates, groups, and rejects, all form an

1. The Argentine writer Tomás Eloy Martínez (1934–2010) attributes this quotation to Rama in "Por qué están los que están" ("Why Those Here Are Here"), an article which appeared in the *ADN* supplement to the Argentine newspaper *La Nación*, March 5, 2008. Cited from *La Nación*'s website (http://adncultura.lanacion.com.ar/nota.asp?nota_id=993112&origen=relacionadas). Accessed July 21, 2008.

effort to account for the current state of literature. At the same time he turns his gaze toward a future that he himself has prefigured and announced. If one of the writers he selects endures in the collective imagination, if this writer transcends the barrier of physical existence through his work, the triumph will always be shared between the popular writer and the one who discovers, shapes, interprets, and presents him.

Throughout the history of Latin American fiction, more than a few collections of stories have sought to illustrate the present (the historical, political, social, economic, technological present, and so on) through a wide range of thematic axes. However, the number of anthologies diminishes if one seeks an articulation of the regional body of contemporary authors who represent a given historical moment. One of the most cited and read of these collections, *Del cuento hispanoamericano: Antología critica-histórica (The Spanish-American Short Story: A Critical Anthology)*, edited by the American critic Seymour Menton (1927), offers a panoramic view of the future of the Latin American story in an effective format for the university student. Menton's anthology fulfills the disseminating function of these projects through its academic framework. It arranges authors from different countries according to the different literary movements to which the critical canon has assigned them. In this text, Menton takes an X-ray of the formal and thematic evolution of the short story in our countries. As Julio Ortega (1942) points out, he "sums up a nation, sometimes even the region, with a story."[2] As such, Menton's interest or focus does not center around the present as a rupture from something in the past, but rather as something based on what is continuous and common to the whole historic process.

2. Julio Ortega (ed.), *El muro y la intemperie. El nuevo cuento latinoamericano*, (New Hampshire: Ediciones del Norte, 1989), pp. iv–v.

This isn't the case with *Onda y escritura, jóvenes de 20 a 33* (*Wave and Writing, Young Writers Ages 20 to 33,* 1971) edited by Margo Glanz (1930). Though it only accounts for the Mexican scene, stemming from a famous story ("¿Cuál es la onda?", or "What's the Wave?") by Jose Agustín (1944), it names and defines a literary vanguard movement ("La Onda," or "The Wave") denied by its supposed members, even up to the present, as Agustín himself testifies in his article, "La Onda que nunca existió" ("The Wave That Never Existed"):

> This wasn't an articulated, coordinated literary movement like those of the stridentists, the surrealists, existentialists, beats, or nadaists. We weren't even a group like the Contemporaries, since [Gustavo] Sainz and Parménides [García Saldaña] were never friends, and they dealt with each other very little. We never met to draft a manifesto for "La Onda;" we never fired our canons. We didn't sign ourselves up to be literary models, not even remotely. We wrote books for the sake of writing them. But it's true that we shared a generational spirit, which is why our first enthusiastic readers were young people our age who found reflections of themselves in our books.[3]

If Glantz delimits one thing very successfully, it's a chronological framework. That is, the anthology groups these new authors—and, by extension, the audience to whom this text was primarily directed—within a manageable, thirteen-year range (from ages 20 to 33), which

3. José Agustín, "La Onda que nunca existió" in *Revista de Crítica Literaria Latinoamericana* 59 (2004): 13–14.

leaves no doubt about the youth of its participants. (When it was published, Agustín and García Saldaña were 27 and Sainz was 31.)

Defining a period of time, marking the limits of what the anthologist considers *new* or *young* in literary terms always risks the weakness of seeming arbitrary. This is why two things happen in most of the anthologies that came after Glantz's: first, they are extremely careful about using terms like "generation," "new," and "youth," and second, they tend to establish chronological boundaries that they never can respect completely. I refer here to Glantz's valuable precedent to point out one of my main objectives in making this selection: the fundamental necessity of establishing an age range, not because I disbelieve in the validity of objections to the relativity of concepts like "the new" and "the young," but rather, because it seems preferable to assume this methodological limitation in the effort to capture something that by nature seems slippery and fleeting, particularly in a world whose habits and values have radically changed through technology, a world marked by the end of utopias of political and social transformations.

So I am talking about the way that writers face *the act of writing*—what Agustín calls a "generational spirit"—within a group of Latin American writers born just after the Paris May of 1968 and the student massacre in Tlatelolco; educated under the framework of military dictatorships in Argentina, Bolivia, Brazil, Chile, Cuba, the Dominican Republic, El Salvador, Ecuador, Guatemala, Honduras, Nicaragua, Panama, Paraguay, Peru, and Uruguay; who as teenagers and young adults witnessed the fall of the Berlin Wall, the massacre in Tiananmen Square, the Srebrenica massacre, the fall of perestroika and the collapse of the Soviet Union, the end of the Cold War, and armed subversion and military repression in South America; who witnessed the rise of the internet, Kurt Cobain's suicide, the prolonged, methodical murders of women in Ciudad Juárez, the height of electronic music, the attacks on the World Trade Center, terrorist attacks in Spain and the U.K., the Palestinian-Israeli conflict, the Guantánamo prison, the Darfur genocide, the election of the first black president of the United States, the revolutions and popular uprisings of the Arab Spring, the occupation of many cities' parks and streets by citizens angry at the current state of affairs, and, among many armed conflicts, the Soviet and U.S. invasions of Afghanistan, as well as the U.S. invasion of Iraq with an international coalition of countries.

The age range in this anthology—published writers born between 1970 and 1980—was based on two premises which I will attempt to explain in the course of this prologue. The first is to differentiate these writers from those included in the anthologies *McOndo* (1996), *Líneas Aéreas* (*Airlines,* 1997), and *Se habla español* (*Spanish Spoken Here,* 2000). These writers' testimonies, read at a literary conference in Seville, appeared in the book *Palabra de América*[4] (*Word from America*, 2003). Together, these anthologies comprise a wonderful collection of Latin American writers, most of whom were born in the 1960s and who were definitely young when these anthologies came out.

The second premise is associated with the title of this volume, for which I alone am responsible and which, just like contents of this introduction, does not necessarily represent the opinion of its authors. *The Future Is Not Ours* emerges in the first place as a response to a series of misconceptions associated with a demagogic idea, a slogan

---

4. The compilation *Palabra de América* contains the speeches given at this literary conference in Seville by twelve Latin American writers, the majority of them born in the 1960s. However, it's necessary to note here that some of the authors included in *The Future Is Not Ours* also appeared on this list. The main reason is that those workshops defined their chronological frameworks as flexibly as possible. (In general, 1960 was the cut-off birth date.)

proclaimed and repeated to the point of exhaustion, that the future belongs to the young. This chorus, poorly disguised as sincere hope, aspires to justify and tends to cover up a bleak present: a time catastrophic in terms of equality and social justice, sinister with respect to human rights, apocalyptic for the ecological health of the planet, cynical toward those least favored by the neoliberal fundamentalism of a market currently in free fall.

The Future Is Not Ours also emerges as a response to anticipated questions about the literary future that become inevitable with a changing of the guard. Questions about the future have formed the backbone of the brief but intense history of generational anthologies in Latin America. Concerns about the transcendence or endurance of the author were already present in *Novísimos narradores hispanoamericanos en Marcha (The Marcha Anthology of New Latin American Novelists,* 1981), Ángel Rama's precursory selection. Similarly, Julio Ortega's two anthological projects—*El muro y la intemperie. El nuevo cuento latinoamericano* (*The Wall and the Open Air: New Latin American Stories,* 1989) and *Antología del cuento latinoamericano del siglo XXI: Las horas y las hordas* (*Anthology of the Twenty-First Century Latin American Story: The Hours and the Hordes*, 1997)—propose a future anticipated by the present, discovered in the new sensibilities of the end of the millennium.

It is interesting to note how Ortega introduces the second volume to his readers:

> This anthology begins with the conviction that the future is already here and it has come early; it rushes into recent texts that open the scenes where we begin to read what we will be. This doesn't refer to a mere technological futurism, which is a calculation of possibilities, but rather, it refers to an end-of-century sensibility

> which encompasses new subjectivities, restless for the future.[5]

Ortega optimistically views this projection of the verbalized future, three years from the turn of the millennium, through stories that

> come out of crises of national representation and move toward the intermediary space of what is now called "the new internationalism," or the notion of a more diverse and more international world, one required of networks of solidarity able to resist the new hegemonies.[6]

Although Ortega generously observes the appearance of this new multi-genre, multinational creative space, the immediate future proved to be less comfortable than he foresaw. In 1996, *McOndo* was published, an anthology compiled and introduced by two Chilean writers, Alberto Fuguet (1964) and Sergio Gómez (1962). The book had a healthy, provocative spirit and a good selection of stories, though it was limited by a theoretical proposal that was not entirely solid and that stuttered somewhat in its attempt to voice the true thematic, formal, and linguistic change that Latin American literature was experiencing in the 1990s. In *McOndo*, the "restlessness for the future" that Ortega talks about appears almost exclusively bound to the figure of the U.S. as a totem or a concave mirror in which the Latin American writer of the twenty-first century would have to be reflected.

---

5. Julio Ortega (ed.), *Antología del cuento latinoamericano del siglo XXI: Las horas y las hordas* (Mexico: Siglo XXI Editores, 1997), 11.

6. Ortega, *Antología*, 12–13

What Fuguet and Gómez called the country of "McOndo" was an energetic response, not so much to Gabriel García Márquez's (1927) literary Macondo, as to his epigones, who up to the present sell a bastard version of magical realism that combines magic, folklore, and miraculous cooking to go. The principal idea of *McOndo* hasn't ceased to be interesting and even has proved valuable in overcoming what Eduardo Becerra calls "the stagnant situation of a fixed Latin American landscape, formed in part by its own narrative some time ago." However, *McOndo's* approach staggers and ends up collapsing because "it responds to Macondian homogenization with an equally uniform vision of a Latin America whose physiognomy is too close to that of any U.S. city."[7]

McOndo could have been a real shot at stylistic and thematic renewal, a sharp reflection on new ways of narrating and expressing the contradictions that an aggressive modernity was generating on the Latin American continent. Instead, it ended up being an inoffensive sham of precisely what Fuguet and Gómez sought to criticize. If the worst Latin American magical realism ends up reduced to exoticism-on-demand for foreign consumers and American and European Spanish departments, "McOndo" replaces this figure, deformed by a magic wand, with an excluding Latin American reality consisting of the lounge and the mall:

> A few years ago, the young writer's dilemma was to choose between picking up a pencil or a gun. Now it seems that the most distressing thing about writing is choosing between Windows 95 or a Macintosh. [. . .] In McOndo, there are McDonald's, Mac computers and

7. Eduardo Becerra (ed.), *Líneas aéreas*, (Madrid, Lengua de Trapo, 1997) xxii.

> condos, and amen to five-star hotels built with laundered money and gigantic malls. [. . .] While we're at it, let's say that McOndo is MTV Latino, but in print.[8]

With *Se habla español*, Fuguet repeats this offering, now accompanied by the Bolivian writer Edmundo Paz Soldán (1967). The book consolidates many of the writers that had appeared already in *McOndo* as well as *Líneas Aéreas*.[9] Fuguet and Paz Soldán make the selection's thematic character clear from the start—the objective is to create "an anthology about the United States, yes, but [written] in Spanish"[10]—and it puts forth a fairly specific idea of what the authors seek to demonstrate:

> The idea of this anthology was to express the scent (the perfume, let's say) of the times. To write stories or texts that in one way or another would capture the present *zeitgeist*. Sign o' the Times, in the words of Prince. A collection that would smell like French fries, buttered popcorn, and Sloppy Joes, but also like burritos, Goya

8. Sergio Gómez and Alberto Fuguet, eds., *McOndo*, (Barcelona: Mondadori, 1996), 13, 15, and 16.

9. Some of the Mexican and Columbian participants in these anthologies were later included in two groups that aren't discussed in this prologue: *Crack* in Mexico and *Nueva Ola* (New Wave) in Colombia. Closer to advertisements than serious formulations of literary movements, much more attentive to their impact and the media's agenda than they were to a need for expression or the discovery of a shared sensibility, deeply infatuated with the patronage of the recognized writers who would publicly validate a ghost movement ready to increase the sales of novels in Spanish bookstores—literally, *at any cost*—*Crack* and *Nueva Ola* can't be considered seriously in this text.

10. Alberto Fuguet and Edmundo Paz Soldán, eds., *Se habla español. Voces latinas en USA* (Miami: Alfaguara, 2000), 14.

products, mango-guava smoothies and *dulce de leche* Häagen-Dazs.[11]

Although *Se habla español* radically washes its hands of the criticism of magical realism that had been taken as a personal attack on García Márquez, thanks to a certain ambivalence in *McOndo's* prologue and great deal of journalistic and academic hostility, it is difficult not to see this selection as a continuation of Fuguet's first anthology. "The United States—let's face it—is everywhere,"[12] announces an introduction that uses a somewhat forced combination of Spanish and English to reinforce the unavoidable relationship between "America (you already know which America)" and the "Latin America which has been lost/trapped/seduced"[13] by it.

For all of their qualities and defects, however, it's necessary to emphasize and recognize an unquestionable fact: *McOndo,* as well as *Líneas aéreas* and *Se habla español,* shaped a generation of Latin American (and Spanish) writers, with their own gaze, though with a different fortune, who could write and describe a literary world now distanced from limiting national boundaries. The McOndo writers' fruitful alliances with other media and genres broadened the spectrum of fiction for those of us who came afterward, eager and attentive.[14] Before them, *The Future Is Not Ours* announces itself, here

11. Fuguet and Paz Soldán, *Se habla español,* 15.

12. Ibid., 14.

13. Ibid., 14 and 17.

14. Here and elsewhere in the text I use the first person plural (we, us) because *The Future Is Not Ours* has two parts, created and conceived of by writers. The first part is available free on the web. It was published in August 2008 in the Colombian magazine *Pie de Página* and can be found here: http://www.piedepagina.com/redux/category/especiales/el-futuro-no-es-nuestro/.

and now, with a scalpel in its hand and the happy certainty that in literature, as in all art, without rupture, there is no relief.

2.

Certainly, one of our greatest paradoxes as a group is that, above all, our fractures are internal. Something of this seminal disintegration, this forced isolation, the somewhat cynical disillusionment that begins right at our door has been described by the writer Tryno Maldonado (1977) in his prologue to *Grandes hits, vol. 1. Nueva generación de narradores mexicanos (Greatest Hits, Volume 1. The New Generation of Mexican Novelists,* 2008):

> The writers in this anthology [belong to] [. . .] a generation full of disillusionment that has equipped itself with cynicism and indifference to avoid being disappointed again; a generation that no longer believes in anything because its entire life has occurred through deceit; a generation raised by its country through large doses of unfulfilled promises, some larger than others, like an endless joke.[15]

In many of the stories in *The Future Is Not Ours,* one can recognize the rather nihilistic conviction with which each writer confronts the disillusionment that Maldonado refers to. However, it is possible to find different styles and themes and multiple influences—not just literary—in the writers included in this collection, just as it

15. Tryno Maldonado (ed.), *Grandes hits, vol. 1. Nueva generación de narradores mexicanos* (Oaxaca: Almadía, 2008), 12.

also is possible to find close connections between them. It is true, for instance, that cynicism, indifference, and individualism are present, directly or obliquely, in many of these authors' works, to the point that these tendencies feel like a sort of unity. On the basis of these stories, however, it is possible to add that the core motives and concerns of the Latin American literary tradition haven't essentially changed.

For instance, in many of these stories, different manifestations of violence, whether in interpersonal relationships or in the difficult process of cultural, social, and political coexistence in the highly unequal nations, are what form or complement the general narrative crux. In the first case, violence arises through the process of human development and growth, and it tends to manifest itself as much in an early discovery of sexuality as in the sudden and painful appearance of death. This is the case with "Fifteen Flowers" by Federico Falco, a moving and melancholy story about the loss of innocence among a group of adolescents in the Argentine provinces. In "The Last Corrido" by Juan Gabriel Vásquez, one can observe the theme of lost innocence from another perspective. As in a *Künstlerroman,* the tragic family story of a famous Mexican corrido band on tour in Spain allows Vásquez to approach the theme of the artistic education of a young singer and his inevitable parricidal confrontation with his uncle and master. In the second case, daily, routine, and generalized violence is born from class conflicts, racial hatred and community segregation in all of their ugly aspects. This kind of violence arose from the social deterioration produced by waves of migration from the country to the city in many Latin American countries in the 1970s, and it was intensified by poverty, drug trafficking, and political repression. It is present in different forms and on different scales in stories by Ronald Flores, Daniel Alarcón, Alejandro Zambra, Yolanda Arroyo Pizarro, and Santiago Roncagliolo.

With "Any Old Story," Flores takes up the somewhat exacerbated realism of witness literature while eluding its usual elegiac tone and moral weightiness, through the story of a migrant resigned to the fury of a bursting, chaotic Guatemala City. Alarcón's story, "Lima, Perú, July 28, 1979," narrates the beginnings of the subversive Shining Path movement through an intriguing story of a multiple pursuit that involves strange, gutted dogs hanging from the light posts of Lima. The protagonists of "34" by Alejandro Zambra are adolescents who have been subtly divested of their names and identities in Chile's most prestigious high school during the military dictatorship. The teachers ("Frustrated, stupid. Fawning fans of Pinochet. Pieces of shit") call them by their number on the class list, and even among themselves, the students call each other by the number that identifies them. Zambra's allegorical story alludes to a society partially dehumanized by political violence and condemned to failure ("We knew that tomorrow his failure would be ours") in which the collective memory is a hindrance to progress ("It's not healthy to remain in the past"). In "Pillage," by Yolanda Arroyo Pizarro, the brutal rape of a girl fascinates and paralyzes a man who observes her without daring to help. The story carries a strong allegorical charge, as chilling and powerful as a punch, and it depicts a society where violence is so pervasive that it becomes normal and turns into a public show. Roncagliolo, in "A Desert Full of Water," takes on the insurmountable breach that separates the rich from the poor and the powerful from the miserable in a typical Latin American society divided by racism, but he does this with a colloquial tone and a good dose of humor and cynicism.

Eroticism is another predominant theme in many of these stories. This isn't far removed from the matrix of violence, of course, as the sexuality in these texts is permeated by the ambiguous, the strange, the anomalous, and the sordid. It is, therefore, a freer, less guilty sexuality that sharply questions the traditional roles of men and women in conservative, phallocentric societies that resent and sabotage any change. "Sun-Woo," by Oliverio Coelho, is very much in line with a paradigmatic story like "Putas asesinas" ("Killer Whores") by Roberto Bolaño (1953–2000). It narrates the story of Elías Garcilazo, a writer in decline whose strange and perverse adventure with a mysterious Korean woman puts him at the brink of an abyss.

Although there aren't major correspondences in the prose styles of Giovanna Rivero and Lina Meruane—the former tends toward quick, short, and direct phrasing, and the latter's prose breathes with an elegant lyricism—the world of feminine intimacy is expressed allegorically through hair removal and overt allusions to lesbianism in "Twin Beds" (Rivero) and "Razor Blades" (Meruane.) The themes of incest and guilt are present in the story "Family Tree," by Andrea Jeftanovic, and the conflicts and intrigues of romantic relationships are focused through different prisms in the stories of María del Carmen Pérez Cuadra, Ariadna Vásquez, and Antonio Ortuño. "Without Artificial Light," by Pérez Cuadra, is a stark story that confronts men and women and exhibits and rehabilitates a certain feminine perspective. "Shipwrecked on Naxos," by Vásquez, on the other hand, uses a fragmented and relatively complex structure to reformulate the Greek myth of Ariadne and Theseus in a dark Mexico where the protagonist, Ariadne, a submissive drug dealer who accepts her partner's abuse, meditates with a certain cynicism on her life. "Pseudoephedrine," by Ortuño, has the form and jocular tone of a sitcom about insecurity and jealous passion.

The third group of stories in this anthology includes those that resist classification and further expand this book's aesthetic diversity. "Chicken Soup," by Ignacio Alcuri, is the direct child of comic strips, sitcoms, and British nonsense movies, with its deliberately prosaic tone and its humor made up of recited gags, dialogues, and situations that exploit the absurd. "On the Steppe," by Samanta Schweblin, a strangely suggestive story, plays with an elusive element, with hidden information, to create a fantastic plot and a horror story simultaneously. "Fish Spine," by Santiago Nazarian, is a highly polished exercise in style, minimalistic and highly symbolic. "Variation on Themes by Murakami and Tsau Hseuh-Chin," by Tryno Maldonado, is a children's story for adults, a dark fable that plays formally and thematically with the themes of repetition and doubles. "Hypothetically," by Antonio Ungar, explores and confronts the wicked world of two English brothers made idiots by alcohol with that of a young South American immigrant who spies on them while he reflects on his own miseries. "Hurricane," by Ena Lucía Portela, draws parallels between the enormous, powerful storm and the decadent situation in Cuba, and presents a somewhat cynical young woman who makes a vital decision. "Boxer," by Carlos Wynter, explores the world of a boxer intrigued by his dreams and his existential conflicts. "Love, You Belong to Another Port," by Slavko Zupcic, is almost a detective story, in which a writer investigates the confusing traces of his possible Yugoslavian father. Similarly, "Wolf to Man," by Inés Bortagaray, uses a metatextual narrative that interweaves footnotes with a journalistic report to play with the reader, ironically and humorously, in its attempt to unveil the life of a Uruguayan ex-guerilla who supposedly corresponded with Fidel Castro.

3.

Although, as one can see, the essential motives of the literary tradition have not radically changed between the last generations of Latin American writers, a formal and thematic certainty has consolidated that unites and identifies us beyond our desires and our reluctances: overcoming the so-called *totalizing novel,* or in other words, the death of this idea, so rooted in the Latin American writers of the Boom, of the novel as a genre committed to explaining an era in its totality and faithfully spanning our countries' tragicomic history.

Of course, we are not at all talking about renouncing the historical past as a literary topic. What has changed is the literary *form*, and moreover, the writer's foundational ambition to legitimize or distort an origin which is no longer vital for us. Neither our roots nor our traditions, much less concepts as outdated as nationality or country, now limit our unconditional pact with fiction. At the same time, it no longer seems crazy or unserious to treat historical themes (national heroes and dictators, armed conflicts and revolutions) through genres previously underrated because of their formulaic character and popular roots, such as the detective novel or science fiction. The writers who have opened this door, with talent and without inhibition, with character and a deep love for literature (without a capital L), have names and are referenced almost unanimously by the members of this anthology. Among many others who I'm failing to mention are five men: Augusto Monterroso (1921–2003), Jorge Ibargüengoitia (1928–1983), Manuel Puig (1932–1990), Ricardo Piglia (1940), and Roberto Bolaño (1953–2003), and two women: Clarice Lispector (1920–1977) and Diamela Eltit (1949).

Finally, one of the fundamental purposes of this literary offering, comprised of many writers who use electronic means—blogs, personal web pages, social networks, electronic publishing, TV, email, and so on—is to fight the internal editorial isolation in which the region is submerged. (It's very difficult, for instance, for an Ecuadorian or a Uruguayan to read a book published by a Paraguayan or a Guatemalan.) This collection seeks to recover the active exchange with the reader who gives literature its only pertinent fire.

Now that the world stands by and watches, undaunted, the compulsory reduction of literature. Now that the written word is losing space and the false apocalyptic cult of the death of the press is spreading. Now that publishers, agents, and writers see the need to adapt, half-smiling, to the pragmatic logic of the market. (One would have to ask the great Cormac McCarthy (1933)—an idol to many of us—what he really thinks of Oprah Winfrey.) Now, finally, that "the greatest danger to the novel is not the cult of images (forcing people in too many places to consider only *telenovelas*—soap operas—novels) nor a technological disdain for the written word, and not even the cultural isolation between Latin American countries, but rather an educational disaster, strengthened by economic collapse and the neoliberal contempt for the humanities,"[16] as Carlos Monsiváis (1938–2010) signaled, *The Future Is Not Ours* aspires to retrace the first steps of the productive dialogue, of the seminal alliance, of the marvelous pact between writers and readers that forged maturity and modernity in the creative process as an open, interactive, and reciprocal matter.

We want to be read, yes, but without the incentives or extraliterary conditions imposed by a market that stigmatizes and simplifies the differences between us. We want to be read, of course, but without allowing the market to place the burden on our shoulders of the wonderful and undoubtedly formative literary past that belongs to the Boom writers, the beloved monsters of our literary apprenticeship. We don't expect your benevolence or delicacy, but rather your complicity and sincere interest on the pleasant or nightmarish journey through *your* reading.

The window is now open: without onomatopoeias or catchy prefixes. Without rock-star marketing or the posing of an ultra-hip

---

16. Carlos Monsiváis, "Entre la imprenta y el zapping," in *Babelia*, the cultural supplement to the Spanish newspaper *El País*, July 19, 2008. Cited from the web page of *El País* (http://www.elpais.com/articulo/narrativa/imprenta/zapping/elpepuculbab/20080719elpbabnar?5/Tes). Accessed July 24, 2008.

writer who looks-but-doesn't-look at the glitter of the flashes. We invite you to drop by our little house, stealing the title of a war movie by the forgotten Russian master Elem Klimov (1933–2003):

Come and See, dear reader, *ven y mira,* here we are: with our backs to the future, narrating the collapse.

Diego Trelles Paz
Binghamton, New York
December 2008

The Future Is Not Ours

SUN-WOO
BY OLIVERIO COELHO (ARGENTINA)

Elías Garcilazo's life, like that of any Latin American writer from a comfortable family, unfolded to his fortieth year through exclusive parties and trips to the old continent. The works he had published to that date were copious and mediocre, though his delicate manners and shrewd answers in the interviews (that he not only granted, but also arranged) placed him in the second tier of national writers, those who were capable of winning a municipal prize or negotiating a spot on the cover of a cultural supplement.

Until that point he had suffered no pain in his romantic life, which he cultivated with the cynicism and parodied elegance bestowed on him by his Italian shoes and tailored suits. Nearly always, and sooner rather than later, women succumbed to the attraction of this dandy who found, in the cruelty of subtle abandonment, a happy reward for the price of seduction.

On the eve of his first translation into French he went to Paris, where he signed the few copies of his works that were available in a couple of bookstores in the Latin Quarter. To ease his disappointment at the lack of enthusiasm in the specialty press—the translation only put his book's insignificance into relief—he extended his journey to the Far East.

He landed in Seoul one humid summer day. The airport's futuristic architecture impressed him less than the swarm of pale, shapely women. He suspected immediately that this Asian peninsula could entertain his voyeuristic instincts. He left his luggage in a hotel bedroom whose brilliant fabrics and vacuous lighting simulated a superior luxury. As if this sham of wealth had expelled him toward the city, he found himself walking through a fog that a profusion of glowing signs turned phosphorescent. The Apgujeong zone, on the banks of the Han River, turned out to be a flawless condominium of ladies who showed their legs but held a twin secret in their elusive gazes: chastity and cruelty.

He felt hungry after walking for a while. In the doors of various restaurants, he identified the prices of a few plates whose ingredients he couldn't decipher, despite the photos that accompanied the menus. A sudden miserly urge paralyzed him. This was the first incursion of Asia in his character: he began to save what he had squandered his whole life.

He took a while to choose a restaurant. Exhausted, he leaned toward the one that seemed the least expensive. He located a mat on the floor and took a seat at a low table, crossing his legs. He extracted the chopsticks and a spoon from a small glass case. He watched how the waitress lit a burner in the middle of the table and, without looking, laid out the ingredients to cook. Elías determined immediately that this ceremonial modesty, so much like the mercy that he'd been breathing since his arrival, really formed the spine of these people's actions. In solitude or through the contingencies of apathetic marriages, their social masks revealed themselves through this ambiguous drive.

His vanity swelled when he confirmed, through an epiphany, that the writer he thought the French had killed with their indifference still lived. Any other writer would have looked for his notebook;

Elías, however, looked for a mirror and encountered the image of a girl with fine features and perfect legs who was preparing to sit at a nearby table. The cold halo of vice around her big brown eyes set her apart from the other Asian women he had seen. The mask of modesty glittered in her with a sensuality that was at once marginal and servile, like the geishas'.

Elías considered himself entitled to his good fortune, and he addressed her with a few words in English. Through he believed his English to be irreproachably British, he feared that on speaking the distance between them would be accentuated, and rather than seduce her, he would end up scaring her away. Sun-Woo's answer to all that he said was a smile. But when she stood up to pay, Elías understood, as their gazes met, that this woman of indeterminate age, in short jean shorts that exposed the pale length of her perfect legs, was waiting for him.

He followed her through the street, a little disconcerted. He couldn't catch up with her, as if this phosphorescent, humid city exposed the shadow of mediocrity underlying his Argentine grace. Perhaps he began his pursuit through a mere misunderstanding. He stopped and let her gain distance. She moved her hips lightly, like a classical ballerina. At the stoplight she turned around and seemed to suggest, with a face Elías couldn't quite decipher—was it a sidelong glance or a smile?—that he catch up to her.

He walked at her side. His cloying English proved inadequate against the lethargy that Sun-Woo, recently awoken, seemed to be expiating after a night of sex, drugs, and alcohol. They abandoned the avenue and went down a street teeming with shops and restaurants that were closing.

They stopped at a door that led into a grey building indistinguishable from the chaotic architectural mass. She invited him in. Elías wavered at her feminine promise: perhaps because they shared no common language, her characteristics led him to think that she might be a high-end whore in disguise.

The one-room apartment on the first floor had a miserable outward appearance and a sophisticated interior. The minimalist furniture, the absence of personal objects or signs of an inhabitant, established it as the refuge of someone who was neutral and prosperous. The sounds of neighboring apartments seemed like emanations from a parallel world, a jumble of promiscuity and overcrowding.

She sat on the marble countertop and crossed her legs. She lit a cigarette and with her free hand signaled an acrylic shelf: whiskey, vodka, yakju, fruit wine, and cheongju. Elías, following an impulse that ran contrary to that finger, threw himself at Sun-Woo: her tight mouth melted in a long kiss. The tentacle of her tongue yielded a thick saliva, a kind of marine syrup, and her tongue squeezed more than it rubbed or caressed.

He entered Sun-Woo slowly. He penetrated her dense hair and immediately felt an estuary of pleats that molded to his sex and provided a splendid glide. She accompanied his work with sharp moans, and her back writhed in undulations that extended to her small breasts. With each orgasm, her moans intensified rather than diminished, and although Elías considered himself a marathoner who could withstand any woman's intensity, after an hour he encouraged the end of her pleasure. Sun-Woo immediately got down from the marble, kneeled trembling, washed the tip of his penis with her tongue and gently caressed his testicles. He got excited again, observing her rough, tiny feet that, through the tiny movement of their toes, seemed to accompany or celebrate each stab of his new erection.

He woke up on the floor. It took him a while to remember where he was. Because of his drowsiness, he presumed that he had slept too much. He remembered his arrival, and something told him that the decision to surrender to this woman had been absurd. There were no traces of Sun-Woo, no paper with a phone number or an address.

While he bathed, he supposed that the only way to see her again was to hole up in the apartment: to mutiny. After a while he understood that was unnecessary. The door was locked and the windows sealed, which indicated she would come back sometime soon to free him or exploit his vigor again. The idea turned out to be a soothing one, though the situation had the potential to turn into a nightmare whose author, strangely, seemed to be his vanity. He remembered the moment when, about to brave the fourth fuck, with a glass of Jack Daniel's in his hand, he toyed with the idea of turning Sun-Woo into his nurse. A writer with a personal nurse was, in the end, more picturesque than a solitary, brilliant writer.

He heard steps in the apartment upstairs. Screams spread through the hallway; a series of doors opened and slammed shut; there was a rush down the stairs, as if cattle were descending. He thought he might make some noise, so that someone would rescue him, but it was too early to consider his enclosure a planned imprisonment. Besides, such an attitude didn't correspond with what Sun-Woo had offered him during one unforgettable night, without needing words to mediate. He discarded the idea of becoming a traitor. When the moment arrived, if she didn't come back in a few hours, he would break a window and hurl himself out. He wouldn't be betraying her, so much as deserting her. In every great writer, Elías told himself, suddenly absorbed by his situation, there was a deserter.

Several hours passed; he fell asleep again. He woke up thirsty and bent over to drink water from the tap; he poked around the fridge and found provisions for a week.

Contrary to all his calculations, his anxiety diminished after the first day. For a moment he hoped no one would come back for him. Or if

Sun-Woo came, that she would limit her visit to the exchange of pleasures. He didn't despair even after he discovered that a small caged balcony outside the window prohibited what, until that moment, had been his only means of escape. Only the thought that the hotel staff, with no sign of his whereabouts, would vacate his room and appropriate his suits convinced him that he'd lost something in his imprisonment.

It happened while he was watching TV. Accustomed to the neighbors' noises and the omens of steps and keys rattling in the hallway, it took him some time to understand that Sun-Woo had returned. She had another hairstyle; she wore makeup and clothes that, by the texture of their fabric and cut, seemed expensive. Elías invented a few friendly words to make her understand that he had been confined. She smiled as though she were looking at a baby, set her colored leather Gucci purse on the marble countertop, examined the freezer, and, as if its contents and her desire had some connection, she undressed. She wore white lace lingerie that Elías tore off with a violence that ran counter to his hedonistic principles. Without any further preamble, Sun-Woo slid a hand between his legs and worked. This time their coupling was slow, and while Elías lie underneath Sun-Woo, holding her thrusting hips and glancing at the TV, he thought with some sadness that after this act he would be free.

They lay naked on the floor for an indefinite time. Every now and then Sun-Woo intoned something in Korean, and he annotated what she said with some absurdity in Spanish. And if no one remembered him outside? A reader, two readers, ridiculous numbers. Perhaps at this moment no one in the world was reading one of his books. He let out a bitter laugh: he had no time left to be a genius. Sun-Woo nodded, as if she understood. Forty years. Roberto Bolaño died at fifty. Ten years were not enough to cultivate a genius's submissive state and die victim to an absurd disease. Ten years were not enough for his writing to warm his death. If he couldn't be a genius, he at least could extend his life expectancy by giving up writing. He'd never thought of it before, but he could choose to give up writing and live anonymously.

Sun-Woo left the bathroom dressed, drank one last glass of red wine, and said goodbye to Elías discreetly, as if she were addressing someone who had just crossed the street. He had barely been able to murmur that he needed his luggage at the hotel when the door closed. A jingle of the keys and the subsequent sound of the bolt suggested his imprisonment would be prolonged. He remained in the middle of the dining area, confused. He discarded the idea of getting dressed and lay down on the floor.

With the days of confinement, the apartment's geometry weakened. Elías discerned a hollow design behind its limpid minimalism. He presumed that with each visit Sun-Woo took something away. In the same way that she could remove objects and furniture secretly to fashion his surroundings into a friendly void, she also could have taken his only clothes. He was surprised: even without clothes, he didn't feel naked. He assumed that his suits and Italian shoes had already been distributed among the hotel staff. As soon as Sun-Woo returned, he would explain his situation before submitting to any erotic diversion. He couldn't understand whether his confinement was a prize or if it was a punishment whose encounters represented the positive part of a sinister whole. His sexual tributes might be the beginning of an unclassifiable sacrifice.

Through the window he observed the wire mesh that sealed the small balcony. He flexed his legs and lowered himself toward the floor, slowly, as if he were sinking in a surface of hot sand. He fixed his gaze on the TV. Something in his conscience tempered the certainty that he was slowly paying a sentence for sins he had committed long ago. He flipped through several channels, and on one of the Korean soap operas he thought he recognized Sun-Woo: the coveted features of the actress who played the melodrama's demented wife almost coincided with those of his Asian "nurse."

Elías was sleeping with his arms wide open in the middle of the apartment when the third visit took place. He felt the pressure of a mouth between his legs. He tried to separate his eyelids, but the darkness was absolute. As soon as he tried to raise his hands to remove the blindfold pressing his temples, someone quickly took his wrists and bound them with pantyhose. A few seconds later, four feminine hands ran over his body in a game teeming with caresses. The arc of sighs grew when the two strangers joined their mouths around his sex and sucked together. He felt startlingly excited at the innovation and couldn't contain a stampede. A sudden, grave silence spread through the air. Afterward the women argued, upset, as if they blamed each other for the incident. Elías deduced from the pitch of their voices that they were mature women and that therefore Sun-Woo was not among them. For the first time during his imprisonment, he was afraid. Since he was young he had associated the cruelty of false seduction with the contagious scent of veteran women. After age fifty, women took their revenge on helpless men for the humiliation they had suffered through their catastrophic marriages.

"Sun-Woo?" he babbled.

He heard giggles around him. There weren't two, but rather three women. The third hadn't intervened yet.

"Sun-Woo?"

Laughter, then a punitive echo of high heels echoing through the hollow space of the apartment.

He wanted to get up. Sun-Woo had abandoned him, or worse, had offered him like an exotic animal to three divorcées who were eager to rent a passing pleasure. His helplessness weighed on him. He felt a calf brush against his cheek. He asked himself whether it might be his own leg. He thought of biting it, but it was gone.

The door slammed.

On the floor, alone again.

They had forgotten to untie and clean him.

He slithered a little; he turned; he rubbed against the floor as if he were trying to erase a stain. Suddenly he stopped, aware of his absurdity. He was naked; no one saw him. How long had it been since he had bathed? How long since he had opened a book? How long since he had cried? He had never cried for a woman in his life. Why didn't he get up? He heard a little laugh. One of the women had remained in the apartment. He recoiled, fearing it was one of the divorcées. Through an ebbing caress and the watery flavor of her mouth he recognized her: Sun-Woo had returned. How could he have thought she would abandon or surrender him? At most she had allowed herself to share her gift with two friends without consulting him first. As soon as she untied him, Elías kissed and embraced her with boundless tenderness. Though Sun-Woo first drank from this fountain of affection, she checked her impulse and pretended to have chores to do in the bathroom.

When she returned, he embraced her and spilled a few tears on her shoulder. It was as if, through his sobs, he was cured of the twenty years he had dedicated to the fantasy of being a writer. He felt like a new man: he left behind the stranger's caprices, the conformism, the irony.

As happened with the two guests before, his excitement on entering Sun-Woo and at feeling her legs grip and draw him in was so great that after a few impassioned charges he couldn't delay his release. She opened her eyes halfway. She blinked, incredulous. She avoided looking at the body that covered her and sighed like a corralled animal.

She rejected his solemn kisses, adjusted the lock her legs formed, and increased the pressure until something cracked. She pushed Elías's body aside with her knees and the soles of her feet, and she locked herself in the bathroom.

He stood and waited for what seemed like an eternity, due to the stabbing pain in one of his hips. As soon as he saw Sun-Woo leave the bathroom dressed, made up, and in high heels, he rushed toward her, limping. She dodged him and scampered to the other end of the apartment. He went after her, groping his hip with one hand and holding an imaginary cane with the other. With the same skill she slipped away. The skirmish went on a while. Sun-Woo's high-pitched laugh held a mysterious charm, as if the scene's perversion had rejuvenated her.

Elías surrendered. He needed to catch his breath, and the pain in his hip was growing. From the floor he observed the sculpted figure of an exterminating angel. She returned his gaze and looked at him at length, standing, with a mixture of disgust, modesty, and piety. She felt a supreme pleasure when Elías's bad leg trembled and convulsed, as if it were trying to free itself from the writer's corrupted organism. Then she left. He squeezed his eyes shut and paid attention to the light click of high heels fading in the distance. When he understood that this time Sun-Woo hadn't locked the door, he knelt down to cry.

FIFTEEN FLOWERS
BY FEDERICO FALCO (ARGENTINA)

to Lilia Lardone

Summer was ending. The air already smelled like smoke, but it still looked clear, sunny. The women swept their sidewalks and burned the first dry leaves on the corners. When classes began, so did the girls' fifteenth birthday parties. It hadn't been long since I'd seen my first dead body. Tolchi Pereno threw herself under the train because she was pregnant. We sat at the same desk, and during geography class she burst out crying, though no one had said anything to her. Blanquita Calzolari had called on Tano Buriolo to present his homework, and Tano tried to explain that thing about meridians and parallels.

They say that meridians are lines that divide the world into halves, Tano said, and Blanquita Calzolari agreed.

They say that the two halves are equal and the dividing line is a very fine line, so fine that you can't see it, Tano said, and Blanquita Calzolari agreed.

They say that the parallels are the same lines, but in reverse. They say that if you change hemispheres and you pass over a meridian or parallel, it sends shivers down your back. Blanquita Calzolari lifted her gaze, her eyes suddenly alert.

Who says that? she asked.

Tano Buriolo retorted immediately, The wise say so.

No, that's wrong, Blanquita Calzolari declared. Return to your seat. Then Tolchi Pereno burst out crying. Blanquita looked at her and asked what happened.

Nothing happened, Tolchi said. I'm having a nervous attack, that's all, she said, and she started to scream and took my hand, which was next to hers, and rested it on her chest.

Feel this, feel this, she said. Feel how my nerves are turning over inside.

I noticed the edge of her bra under her knit sweater and something like termites over Tolchi's heart. I blushed.

Go drink a glass of water and come back, Blanquita Calzolari said.

Tolchi let my hand go and kept hiccupping in silence, sitting on her bench. We looked at her. She got up and left and returned after a while with red eyes and a swollen face. Early that evening, she threw herself under the train. Not many trains pass through here. Tolchi must have waited, crouched next to the tracks, until a train came and she could throw herself under it. The engineer swears he didn't see her. He was distracted; if he hadn't been distracted, he would have blown the whistle, he always scares suicides with the train whistle. Sometimes I think about Tolchi, how fervently she must have wished for the train to come, for it to come, for it to come, having already decided to kill herself. At first no one knew it was her. The firefighters' siren went off; we were at Serasio's bar, playing pinball. We ran out after the fire engine. Before we got there, a policeman stopped us, but we paid no mind and continued. The Tambu twins' father, who was a fireman, told us that, by far, gathering up Tolchi had been the worst thing he had to do in his life. He wouldn't wish it on anyone. We were about ten meters away; they didn't let us get any closer. All the same, we saw. At first no one knew who it was; then after a while they began to say that it was Tolchi, that she had thrown herself under the train because she was pregnant. They came and asked us, we told them that we knew nothing. It was true, we knew nothing; still, people talked and someone said that earlier in the afternoon Tolchi had burst out crying while Tano Buriolo explained the meridians and parallels, and she made me touch her tits. They gossiped, saying Tano was the father or I was. Even now they say it. It was a Tuesday. On Wednesday Stella Maris de Manccini, the acting vice-principal, came to visit our class. She gave us a talk about the value of life and the morality and responsibility of being alive. She wrote it on the chalkboard: The responsibility of being alive. While she talked, she sweated under her armpits and stained her blouse. The words wouldn't come out. The Ministry had sent her, she didn't want to have to explain all this to us. A few people tried to give us the day off for the wake, but the Parents' Association opposed it. They were afraid of a contagious effect, they thought that if they lent too much importance to Tolchi, suicide might seem attractive to us. So we didn't get the day off. They brought in an educational psychologist who gave a talk for the parents at the high school one night, and they say a lot of people went. That same night Father Porto also talked. We never really found out what they told our parents, but from then on they began to treat us more carefully. Papa came back from the talk and hid his hunting rifle. He used to always keep it in a wardrobe in the shed, and after the talk it disappeared.

I remember Martín Besone saying that it was impossible to pick up all of her, that in the end they had to clean the tracks with a hose, and the last little pieces of Tolchi remained in the rocks between the ties, and the street dogs in the neighborhood went to lick her up. We told him not to talk anymore, and he immediately fell silent. Tolchi's mother made a wooden cross and put it on the edge of the tracks, right where it happened. Each month, on the day, she brought fresh flowers.

Afterward, Blanquita Calzolari forgot about meridians and parallels and made us do a group project about the five continents. My group was assigned Africa. We had to research the tribes and areas of the planet where man had never yet set foot. Fernandito Giraudo had a subscription to *Very Interesting*; we took a ton of things out of there and made the rest up. I invented a tribe of hunters that left the jungle once a year and walked thousands of kilometers, until they arrived at the edge of a city. Then they waited for night to fall, and under the cloak of shadows they entered the city, carrying a chosen child, and they left him as a sacrifice in the parking lot of a mall. I liked to imagine that boy there, alone in the middle of the big steel and glass buildings. Blanquita Calzolari believed it; she was very interested in the topic and gave us an A+. She was tired already, at that time, Blanquita Calzolari, and she was the only one, besides Stella Maris de Manccini, who talked with us about Tolchi. One day Blanquita Calzolari was explaining something to us and her denture came unglued. She didn't even give us time to laugh; she sat down at her desk, took it out, applied Corega glue, and put it back in no time. She held her face between her hands and rubbed her eyes. I've never seen a woman so tired. She was old enough to retire, but the government paperwork hadn't arrived, and it was all the same to her. Fifteen or twenty days had passed since everything with Tolchi; we never guessed Blanquita Calzolari would come out with that. She started to talk. At the beginning it seemed like she was talking about anything, that she'd lost her mind. She told us about the time when she was a little girl. She woke up at four in the morning to go to the pasture to find the cows to milk. She had a younger brother who was a sleepwalker. She found him walking around the farm, and she was scared, she thought her brother was a ghost. Blanquita let out a scream from the shock and it woke up her brother, who had been disturbed ever since. She had to take care of her brother herself until he died young from heart failure. But it was never a burden. She loved him, he was her brother, how could it have ever been a burden? She told us about her alcoholic father who beat the animals. She'd been given a puppy, but her father lashed its back with a whip; the dog bit him and escaped the farm. It went to live with a neighbor's dogs; they went wild, attacked as a pack, and had to be killed with a rifle. She told us about her marriage. After two months she realized she wasn't in love with her husband; she had only gotten married to run away from her family. She told us how she would have liked to get out, travel, see and understand the world, but she didn't have enough money, so she had to resign herself to being a history and geography teacher. In the mornings she worked as a checker at the Co-operative supermarket, and in the afternoons she went to the community college in Villa María to study to become a teacher, but even with that, she had three boys and raised them and they turned out to be good boys. She told us how cold it was in the shelter on the side of the road where she waited for the bus, and about how she fell in love with a classmate at the college. They would meet at a hotel near the Villa María Terminal, when classes got out. She stayed with her husband, he was a good man, she felt bad, but one day her husband died from thrombosis, because he ate a lot of salami and had uric acid and high cholesterol. Blanquita thought that God was just and things had worked themselves out. During her husband's wake, Blanquita went to the phone booth, placed a call, and talked with her classmate, and he told her, there, on the phone, that he only wanted her in the hotel, in front of the Terminal, and he didn't want anything else with her. That's life, Blanquita Calzolari said, and yet she hadn't thrown herself under any train, no, she had not. Just then we realized that she was talking about Tolchi Pereno. Afterward, though there was still time before recess, Blanquita Calzolari told us to go, to leave her alone, she was giving us the hour free. We went out to the schoolyard without saying a word, and she remained sitting at her desk. I saw her fix her hair and, with a finger, make sure the denture was in her palate.

◆

Soon after, the good times came. Tolchi brought us closer together as a group. Before, the girls wouldn't look at us, they hung out with the guys in fourth year, fifth year. They had cookouts at the Ezquinos' house and didn't invite us, only the girls went with the older guys. Neto Paladizini started dating Belkys Ezquino and old Ezquino paid him to go sleep with a hooker instead and keep his hands off Belkys. But as for Tolchi Pereno, the people said that Tano Buriolo or I had gotten her pregnant. It didn't matter which—it was one of us. And we were the ones who had gone up to the train tracks to see the body. The guys from fourth and fifth year didn't go. And Stella Maris de Manccini and Blanquita Calzolari had talked to us. They began to look at us with different eyes. Bichín Peirano was still perfecting his secret plan with the cow hormones and suddenly it was ready. We tried it a couple of times. Bichín learned from his father, who was a veterinarian and injected the cows so they'd all be in heat at the same time. We put it in Carinita Plaza's maté water while we were studying Language and Literature that summer. It had no effect. She broke out in a rash, but it didn't turn her on. Bichín thought we were short on hormones, that's what happened. We got a hold of Telesita Currido, who was old and wasn't pretty, but was sort of an idiot, and every time one of us asked her to show us her panties she opened her robe and showed us. We gave her a bottle of pure hormones to drink. We took her to a construction site, made a circle, and started to applaud. Telesita showed us her panties a couple times and fell asleep. They say that the next day they found her rubbing up against the netting of a henhouse; we never knew if it had been our concoction or just craziness. After Tolchi, we didn't need the hormones. Instead, we bore a tragic burden. The guys from fourth and fifth year didn't have this advantage. Tano Buriolo slept with Noemí Orozco, they were the first, in the athletic courts, behind the school, under the stairs. They lay down some cardboard and jackets. Noemí bled a lot, she stained the cardboard, she stained the jackets. They were scared but they kept going. That day, at recess, we all talked about the blood. The girls asked how it felt. Noemí said it felt fine, she wasn't nauseous or anything. To get the blood out of the jacket we used hydrogen peroxide from the first aid kit; we asked the janitor for it. Belkys invited me to her house and we started to try. Belkys thought that I knew how to do it, that I had gotten Tolchi pregnant. I didn't know how but I didn't tell her anything; she could think what she wanted. I found out immediately that Belkys was an expert. She taught me. She was the first girl I saw; I was shocked by so much hair. I didn't know there could be so much. She told me not to be stupid, how could it shock me, it was so soft, and she showed me. That time I didn't last, I came right away. The next time Belkys said that we were doing well, she was about to come, too. She let me know right before. I'm coming, she whispered in my ear, but all the same I was frightened by how it came out of her. She hugged her shoulders and started to cry. A lot. I thought I did something wrong, I held still. Don't stop, don't stop, it's not you, she said without stopping crying. After a while she calmed down and lay at my side. I asked if she was ok. She said yes. She told me that when she was a little girl, a farmhand had gotten hold of her, and she cried when she remembered. It wasn't my fault; I shouldn't let it bother me. Belkys. She always cries when she finishes, because she remembers the farmhand. Poor thing. It frightened me and we didn't try again for a week. But we kept going. Behind the doors and in the little map room and in the lab. The walls of the lab were lined with entomological boxes, and in the closets and above the closets there were embalmed foxes and owls and herons and a Styrofoam box with a dried toad cut open and pinned down and a skeleton whose jawbone had been stolen and a hand and a fetus in formaldehyde. We opened the jar; the fetus floated and the tip of its little head protruded like a soccer ball that had fallen in a water tank. We touched it with our fingers. Although it looked soft like a baby's little head, it was hard because the formaldehyde had dried it out.

Within a month, Belkys was pregnant. We talked about it a lot, and she promised me she wouldn't throw herself under a train. I trusted her, but the others didn't, so they kept vigil over her, and her father went and talked with the engineer and told him never to drive through town distracted again, because it was dangerous. The engineer promised he'd be careful. Stella Maris de Manccini clarified that nothing against the law had happened but she talked about being a bad example. They wrote Belkys up and didn't excuse her absences. In the end they neither threw her out of school nor let her off the hook. The Parents' Association said something had to be done, but they didn't do anything. They took us to talk with Father Porto. He said while it was still a sin, it would be best to live together, since getting married so young would ruin our lives. He made us confess and absolved us. At that time a fundraising drive to build a new church had begun and Belkys's father had donated a lot of money. One day a crane came with a team of engineers, and they dynamited the bell tower and the old part of the church. It was an implosion, not an explosion. At school they explained the difference to us. We went to see, each one with their group, Belkys with the girls in her class and I with my friends. A dust cloud rose and rained dirt for four blocks around. They say that from far away it looked like an atom bomb, but a really small one. The dust settled and little by little the sky appeared again between the bricks and dry mortar. Then it started to rain little papers. They glided in the wind; they landed as if they were leaves when autumn gets hold of the trees. But they were little yellow papers, barely folded, with writing. Papa ran and caught a few that were still in the air. He read them and burst out laughing. Papa's friends hunted for papers in the air, too. They climbed the ruins to reach them, they traded them among themselves. Their faces turned gray from the falling talc. Their eyes stood out, the edges of them, pink. The little papers were left from the time the church was built, when Papa and his friends were seven or eight years old. During their lunch break, the bricklayers slept, and just to cause trouble, Papa and his friends lifted the fresh bricks, and between the bricks and mortar hid little messages for God, things that they asked him for. Papa found some of his messages and found some from others. He recognized their handwriting. He went to look for the others and said: This must be yours. Three or four were from friends who had already died. Papa burned them. I asked him what the little papers said, and he refused to tell me.

The Cabrera church had to be torn down because it was sinking. The foundation was poorly made; it couldn't support the building's weight. The tiles were splitting, dirt was embedded in the baseboards, and you could see the sky through the cracks in the roof. The sunbeams entered through the cracks and lit the inside. From noon to one the sun shone just above the altar, and it seemed like an angel was descending. There was no way to save the church. So the archbishop's office decided to demolish it and build a new one.

Belkys's father lent us a little house, and we went to live together. At the time that we moved in, I met up with my father at Mass. He waited for me at the doors. We have to talk, he said. We went out for a drive in his pick-up truck. Papa said I was grown up now, I had a baby on the way, I had to be able to feed it. He proposed that I go work with him at his business in the afternoons, after school. He would give me a salary. I said I didn't know, since I didn't like to deal with customers and I didn't want to sell hardware all my life.

Think about it, Papa said. You don't have to decide right now, there's still time.

We got quiet and kept driving. Every time we saw a new car, Papa told me who it belonged to.

That's the Gugliermis', they sold the Renault, they traded it in for a Peugeot.

That's the Espinas', it's imported, zero kilometers on it. You can't get the parts; if it breaks they'll have to send it back, to the henhouse.

That's the widow Lamónica's, she bought it with her insurance payment.

Papa talked, and all of a sudden I realized he'd grown old. His hair was grey and so was the hair that stuck out through his collar. I remembered one weekend when we went to the mountains, to Santa Rosa. We were at the river, a car stopped, one of the Cabreras got out and went up to my father. He asked if Papa knew about Mustín Puchino. Papa said no. The man told us that a tank of solvent exploded near Mustín, that ninety percent of his body was burned and he was in intensive care, they were waiting for him to die. We carried the folding chairs to the truck, got our bags, and left. That was the first time I saw Papa cry. He drove and the tears fell. Mustín was his best friend. He had been a bank teller, but they fired him, and Mustín started doing experiments to manufacture peanut oil. He set up a laboratory in his living room. Three or four tanks painted silver, connected by pipes. At some point he did something wrong. He died after two days. His little papers were among those that Papa burned when they imploded the church.

Now that I'm grown up, will you lend me the truck? I asked Papa then.

He didn't even blink.

No, I already told you no. I won't lend it to you until you have your license, he said.

We might need it in an emergency. For Belkys, I insisted.

Call me and I'll come get you.

Tano's father lends him the car.

I don't give a damn what the Buriolos do, Papa said and parked in front of the house.

I got out without saying goodbye.

The year I started high school I made friends with Fata Buriolo, Tano's cousin. Fata was big and tall, and the guys said he was retarded. He didn't seem that stupid when I looked at him. Fata did poorly in school, he hardly ever passed his classes. Our classmates started saying Fata's father had to teach him to jerk off; he was too retarded to do it himself. I asked him and he said it wasn't true, and to prove it we started to touch ourselves and show each other how, to be sure of what to do when we were with a girl for real. Fata had a dog named Flecha, and Fata had the habit of rolling over, with the cum still in his hand, and calling Flecha over and letting him eat it. Flecha licked it right up. Fata said you could give a dog candy and he wouldn't like it so much. I tried giving my cum to other dogs to eat, but they just came over, smelled my hand, and left. Only Flecha had this preference. Fata and I did this for a while. We didn't tell anyone since we realized people wouldn't understand. At school we acted like we weren't such good friends. We saw each other outside school, I went to his house or he came to mine. Fata was my best friend when I was in first year. Then he repeated the grade and he himself began to say he was retarded, that school wasn't for him, that he should quit and go work in the fields. My mother asked me to go talk with him, to talk him into continuing. His mother asked my mother. I went, and Fata confessed to me that as a boy he believed that the doves in the cemetery were Holy Spirits, and he went to hunt them with a slingshot; he filled a bag with dead Holy Spirits and threw them in the priest's yard. He made me promise I'd never tell anyone. It was going to be our secret. I swore I wouldn't.

But I don't understand what the Holy Spirit has to do with leaving high school, I said.

Can't you see I've always been dumb? Fata answered. How could I have thought doves were Holy Spirits? There's something wrong with my head, it won't let me finish high school.

Fata went to work in the fields. His father bought him a harvester. He threshed the whole day; he slept alone in a little trailer in the middle of the field, and we stopped seeing each other. One afternoon, Belkys wasn't home, and there was a knock at the door. I went to open the door; it was Fata. I let him in and offered him wine, vermouth, Gancia. He took the wine. He sat down, gripped the glass with one hand, and emptied it. The other hand hung limp; he had to prop it on the table. I noticed the hand didn't look right. It was fat, purple. I asked him what happened, and he said it got caught in an angle grinder. They saved it, but it wound up just like that, half lame, it wasn't good for much. Then he asked if I was home alone. I said yes, and he burst out crying. At first I thought he was crying because of his hand, he talked and I didn't understand the words, until I understood and realized he was crying because of Belkys. He said how could I do this to him, cheat on him with Belkys, he was so in love with me and not a night passed when he didn't think of me, alone in his little trailer, in the middle of the fields. I told him I was sorry, I gave him a little more wine, just a little, because I noticed he was almost drunk. When he calmed down, I asked him to leave and never come back.

◆

Belkys was sad; I was worried. Her belly showed, her feet were swollen, we went to the doctor and the doctor said that was normal. Her birthday came and she didn't want to celebrate. Ever since she'd reached the age of reason, she'd dreamed of it, her fifteenth birthday. She never imagined that before she turned fifteen I would get her pregnant. Since she was twelve she'd been planning the dress and the decorations for the hall. She showed me the drawings she made in a notebook. Belkys's father was going to ask the Belgrano Club to lend them the basketball court. Instead of using the club's tables, they were going to rent round tables with white tablecloths from Villa María. They were going to cover the chairs with white fabric, too. So the fabric wouldn't slide off, they'd have to tie it with pink ribbons in the back. Belkys planned to use the basketball hoops as plant holders and place two big ferns inside that would hang and cover the hoops. The dance floor would be in the middle, with a rented mirror ball, and in the invitations they would require the men to wear jackets and ties. First would come the dinner, for the relatives, friends of her father, and acquaintances they had to invite. She planned to invite us, her classmates, afterward, for the toast and dance. At dinner they would serve antipasti with *vittel tonè*, beef tongue, salami, and potato salad, baked chicken as the main dish, and ice cream for dessert. For the toast there would be a table of sweets, with cakes, pies, and little treats that her mother and aunts would cook. They would turn off the lights and she and her father would dance the waltz in the middle of the dance floor, alone, illuminated by a spotlight. Just before the waltz ended, fifteen of her best friends would come in from the sides, each one with a white rose in her hand. Then the DJ would put on the Trío San Javier song, "Fifteen Springs," the one that goes, *You have to live through fifteen springs, Fifteen fresh flowers to bring you joy*, and one by one her friends would hand her the roses. Belkys told me all of this at night. We turned out the light and talked. Sometimes she cried. Sometimes she forgot that she wouldn't be able to have the party, and she talked like she still had to get things ready, like she still had a year or more left. But she didn't. The day arrived. Belkys didn't want to go to school. I understood, she stayed home, sprawled on the bed. In the afternoon her closest friends came over to comfort her a little. The Farmers' Co-operative sent a bouquet of flowers, since her father was president of the assembly. The boys in the class all put in a little and bought her a pink wool hat and a pair of gloves to match. Fernandito Giraudo was in charge of collecting the money and buying the gift. He had good taste and knew what people wore, since he read a lot of magazines and always kept up with the latest fashions. He checked with me first, he said: Hat and gloves, the latest style. It was a practical gift, Belkys could use it while she was pregnant, and once the baby was born, she could still use it. That night the doorbell rang. They gave her the present wrapped in a lot of paper. Belkys thanked them and set it aside. I invited them to drink a Gancia with soda. They drank it and left right away. We weren't used to this. We couldn't talk about men's things in front of Belkys.

When would I wear a hat in this hot, shitty town! Belkys said right after they left.

She kept the hat and gloves in the closet, I never saw them again. I bought her cowboy boots. They were also in style, I knew she'd like them. They made her happy, and though she said I shouldn't have spent so much since we needed to save up for the baby, she wore them a lot to school. She didn't want to go out with her belly, so people wouldn't talk, so she wore them in the house, too.

Every time a girl turned fifteen, she requested a Mass and carried up the offering. After the Mass, she had a photo taken in front of the church, sitting next to a statue of the Virgin on a little grassy hill. For the photos they called Red, the only photographer, as well as the only communist, in town. The seamstress came, too, so the girl's dress turned out right, and the hairdresser came in case her hair needed touching up. After the picture, the party happened. But the year we turned fifteen was the year that Father Porto had the church demolished. They put the statue of the Virgin in storage, along with Saint Roch and his dog and the Sacred Heart and covered all of them with nylon. The Masses were held in the municipal warehouse. It wouldn't have occurred to anyone to take a picture in front of the warehouse. Since the girls didn't have anywhere to take the picture, the Parents' Association from the school made an agreement and constructed a monument in the corner of the plaza with their own funds. Father Porto handed over the Virgin, and they installed her there. It was the monument for the fifteenth birthday photos. It was only used for that. Belkys didn't throw a party and she hadn't asked for a Mass, but to me it seemed unfair that she should go without a photo. I asked my mother to lend me the camera. We waited until late one night and went to the plaza. We wasted the first photo, I forgot the flash. The second came out well. Since it was cold, Belkys put on her winter jacket, and she almost doesn't look pregnant. She's wearing a long skirt in the photo, the cowboy boots, and she's standing next to the Virgin in the middle of the monument.

When I moved in with Belkys, Papa started coming by the house when Mass let out. He honked the horn without getting out of the truck and invited me to drink a glass of wine at the Italian Society. He always goes to Mass on Sunday mornings. According to him, the Saturday evening Mass doesn't count. He never sits. He stands in the back, and every now and then he steps out to smoke a cigarette. When I was little, Papa went with his gang to a bar, El Moderno, after Mass. There were about seven or eight of them, they argued, they shot the breeze. The harvest, the weather, the prices, new cars, and the champion bull that the Aguirrezurretas bought at the Fair and that broke its leg as soon as they took it off the trailer. They pounded the table, they laughed, they added soda to their drinks to stretch them further, and if they ran out of peanuts they gestured to the waiter so he'd bring them more. Over the years they began to thin out, little by little. First Mustín died. Enrique Oncalvo followed, from prostate cancer. Michelo Tiempini, lung cancer, it went into his bones and during his last week he screamed like a pig until Doctor Karakachoff took pity and gave him morphine. Oscarcito Kunsel, who was a singer, from a heart attack in his sleep. The Farmers' Co-operative transferred Coquito Molinero to the Vicuña Mackena plant. And Pancho Miranda was left blind by diabetes; his wife took care of him and some Sundays she let him go to the bar but most Sundays she didn't. In the end there were three of them left in the gang, Jorgito Piazza, Osvaldo Fava, and Papa. Their bar, El Moderno, was sold. Since it was by the highway, they put a gas station there. People began to go to the bar at the Terminal or the Italian Society. Papa went, too, but less, just every once in a while. Sometimes he got together with Jorgito and Osvaldo; they parked the truck at the service station and talked for a while by the gas pumps. Otherwise, he came by the house and honked the horn.

Let's go have a glass of wine, he called from the window.

We went to the Italian Society and drove around town a few times. We went up and down the boulevard, we passed by the house that Tuti Ponti was building. Papa knew the watchman and said hello. One day he invited us to come in and see the work. We wandered through the labyrinth of bricks and scaffolding.

Why does Tuti want so many rooms, if it's only him and his wife? Papa said.

He has to spend his money on something, the watchman answered.

We said goodbye, Papa started the truck and set off as if to take me home. Before we got there, he asked if I didn't want to invite Belkys to have lunch with them, Mama had made baked chicken. Since I hadn't mentioned anything at home, I told him not that day, but any other Sunday, we would go.

◆

We didn't sleep well. Belkys tossed and turned, she complained, her back hurt, she couldn't find a comfortable position. Springtime arrived, and with it, the second big wave of fifteenth birthdays came. Most girls in our class had birthdays in September, there weren't enough weekends to throw parties. Belkys didn't want to go to any, and I had to stay home with her. Mondays, at school, the boys told me. Noemí Orozco's party was the biggest of all. Her father was the bank manager, they came from out of town, from Rosario, they had other customs. Noemí was an only child, so they went all out. They rented a tent and put it up in the soccer field. The tent was white, and inside they decorated it with pink tulle and lilac crepe paper.

Noemí attended Mass in a more or less normal dress, she had her photo taken in this dress by the fifteenth birthday monument. But afterward she changed. She went to the party in other clothes, white jeans that showed her panties and a red bra with nothing else on top. Around her neck she hung a chain with a big iron key. When the waltz came, Noemí danced the first half with her father, stopped the music, then called Tano Buriolo, who was now her official boyfriend, and danced the other half with him. They didn't play the fifteen springs song, they played other music, rock, because Noemí liked rock. At three in the morning they turned down the lights and something like twenty waiters came in holding kebabs in the air. On the tip of each skewer was an apple filled with alcohol, lit on fire. They set the skewers on a table, put out the apples, and the people went and served themselves meat directly from the skewers. When it was time for the cake, they formed a circle and Noemí and Tano kissed in the middle of the dance floor. Noemí took off the chain with the iron key and hung it on Tano's neck. The next day the town was sizzling with gossip. The women were scandalized by the bra. Most scandalized of all was Tano Buriolo's mother, who forbade her son from setting foot in the Orozcos' house again. Red hung a few photos from the party in the windows of his shop. The boys came out of the primary school, walked by the shop, and stopped to look at Noemí Orozco's red bra. Someone drew a penis on the glass with white-out. Red erased it right away, but people still found out.

Belkys thought that Noemí was begging for attention and trying to win points for the fifteenth birthday dance. Between Christmas and New Year's, the Belgrano Club organized the dance. The girls who turned fifteen during the year present themselves with their best dresses, parade in on their fathers' arms, and dance the waltz, and then they elect the queen. It's turned into a benefit also. The money from the tickets and the cantina goes to the hospital. The queen is selected by a jury of men. There's the mayor and the secretary of public works, Father Porto, Belkys's father, because he's the president of the assembly of the Farmers' Co-operative, Padilla the hair stylist, Dr. Karakachoff, and Noemí's father, for being the bank manager. If the harvest has been good, they invite some entertainment personality to preside. Someone from Córdoba, a radio announcer. If it hasn't been a good year, it stays how it is and the president is chosen by rotation. Belkys's theory was that, with a little luck, Noemí would get her father chosen president. The president has a double vote. If you added to this the good impression that the red bra made on the men, she would be queen. Belkys explained these things to me at night with the lights out. Sometimes I would doze off, but she would elbow me and continue telling me about Noemí Orozco's plotting and schemes. So as not to get bored, I would rest my head on Belkys's belly. I tried to hear the baby's heartbeats or if it kicked. Every time it seemed the baby moved, I told Belkys. There, it just moved! I said. Sometimes Belkys answered, Yes, it moved, and sometimes she answered, No, it was only her, she had gas. Sometimes she burst out crying because she'd wound up pregnant and wouldn't be able to present herself at the dance.

◆

Tano Buriolo's father was a mechanic, he'd liked working with tools since he was a boy. At one time he had a little coupe; he fixed it up to race, and he did well, but he was cheated on once. He got angry and didn't want to race anymore. He'd lent Tano the car since he turned twelve years old. Tano used it on the weekends, mostly. We went to dance at the Ruinas Disco in Perdices, or at The Rancho in Deheza. Sometimes Tano got tipsy and someone drove back for him.

Other times he drove. Every time he crashed, he did the same thing. He stopped someone on the road, asked them to take him home, wrote a note to his father telling him where he left the car, and disappeared for a couple days. He'd hide out at a friend's house until his father's mood had passed. Then he came home. The time we went with him and the car flipped over, Tano went to Pamela Caudana's house, since she was alone; her family had gone on vacation. Our classmates knew he was there, and we went to visit him secretly. I still don't understand how the car flipped. There were nine of us in Tano's father's Falcon. We came up the road slowly. Tano was wasted, and we told him, Slow, Tano, slow. Even with that, we all flipped over on the curve in front of the Cavigliasos' farm. Tonito Mazzuco ended up on top of me, crushing me.

What do I do? What do I do? I screamed. We couldn't get out because the doors were stuck.

Should I break the window? Tonito asked.

We could hear Tano's voice from the front:

Break it and I'll kick the shit out of you. Open it with the handle.

Tonito turned the handle until the window was down, and we climbed out. Tano stopped a car and told us to wait for him there, that he was going to get help and he'd be right back, but we knew what he had planned. He went home, left a note for his father, and hid at Pamela Caudana's house. Oscar Manfioti, who had gone out hunting, picked us up. The police came, and no one was left. There was only the Falcon, with its four wheels facing up and its windows intact.

In October, Tano got into an accident with the Insquieta boy and came to hide at our house. He rang the doorbell early in the morning. We were the only ones who didn't live with our parents, and Belkys thought it would be all right to put him up for a few days. We threw a mattress in the living room and explained how to use the bathroom faucet, which was tricky, it stuck. By ten in the morning our classmates already knew he was with us. Little by little they came over, discreetly. Tano hadn't really told us how the accident happened, but when they came and told us the Insquieta boy was interned at the clinic, I took Tano into the bedroom and asked him to explain. He sat at the end of the bed, he took his head in his hands. Why did I pick him up! Why did I pick him up! he said over and over. The Insquieta boy wasn't our friend, he was in first year. Tano said he left the dance early and came back only because he had fought with Noemí and felt insulted. He went out to the car. While he waited for it to warm up, the Insquieta boy came up to him and asked if he was going to Cabrera. Tano said yes, and the Insquieta boy asked if he could take him. After that, Tano didn't remember very well. They drove along the highway; they didn't talk because they weren't friends. He must have fallen asleep. He crashed into a couple of trees near the dump. They spun around twice and ended up in the gorge, with the car lying on its side. Tano got up right away, he wasn't hurt, but the Insquieta boy was covered with blood. Tano left him there, stopped a car, went home, wrote a note to his father, and came to hide with Belkys and me. I asked him if the Insquieta boy's situation was serious. He said he didn't know. He said the Insquieta boy looked like he was sleeping.

It looked like he was sleeping, except for the blood and the cut on his forehead, he said.

The Tambu twins came, their father was among those who removed the Insquieta boy from the car. They told Tano that the Insquieta boy's father was looking to beat him to a pulp, that he wouldn't get out of this. The first year students, the Insquieta boy's classmates, had gotten together in front of the Mayo Clinic. They waited to see if Dr. Karakachoff would say something. The girls prayed the rosary, sitting on the fence of the house next door. We decided that we'd have to hide Tano well. We told our classmates not to even think about setting foot in our house. We didn't want to call attention to ourselves. Belkys took the folding chair out to the sidewalk and sat in the sun, reading magazines, as if nothing had happened. We shut Tano up in the bedroom. If someone came he could escape through the window. And we waited.

Around two in the afternoon Noemí Orozco came and shut herself up with Tano in the bedroom. She came out after a while; her face was full of tears. She told us that the Insquieta boy was brain dead. It was a matter of hours. Old Insquieta was going around with a revolver, searching for Tano. The first year students wanted to scare him shitless. Belkys gave her a glass of water, calmed her down, and asked what she was going to do. Noemí said her place was at Tano's side. He was the love of her life, in good times and bad. She went back to the bedroom, and we listened to them talk and cry. Tano's steps went from one side to another and the bed frame made a noise every time he fell on it. After a while Papa came by in the truck, parked in front of the house, and honked the horn. I went outside quickly; I didn't want him to come in.

Look at what this friend of yours has done, he said. That's why we can't give you cars, you little brats. Ruined these people's lives.

I didn't know how to answer. I leaned on the door of the truck and said nothing.

They say somewhere around here, Papa continued, he's gone into hiding, at a house in town, in one of his friends' houses. You wouldn't have him here, would you?

I looked at him.

No, Papa, how could you think that, the house is too small, I said.

Of course, of course, that's what I thought, where would you put him, when the house is so small. Well, I'll let you go, he said and started the truck again. Say hi to Belkys.

Bye, Papa, bye, I said and went back inside. Noemí was looking out the bedroom door. She asked me what Papa had said, and I told her he said nothing. There was no news.

The four of us were shut inside all afternoon. Tano and Noemí in the bedroom, Belkys and I in the kitchen. Belkys decided to make a cake. We didn't talk, we listened to Tano and Noemí in the bedroom. At one point they went to bed together. I turned the radio up loud, to cover it up.

Night fell. There was a knock on the door. It was Fata Buriolo. I hadn't seen him since the time he said he was in love with me. I opened the door a crack but didn't let him in.

Is my cousin here? he asked. He still had the lame hand and it hung from his side. I didn't answer.

Open up, I already know he's here, he told me.

The five of us sat around the table. Fata at the head. He seemed bigger than us, more sure of himself.

The Insquieta boy died, he said. And his father is looking for Tano, and so are the Insquietas and the police. I'm sure he'll go to jail for this. He didn't even try to help the boy.

Noemí burst out crying. Belkys passed her a handkerchief and rubbed her back.

It's dangerous for you to hide him here, Fata continued. A lot of people already know; they're keeping the secret for now, but I think by the end of the night, one of them will crack. They really have it in for you, Tano. The Insquieta boy was a good boy, he played soccer well, he could have been a star. Next month he was going to try out in Córdoba.

Tano lowered his head and acknowledged that yes, the Insquieta boy played soccer better than all of us.

The only solution is for you to disappear, Fata said. I have the trailer in the field to the south, near the stream. If it's all right with you, I can come get you in an hour and you can stay there for a few days. After that, maybe you'll have to take off for Buenos Aires, change your name, leave for where no one knows you.

Tano looked hard at the formica on the table. Noemí cried. Belkys had forgotten about the maté. The four of us agreed that Fata's plan was for the best. For me, it wouldn't be a problem putting Tano up for a few more days, if only his father or the Insquietas were after him, but the police were another story. I had to think about my child, about Belkys, I couldn't get into trouble. Fata came by with the truck very late, around two in the morning. I lent Tano a change of clothes, so he wouldn't leave with what he had on. They were making arrangements for the wake at the funeral parlor. They had already sent the Insquieta boy to Villa María for the autopsy, but in just a little while he'd be coming back. Noemí cried like crazy before Tano got into the truck. We had to pull her off of him. She grabbed his sweatshirt, she hung off his legs, she didn't let him go. Fata said goodbye from a distance. Before he left, Tano gave me a hug that still hurts. I never saw him again. In town they say that he threw himself under a train from guilt, like Tolchi Pereno, but that's pure gossip. Just a little while ago, Fata told me that he's living in Florencio Varela, that he opened an auto parts shop, that like his father, he has a good hand for cars. He's doing well.

◆

Belkys reached her seventh month in the middle of November; it was already hot outside. We fought about everything. About the baby's name, the dirty clothes, food, money. We lived on what Belkys's father gave us. It wasn't much. I didn't want to work with Papa at the hardware store. Every now and then Belkys's mother came and changed our things, bustled around, scolded me for getting her daughter pregnant. One day Noemí Orozco came by the house, she wanted to see Belkys, and Belkys wasn't home just then. She had gone with her mother to buy new pants, because her old ones didn't fit anymore. I offered Noemí a maté. She said, Maté, no, she preferred wine, or whiskey, if I had it. I don't drink whiskey, so there wasn't any in the house. I offered her Gancia and she took wine. She drank two glasses without talking, sitting at the table, leafing through the pages of a magazine, *Being Parents Today*, which a girl at the pharmacy had lent us.

Who got Tolchi pregnant? Noemí asked suddenly. Was it you or was it Tano?

I guessed her intentions, I tried to change the subject and take her mind somewhere else. But she insisted. I had to tell her that it hadn't been me, and I guessed it wasn't Tano, either.

Maybe it was Tano, she told me. He never wanted to tell me, there must have been a reason he was hiding it.

Maybe he didn't want to tell you, so you wouldn't know how stupid we were. I don't think either Tano or I had anything to do with it.

I always asked Tano, and he said that if he had to choose between Tolchi Pereno and me, he'd spend his life with me. What do you think? Am I prettier than Tolchi?

I told her yes, of course, but please not to tell Belkys I said that, because she would get upset. She smiled. She promised she wouldn't tell.

If Tolchi hadn't thrown herself under the train, at least one of Tano's sons would be here today. I could go see him, I could visit him, like a godmother.

If you ask me, it wasn't his, I answered. Who knows what trouble Tolchi had gotten herself into. She didn't hang out with us a lot.

It's not easy, Noemí said. It's not easy being here. My boyfriend left, people know I slept with him, no one else will want me. Tano's mother turned her back on me. She says I led him down the wrong path. Even worse is running into the Insquietas, I don't have the eyes to look at them. If I hadn't fought with Tano that night, none of this would have happened. Do you know why we fought?

I told her no, I didn't know, and she should stop thinking about it, it wasn't worth it. She looked at me.

About something stupid, she said, and she asked if I had more wine. I told her I didn't have any more, but she went to the fridge, looked for a bottle, and poured herself another glass.

Now I'll either be a nun or a whore, I have no other choice, Noemí said.

You can go to Rosario. You have family there; you can transfer and finish high school there.

She shook her head. I can still see her. She was leaning on the kitchen counter and made a sour face, because the wine was strong and scratched her throat.

I don't want to go, she said. What I want is for Tano to come back, to be the queen of the fifteenth birthdays, to marry him, to have a pretty house and three children, two boys and a girl. We were going to name the boys Alfonso and Miguel. We hadn't yet decided if the girl should be Elisa or María Elisa, or Juliana. Tano liked Juliana, but I didn't. What time does Belkys come back?

She should be coming home any minute now; it's been a while since she left. They were going to Co-op to look for pants and then coming right back.

Then I'm going, Noemí said, and she got up and left without giving me a chance to say anything else. The truth is, I thought of it then. I saw that she looked bad, and I thought of it. But I knew the engineer already had been warned to watch the tracks, to drive through town slowly. All the same, it didn't happen that afternoon, it was two days later. She hung herself from a tree in her backyard. Her mother had traveled to Río Cuarto to conduct some studies, and her father was at the bank. Noemí acted like she was leaving for school, came back, and hung herself with her uniform on.

This affected Belkys a lot. It hadn't been that way with Tolchi, since we were only classmates. But Noemí was her best friend. She didn't want to go to the wake or the burial, so people wouldn't see her all swollen by the pregnancy and from crying. I went. Again at school they didn't give us the day off. As a group we skipped class and all went together. Father Porto didn't give speeches or anything, he blessed the coffin and read the usual. At first they said her parents would take her to be buried in Rosario, but in the end they left her here. The Italian Society gave them a niche in their mausoleum. When I got home Belkys asked me how it went. I told her well, it went well. She burst out crying and told me I was insensitive, how could I say it went well. I tried to explain that it was just a way of saying things, but she didn't understand. We went to sleep without talking. At three in the morning her screaming woke me up. Belkys was in the bathroom, she was having contractions. It was too soon, we weren't even in the eighth month yet. It's impossible, I told her, but she told me yes, that's what it was. I ran to the Astronaves' house around the corner to ask them to lend me their phone, and I called Belkys's father. They came right away and took her to the clinic. The Astronaves had already let Karakachoff know, he was there in five minutes. It was as if I were in a dream, and the only thing I said was it's impossible, it's too early, it's impossible, it's too early, it's impossible, it's too early. I sat in the waiting room, in one of the fake leather chairs. Belkys's father smoked outside, and her mother was in the hallway, trying to see what was going on. The people in town were asleep, the only thing you could hear were Belkys's screams. Karakachoff appeared, he took off his glasses and cleaned them with a handkerchief. Then I noticed that it had gone silent. Belkys didn't scream anymore. Karakachoff called me inside. Belkys was sleeping on a gurney, covered with a green sheet. They had sedated her.

It's a girl, Karakachoff told me, but she's very ill. It could be anything. We can only wait now. It's already a miracle that she was born.

After two hours, they let me see her. She looked like the fetus in formaldehyde from the lab at school. She was missing something. She was tiny, with a huge head. She was quiet, her eyes were covered with gauze. Belkys wanted to name her Milagros Noemí. I agreed. Belkys spent her days next to the incubator. Her mother came to take her place, my mother came to take her place, but she didn't want to leave. Karakachoff took me aside every now and then and told me things. Most likely she wasn't a normal baby, she was going to have some handicap. He couldn't tell what yet. We'd have to wait. It could be anything, Karakachoff told me. He gave me a pat on the back and left. Father Porto had already started building the new church, so one day during the lunch hour, while the bricklayers slept, I went into the construction site and wrote a little note to God. I folded it well, lifted a brick, and encrusted it in the fresh mortar and stood there, not really knowing what to do. I left before anyone saw me. In the end, Milagros Noemí lasted a week, no more. We buried her in Belkys's family's vault. After the burial Belkys told me that she wanted to go sleep at her mother's house. It sounded good to me. I didn't go back to our house, either, I went to Mama and Papa's and slept there. Belkys missed class an entire week. On Sunday I packed our things, I separated what her mother and my mother had bought us. I went to give the key back to Belkys's father. I asked if I could see her, if I could talk to her, and he said it would be better not to, what for? I didn't insist, because I agreed. What would I say? Afterward we saw each other at school, and we didn't talk there either, even though we could have, at recess.

◆

My fifteenth birthday fell on a Tuesday. It was drizzling when I woke up. It was cold, especially for December. Boys didn't have fifteenth birthday parties. We used the occasion to have a cookout with our friends. I didn't even tell anyone it was my birthday. A few people remembered and congratulated me at school. The day went by like any other. It rained and it was cold, that was the only difference. The town left the streetlights on all day because with the drizzle you couldn't see anything. It was such a fine drizzle it seemed like mist. But it got you wet. In the morning, Mama offered to make me a cake. I told her no. Papa took me out driving and gave me an envelope. Inside there was money, a lot.

Buy what you want, he said.

I thanked him. Late at night the doorbell rang. It was Fata Buriolo; Mama got the door, I recognized his voice. Mama came to the bedroom to let me know he was looking for me, but I pretended I was asleep, I didn't want to get up. Fata left. We hadn't seen each other since Noemí's wake. In the cemetery I wanted to go up to him and ask about Tano, but he made a gesture from a distance, as if we'd talk later. It wouldn't look good to be seen together. When the burial was through, I couldn't find him anywhere. He disappeared in the crowd. The night of my birthday Mama entered my bedroom and gave me a box wrapped in newspapers.

The Buriolo boy left this for you, she said.

Inside, between wads of paper, were two little white ceramic doves. They were a coffee table decoration, I had already seen them in the shop window at Constantin's hardware store. On one side was a letter folded in quarters, written by hand. Fata told me a few things about Tano. He'd already left for Buenos Aires. A truck driver took him there, hidden in an empty trailer. He had an appointment to get new documents, to change his name. Fata had lent him money. He had also decided not to tell Tano anything about Noemí, and he asked me not to say anything, either, if by some chance Tano got in touch with me. Why tell him? Fata said, he already has enough to worry about. With time, Fata's handwriting had gotten better. It wasn't so disastrous anymore, you could read it. At the end he asked me to burn the letter, so no sign or proof of Tano's whereabouts would remain. Then he wished me a happy birthday and explained that the little ceramic doves were a joke. So that the Holy Spirit may always be with you, he wrote in quotation marks. To see if you remember me every once in a while. I burned the letter, like he'd asked.

For a long time I thought about what to buy with the money that Papa had given me. I finally decided. I wanted a car. I went to the Petitos' dealership, at the bend in the road. I asked one of them to show me the used cars. The cheapest, I told him. There was a Renault that looked nice. If you take care of them, Renaults last. It was green. The body and the motor were good. It needed new upholstery. Here and there it needed new chrome on the fenders, but it wasn't bad for a start. I asked the price. I still needed half.

Ask your father; I'm sure the old man will help you out, one of the Petitos told me, the youngest.

I went to look at it a few afternoons. I got in the Renault at the back of the showroom and sat there. The Petitos didn't say anything.

I wasn't doing anyone any harm. Every now and then they brought me a maté, otherwise, they left me alone. I closed my eyes and imagined I was driving through the streets in town. The shops on Nueve de Julio Street, the sports club, the bank they all paraded past on either side of me. I drove around the plaza, took Santa Fe Street and drove by the old mill. I came back down the boulevard. I drove up the highway, past Cervio's butcher shop; I drove slowly. I had to stop at the light by the bus terminal. I kept going, hugging the pines of the cemetery; I crossed the bridge over the creek, by the smoke cloud from the smoldering dump. After that it was pure highway and I sped up and the town fell back. Then I opened my eyes and I was at the back of the Petitos' showroom again, between the polished, neatly-parked cars, and I saw the youngest Petito buffing the Chevy that they had in front.

I could have asked Papa for the other half. He probably would have given it to me. But I didn't want to.

The end of the year came. Belkys was still fifteen years old, she wasn't pregnant anymore, and she'd gotten thin again, so her father signed her up for the fifteenth birthday dance. I'm guessing she didn't want to go, but they signed her up all the same, as if to cover up the pregnancy or to give her a change of scenery, to get her out of the house and finish recovering. Mama came in one day to tell me before I woke up. She sat on the edge of the bed. She handed me my coffee with milk. She had a dish towel in her hand and smelled like bleach.

Now I can tell you, she said. That girl wasn't right for you. Thank goodness. You would have ruined your life.

God knows what He's doing, she said as she got up.

Belkys entered the dance on her father's arm. They made her the dress she wanted. It looked just like the one in the fashion magazine that she'd shown me a thousand times. The same fabric, the same color. They say she got a lot of applause. She came out as the queen. Her father was the president of the Farmers' Co-operative, he was on the jury, he pulled some strings. Even Father Porto voted for her. Red put the photos on his storefront windows. Belkys is sitting on a throne covered with paper flowers. She's barely smiling. She raises her arm, waves. She's holding the golden scepter, and the crown sits over her long hair—straight, with a few curls.

ON THE STEPPE

BY SAMANTA SCHWEBLIN (ARGENTINA)

Life on the steppe isn't easy: everything is hours apart, and there's nothing to see but this great thicket of dry shrubs. Our house is several kilometers from town, but that's fine. It's comfortable and has all that we need. Pol goes into town three days a week, he sends the farm journals his articles about insects and insecticides, and he goes shopping with the lists I make. In the hours that he's gone, I get ahead on a few things I prefer to do alone. I doubt that Pol wants to know about these things, but when you're desperate, when you've reached the limit, like we have, then the simplest solutions, like candles, incense, any piece of advice clipped from a magazine, seem like reasonable options. As there are many recipes for fertility, and not all seem reliable, I bet only on the most plausible and follow them precisely. I mark down any pertinent details, small changes in Pol or me, in a notebook.

The sun sets late on the steppe, which doesn't leave us much time. You need to have everything ready: the flashlights, the nets. Pol cleans the things while he waits for the hour to arrive. This shaking out the dust, just to get things dirty again a second later, gives things a ritual air, as if even before beginning, one were already planning on how to improve, examining the previous days for any detail that might be corrected, that could lead us to them, or at least to one: our own.

When we're ready, Pol passes me my jacket and scarf; I help him put on his gloves, and we each sling our packs on our shoulders. We leave through the back door and walk into the countryside. The night is cold, but soon the wind dies down. Pol goes ahead; he illuminates the ground with his flashlight. Further out, the fields roll into long hills, and we move toward them. In the hills, the shrubs are small, barely tall enough to hide us, and Pol thinks that's one reason our plan fails every night. But we persist, because several times already we thought that we saw them at dawn, when we were tired. During these nights I almost always hide behind a shrub, clutching my net, and I nod off and dream of things that seem fertile. Pol, on the other hand, turns into a kind of predator. I see him move away, crouched between the plants. He can stay crouched, immobile, for a long time.

I've always asked myself what they really would be like. We talk about it sometimes. I think that they're just like the ones from the city, only more rustic, wilder. But according to Pol, they're definitely different, and although he's as eager as I am, and not a night goes by when neither cold nor exhaustion can convince him to postpone our search another day, he moves suspiciously when we're hidden in the shrubs, as if some wild animal might attack.

Now I'm alone, watching the highway from the kitchen. This morning, like always, we woke up late and ate lunch. Afterward, Pol went to town with the shopping list and his articles for the magazines. But it's late, he should have come back a while ago, and he still hasn't appeared. Then I see the pickup truck. As he pulls in, he gestures from the window so that I come out and help him with the things. He waves and says:

"You won't believe it."

"What?"

He smiles and motions that we should go inside. We carry the bags in, but not all the way to the kitchen, not now that something's happened, now that there's finally something to tell. We leave everything at the door and sit in the armchairs.

"Well," Pol says, rubbing his hands, "I met a couple, they're great."

"Where?"

I ask only to make him keep talking, and then he says something wonderful, something that never would have occurred to me, yet I understand it will change everything.

"They had the same problem," he says. His eyes shine and he knows I'm dying for him to continue—"and they have one, they've had him for a month."

"They have one! They really have one! I can't believe it . . ."

Pol keeps nodding and rubbing his hands.

"We're invited to dinner. Tonight."

I'm happy to see him happy, and I'm happy, too, as if we'd gotten what they did. We hug and kiss and immediately start to get ready.

I bake a cake, and Pol picks out a bottle of wine and his best cigars. He tells me everything he knows while we bathe and get dressed. Arnol and Nabel live some twenty kilometers from here, in a house very similar to ours. Pol saw the house because they drove back together, in a caravan, until Arnol honked the horn to let him know they were turning, and then he saw Nabel point to the house. "They're great," Pol keeps saying, and I feel a certain envy that he already knows so much about them.

"And what's he like? You saw him?"

"They left him at home."

"What do you mean, they left him at home? Alone?"

Pol shrugs. It seems strange to me that this doesn't make him wonder, but I ask for more details while I keep getting ready.

We close up the house as if we won't come back for some time. We bundle up and leave. On the drive, I carry the apple cake on top of my skirt, taking care not to let it tip, and I think of what to say, of everything I want to ask Nabel. What I can ask her when Pol invites Arnol to go smoke a cigar and they leave us alone. So maybe I can talk with her about personal things; maybe Nabel used candles, too, and dreamed of fertile things every now and then, and now that they got him, they can tell us exactly what to do.

We honk the horn when we arrive, and they come out to greet us right away. Arnol is a big man. He's wearing jeans and a red plaid shirt; he greets Pol with a strong embrace, like he was an old friend he hadn't seen for a long time. Nabel leans out behind Arnol and smiles at me. I think we'll get along well. She's also tall, Arnol's size, but skinny, and she dresses almost like him; I feel awkward, having dressed up so much. The inside of the house seems like an old mountain lodge. Wood paneling on the walls and ceiling, a big fireplace in the living room, and animal skins on the floor and on the armchairs. It's well-lit and heated. Really, it's not how I'd decorate my house, but it works for them, and I return Nabel's smile. There's an exquisite smell of roast beef and sauce. It seems like Arnol is the cook; he bustles about the kitchen, moving a few dirty dishes, and tells Nabel to have us sit in the living room. We sit on the sofa. She serves us wine and brings in a tray with some snacks, and soon Arnol joins us. I want to ask questions right away: how they caught him, what he's like, what his name is, if he eats well, if he's already seen a doctor, if he looks as nice as the ones in the city. But the conversation drags on over stupid things. Arnol consults with Pol about insecticides; Pol takes an interest in Arnol's business; then they talk about their trucks, the places they go shopping; they discover that they argued with the same man, the one who works at the gas station, and they agree that he's awful. Then Arnol excuses himself to check on the food. Pol offers to help him, and they leave the room. I make myself comfortable in the sofa, facing Nabel. I know I should say something friendly before asking what's on my mind. I compliment her on the house, and then I ask immediately:

"Is he cute?"

She blushes and smiles. She looks at me as if she were ashamed, and I feel a knot in my stomach, and dying of happiness, I think, "They got him. They got him and he's beautiful."

"I want to see him," I say. I think, "I want to see him now," and sit up tall. I look toward the hallway, waiting for Nabel to say, "This way," and then finally, I'll be able to see him, to hold him.

Then Arnol comes back with the food and invites us to the table.

"So does he sleep all day?" I ask and laugh, as if it were a joke.

"Ana is anxious to meet him," Pol says, and he caresses my hair.

Arnol laughs, but instead of answering, he sets the dish on the table and asks who likes their meat rare and who likes it well done, and soon we're eating again. Nabel is more talkative at dinner. While the men chat, we discover that our lives are similar. Nabel asks me for advice about plants, and then I feel inspired and talk about recipes for fertility. I bring it up as if it were a joke, just a witty remark, but Nabel shows her interest right away, and I discover that she tried them, too.

"And the outings? Hunting all night?" I say, laughing. "The gloves, the backpacks?" For a second, Nabel remains silent, surprised, and then she bursts out laughing with me.

"And the flashlights!" she says, holding her belly. "Those damn batteries that always run out!"

And I, almost in tears:

"And the nets! Pol's net!"

"And Arnol's!" she says. "I can hardly describe it!"

Then the men stop talking: Arnol looks at Nabel; he seems surprised. She hasn't noticed yet: she doubles over with laughter, she pounds the table twice with the palm of her hand, she tries to say something more but can hardly breathe. She looks like she's having fun. I look at Pol—I want to make sure that he's having a good time, too—and then Nabel inhales, laughing so hard she's crying, and says:

"The rifle"—she pounds the table again. "My God, Arnol! If only you'd stopped shooting! We would have found him much sooner . . ."

Arnol looks at Nabel as if he wants to kill her, and then he finally lets out an exaggerated laugh. I look at Pol again; he isn't laughing now. Arnol shrugs his shoulders, resigned, searching for a look of complicity in Pol. After that he gestures as if he were aiming a rifle and firing. Nabel copies him. They do it one more time, aiming at each other, now a little calmer, until they stop laughing.

"Oh, please," Arnol says, and he passes the dish to offer me more meat. "Finally, people we can share this with. Does anyone want seconds?"

"Well, where is he? We want to see him," Pol says, finally.

"You'll see him soon," Arnol says.

"He sleeps a lot," Nabel says.

"All day."

"So then we'll see him sleeping!" Pol says.

"Oh, no, no," Arnol says. "First the dessert Ana made, then a good cup of coffee, and then my Nabel here will get out a few board games. Do you like games of strategy, Pol?"

"But we'd love to see him sleeping."

"No," Arnol says. "I mean, it doesn't make any sense to see him like that. You can see him sleeping any day."

Pol looks at me a second, then he says:

"Well, then, dessert."

I help Nabel clear the table. I take out the cake that Arnol put in the fridge; I carry it to the table and prepare to serve it. Meanwhile, in the kitchen, Nabel busies herself with the coffee.

"The bathroom?" Pol says.

"Oh, the bathroom . . ." Arnol says, and he glances toward the kitchen, maybe looking for Nabel. "It's just that it doesn't work well, and . . ."

Pol waves his hand, to show it doesn't matter.

"Where is it?"

Perhaps involuntarily, Arnol looks toward the hallway. Then Pol gets up and starts walking. Arnol gets up, too.

"I'll go with you."

"It's fine, there's no need," Pol says, already entering the hallway.

Arnol follows him a few steps.

"To the right," he says. "The bathroom door is on the right."

I follow Pol with my gaze until he finally enters the bathroom. Arnol stands behind me for a few seconds, looking toward the hallway.

"Arnol," I say. It's the first time I call him by his name. "Can I serve you?"

"Of course," he says. He looks at me a moment and turns again toward the hall.

"Here you are," I say and slide the first plate toward his place at the table. "Don't worry, he'll take a while."

I smile at Arnol, but he doesn't respond. He returns to the table. He sits in his chair, his back to the hallway. He seems uncomfortable, but finally, he takes his fork and cuts an enormous piece of cake and raises it to his mouth. I look at him, surprised, and keep on serving cake. From the kitchen, Nabel asks how we take our coffee. I'm about to answer, but then I see Pol leave the bathroom silently and cross the hallway to the bedroom. Arnol looks at me, waiting for an answer. I say we love coffee, we'll drink it however she makes it. The light in the bedroom turns on and I hear a muffled noise, like something heavy falling on a carpet. Arnol is about to look toward the hallway, so I say his name:

"Arnol." He looks at me, but he starts to get up.

I hear another noise, and then Pol screams and something falls to the floor, a chair maybe, a heavy piece of furniture falling and things breaking. Arnol runs toward the hallway and grabs the rifle hanging on the wall. I get up to run after Arnol, Pol leaves the room, not letting himself look back. Arnol heads straight at him, but Pol reacts: he knocks the rifle out of Arnol's hands and shoves him aside and runs toward me. I don't understand what's happened, but I let him grab my arm, and we leave. I hear the door close itself slowly behind us, and then I hear it bang open again. Nabel screams. Pol gets into the truck and starts it; I climb in on my side. We put it in reverse, and for a few seconds the headlights illuminate Arnol running toward us.

On the highway, we drive a while in silence, trying to calm down. Pol's shirt is torn; he almost lost his right sleeve, and a few deep scratches bleed on his arm. Soon we approach our house at full speed, and at full speed we drive past it. I look to stop him, but he breathes heavily; his hands grip the wheel. He examines the dark country on either side of the truck and behind us through the rearview mirror. We should slow down. We could die if an animal crosses the road. Then I think that one of them could also cross: our own. But Pol accelerates even faster. From the terror of his lost eyes, it seems like he's counting on that possibility.

TWIN BEDS
BY GIOVANNA RIVERO (BOLIVIA)

The pain of love. Who doesn't know it. The pain of love in your fingertips. Apples rotting when you touched them. Everything rotting. MTV blared at that time, but it didn't make sense of anything. Kenneth Branagh's *Frankenstein* had just been released, and I pressed rewind a thousand times to see the throbbing heart in the orphan monster's hand. The broken chest, an enormous war wound. I took off my blouse to do the same: to break the skin of my chest and pull out my heart, to eat it myself, maybe, and let out a great big belch, just to shock my parents. What the kids did at lunch always made their parents want to retch. On one side, the boy pulls the ugly chicken's wishbone; on the other, the girl makes a wish. He loves me? He loves me not? Cracking bones, that's all.

Then they decided that something was wrong, and someone had to fix it.

"When my daughter was alive, I had breasts just like yours," my roommate said. It was because of the girls in white that we had lost our shame; they used our bodies like quilts that needed to be shaken out every morning to scare off the mites. An eccentricity. Deep down,

I wanted them to tear out my heart. Anyway, they fed us spicy food because the Klonopin had blunted our sense of taste.

"When my girl died," my roommate went on, "my breasts dried out, and they fell off. Look, look . . ." the woman said and lifted her flannel nightgown, which was far too big for her and made her look deranged.

Her nipples were two wilted flowers defeated by grief. Sad nipples. In spite of everything, in spite of the pain of love, I had happy nipples. I liked wearing white T-shirts to share them. My parents didn't like this, either. It's never good for girls to share too much; it works against them, they said, and in a way MTV proved that they were right. Madonna never had a bigger hit than "Like a Virgin." Everything rotted slowly. In some parts of the world, exotic places, worms are an expensive dish.

"Do you think they'll show us a movie tonight?" my roommate asked. Her big nightgown stayed rolled up under her chin. A girl in white came in with the afternoon's cocktail. I had moved on to the yellow pills, but my roommate kept taking the blue ones, drooling on herself in the mornings and recovering a sort of dignity in the afternoon.

"I asked Gio," she said to the girl in white, "if you're going to show us a movie tonight." She pronounced the word "movie" with an "n" at the beginning and without an effort to overcome the imbecility caused by the medicine.

"Pull your nightgown down," the girl in white said. "You look crazy."

My roommate obeyed and stuck out her tongue to take the blue pills. She didn't want any water; she said liquid brought back memories. The girl in white wrinkled her nose. This disgusted the girl in white, this way of expressing the unseen. Losing control wasn't fun, especially when you had to write reports on your depraved charges.

Blood pressure, okay, pupil dilation, okay, nervous reflexes, okay, everything's just fine. "Memories of what?" she asked anyway, exercising those humanoid manners that she had left somewhere outside the gates. There was nothing outside the gates. "Memories of alcohol," my roommate said, as if she were quoting the title of an old tango from an afternoon radio program on one of those stations that had been lost in time. There used to be DJs like that, people who could go out in public without shame after fucking with Mercury, after throwing dirt on your face. They would shit on people like Mercury or Madonna without batting an eye. They deserved to die. But the girls in white did their own thing. "My mouth is watering," my roommate explained again, sending the pills down her throat with the sticky saliva that Klonopin leaves you once you've become its best friend. But the girl in white ordered her to open her mouth again and say, "Aaah," to confirm with her own eyes that she'd swallowed the pills.

"Now it's your turn," she said. Her gaze probed me at the speed of light. "What is this? A party? Button your shirt," she ordered, and she passed me two perfect cylinders the color of ducks, rubber duckies.

The yellow pills traveled down my esophagus. A journey of no return.

Before the girl left with her impeccable whiteness, she explained that yes, they would show us a movie, but only half, and the next day they'd show us the rest, since some of us couldn't handle the medication's side effects and needed to go to bed. Go nighty-night. Sweet dreams. Sweet dreams, souls in agony. Sweet dreams to forget the pain of love.

"*Frankenstein*," I implored.

"Who? What?" The girl in white frowned. The girls in white were easily upset. It was a way of keeping order, a way of making that sure everyone took their medication without saying a word and stretched out their bruised arms for their shots.

"Please, rent *Frankenstein*, the story of the patched man," I begged.

The girl in white said that they were showing a comedy, don't you want to laugh? Forget about patched men. Everyone here is seriously ill.

She finally left, and my roommate started drooling. That afternoon her dignity didn't return. I took off my blouse, raised my arms, and looked at my armpits. The brown hair was too long. I ran my right hand over my left armpit. The hair was soft, but still, it was unacceptable. I could notice it. The pain of love hadn't destroyed my good armpit manners.

"My daughter wasn't nursing then, but my breasts dried up anyway," said the woman who had let her daughter die. The ones who let their children die, they shut them up in homes, where they receive streams of Haldol with open arms, blurring the ceiling, bumping their hips against the walls, drawing hematomas on their wrists because an invisible sadist has said he doesn't love you. Your gums bleed: the girls in white never help you brush your teeth. This woman let her daughter die.

"I want to shave," I said. The only thing I wanted in the world was to shave my armpits. A little of that kind of dignity.

There's a place I don't want to visit. France must be horrible, everyone stinking there. When I was a girl I dreamed of going to Disneyland. My roommate's dead daughter probably dreamed of going to Disneyland, too. At Disney, they say, you go up the roller coaster and raise your arms to scream better. I want to scream like they do in the commercials, without anyone saying, "Look, your armpit hair grew!"

"Shit, all I want is to shave my armpits," I repeated.

In the mornings, I woke up shaking. I would sweat, and the cold breeze would dry my sweat under the sheets. I didn't remember where my hands were to pull up the quilt and wrap myself up. The girls in white locked the doors so that the agonized souls wouldn't try to escape. The nightmares were piled up perfectly in their bedrooms.

One night I dreamed that Frankenstein was my boyfriend. The invisible sadist who swore he wouldn't love me. Love me, my love, love me, even just a little. Frankie smiled without shame. Frankie had borrowed a spirit, and I didn't know whose. Frankie didn't know if he should love me or just fuck me with his dick transplanted from another sadist. I woke up screaming. I screamed until my gums started bleeding again. The girls in white came with their needles and their impeccable discipline. I slept for two days. The nightmares piled up again in some remote region of my brain.

"Shave or tweeze?" my roommate asked. She liked to be precise. All the same, in those twin beds, time was something you could waste. If someone doesn't love you, you can blow away the seconds like soap bubbles; you can spend your whole life popping the bubbles. Nothing will harm you; the bubbles don't hurt; they explode in silence and barely dampen the surfaces where they land.

"Do you have tweezers?" I asked. I was sure my roommate didn't have tweezers. This woman was forty years old and could have been my mother. Mothers never have what their daughters really need. Tweezers, for example.

"No, but nail clippers might work. Tomorrow they cut our nails." She said "nails" with an "m." The saliva was starting to betray her. "But a razor would be better, right?" she said. In the afternoon, her dignity came back slowly, and the words dragged out.

"Yes, a razor would be better. Do you have one?" I asked. The bubbles popped on the ceiling. No one sleeping under lock and key could have a razor. Life denies you these small things. But sometimes it gives them to you. At the end of the hall, a thirteen-year-old boy saw dead people. He spied them through the grate on the air conditioner, and they made faces at him. If someone makes faces at you, answer them. They moved him to a room with a ceiling fan, and then he started to spin like a carousel.

"No, but listen, Gio, let's make a deal." I can't deny that pacts with her worked. This woman asked me for the cotton balls soaked in alcohol that the girls in white left after giving us shots. This woman sucked on these cotton balls like they were candy. In return, sometimes she fixed me up with a blue pill, and I could love Frankenstein just by closing my eyes.

We heard crying coming somewhere in the distance. One of us was throwing a tantrum. Soon the girls in white would go, solicitous, restrained, disciplined to the point of disgust, to fill this person's veins with Haldol.

"A deal? I'm not sure," I said. But I imagined I could also draw a collection of little figures in my pubic hair. Frankie would like it.

"I'll get the razor. I found out they're going to release the guy in the fifth unit. They say he doesn't have insomnia anymore, that he sleeps like an angel. The guy in the fifth unit is my friend." She said "fifth" slowly, with a "v," with that speech defect that hindered our friendship, this thing you could call friendship, those hoarse greetings, "Good morning, Gio. Did you dream of your patched man again?" "Good night, ma'am. Try not to dream about the girl. She's just like Freddy Krueger, deep down. All monsters are the same; don't dream of her." That was friendship.

"The guy in the fifth unit promised me a goodbye present. I can get a razor. You'll like the razor," she said.

"And you'll want some little scoops of ice cream in return." I smiled. My left arm was starting to hurt, and I remembered that I had to lower it. The brown hair would still be there the next day.

"No. I only want to ask you a favor," she said slowly. Her eyes shone like the eyes of a mouse, startled halfway between the kitchen and the dining room.

"A favor . . ."

"Let me touch your nipples." She said "nipples" without effort. Her imbecility had begun to subside; the bubbles flickered above the twin beds.

The cry from the distant room turned into a moan. The girls in white had done their work.

"And tomorrow you'll have your razor," my roommate said. "I promise."

"A razor wouldn't be a bad idea," I answered. "A razor could save your life."

"And get you out of this hell, so you never have to swallow those damn foxes' pills again," she said, overcoming her stupid "f," stretching her hungry hands toward me, like a friendly ghost who wishes you the best. The best of the best.

The yellow dose had given me its usual effect: a pleasant nausea, an acceptance of things, the end of things. I approached her and raised my arms like Madonna, like Frankie, like Krueger, when everything was lost.

Her mouse eyes glittered. One step, two steps. Three steps between the twin beds!

All I wanted in the world was to shave my armpits.

FISH SPINE
BY SANTIAGO NAZARIAN
(BRAZIL)

Hau turned the faucet on with careful fingers. He would have to turn it off after washing his hands. They smelled like fish, fresh fish, like something rotting. Always. Scales on his fingers. He didn't want to contaminate the faucet. He would have to turn it off again, with clean hands. He washed them.

He bent over the sink and felt his back ache. He bent over the sink and felt his spine. He placed his hands on his back; he straightened up before the mirror. He looked into his eyes. He saw himself. No scales. No spine. No reflection of fish in his slanted eyes, in his adolescent face. Hau remained the same, despite his hands.

He took a hand off his back and turned off the faucet. He brought his fingers to his nose. He smelled. Still there. His spine hurt. The fish screamed. His slanted eyes squeezed even tighter before the mirror.

The whole day. Every morning. He helped his parents at their market stall. Knife on spine, fish on ice, lowered eyes, like his voice, though he spoke Portuguese better than they. He wrapped. Newspaper. Black ink. Stained fingers, sinking in the water. Frozen fingers, wrapping the fish, packing the scraps, the end of his adolescence.

Hau spent the whole morning waiting for his reflection in the mirror. His fingers under his nose. Soap, vanilla, to remove a daily life that wasn't his. Only a job. Only family. It wouldn't contaminate his poetry. In his fingers, it wouldn't contaminate his paper. He wrapped. He packed. He folded origami in his free time.

For her. When she passed. She lowered her eyes. She lowered her head. He hoped she didn't see, even if she felt. Even if she felt the smell of the stall miles away. She always passed by in a hurry. She never looked at him. Or maybe it was he who lowered his eyes. And she couldn't perceive him.

They met each other later. In the evening. When she asked him what he did. Or what was he going to do? Philosophy. Together in class, waiting for the entrance exam. Together at the bus stop, waiting for the bus to arrive. And goodnight. Tomorrow I wake up early to help my father.

They didn't go much further. They didn't give each other kisses or caresses, but they said hello. They shook hands and their fingers touched. He hoped his fingers didn't denounce him. The smell of fish. Everything in its place at the end of the day. Until dawn again, when the fish awaited him.

Brushing his teeth, he heard the first birdsongs; he looked at his own reflection in the mirror, foaming at the mouth. He spit. He brought his fingers to his mouth. He no longer felt his spine. At least the pain and smell didn't build up day after day; they disappeared after work without leaving long-term effects. One day his past would erase itself forever. And not even he would remember what fish smelled like.

Perfume. On a Friday night, to see his friends, to see her, until the morning. At a bar, over beers, they would celebrate a birthday. It wasn't his. It wasn't hers. But they would be together, and that was what mattered. He would be on the left, with the boys. Laughing, drinking, distilled, fermented. She would be there in front, with the women, beckoning, perfuming the atmosphere with colorful cocktails. Sitting on the edge of the street, in the gutter, where the market stalls would go up later.

The alcohol opened up his appetite, and the menu opened up his spine, with fish, dried cod, cod cakes, one piece per couple. A piece of provolone. Pies. Ketchup. Mayonnaise. Napkins to clean your fingers.

She pulled off a feat. She only used one. One napkin and she wiped her lipstick. Only one napkin and she handled. The mayonnaise. Ketchup. Provolone, pies, and fish spines, cod cakes. He accompanied the boys; he gathered a mountain of paper. Their napkins with ketchup, mayonnaise. He looked at her and swallowed. He looked at her and everything sweetened. He cleaned his hands on a stack of napkins.

Such women are needed, to make boys behave. Women are needed, so that boys use napkins. To drink a little more, to smile and hide, to hide the fish spines in their teeth. To hide the scales between their fingers. He looked at her and hid behind the paper. A piece, folded, origami.

She was there through it all on the right side of the table. Beside her friends, smiling with composure. The boys mocking. He, working. His fingers for her. His fingers shaking. His fingers working. His sweetened fingers, on paper, transforming into poetry all that he felt.

What did he feel? The gutter calling him. His friends calling for a drink. Beer, fermented, going down the wolves' mouths, fish spines. Hours later he would be there, his fingers frozen. With his fingers in the fish, on that same street, wrapping the women's dinners in paper, the dinners of the mothers, the mothers of their girls.

And poetry would just be black ink. The news would be mayonnaise, stained, on newsprint, on fish spines. He would just be another one. Squinting at the market. Eyes lowered like his voice, quiet.

He would work for the fish, fresh, dead, the true interest of all the women who approached him. They wouldn't sense the perfume on his neck. They wouldn't sense the pain in his spine.

With his fingers working quickly he concluded, though drunk, a job well done. Fish spine. Bar napkin. Origami. Perfect. Figures and poems for her, on a stainless piece of paper. A paper fish. "To dive with you."

She took the fish in her hands, with a smile on her lips. It was lovely. Origami. Her smile. It made the whole market sink beneath the sea and the marine life prevail. She brought it to her mouth, to her lipstick, and kissed it. "Oh, how funny, it even smells like fish."

HYPOTHETICALLY BY ANTONIO UNGAR (COLUMBIA)

1.

Four in the morning. My friend Pierre sits at his desk and watches the wet sidewalk shine through his dirty window. A cup of cold coffee sits atop a book. Pierre has stopped drafting an article on film, and he's bored. His room is on the second floor of a house that's identical to all the others in this damp, dark, miserable neighborhood. Its floor is made of old Formica; its stained walls used to be grey; it has a ramshackle endurance. The bed is undone. A light bulb hangs from a cord above the desk. Through the window, under the city's icy winter, there is a street where the trash builds up and drunks vomit, where the fighting dogs shit and everything freezes fast. Through the window, the city is London: a city of miserable men where it never stops drizzling ice, a city of crazy old ladies who walk endlessly. A city split by a huge, slow, black river.

Pierre is twenty-five, very skinny, hunchbacked, with long hair. Now he plays with the ashtray; he distracts himself thinking of how he will spend the monthly salary he earns writing articles for a mediocre magazine. He imagines the coming winter, the days until spring. Suddenly, he hears a man scream. He pricks up his ears like the poor dog he is: more screams, blows. He stands up, goes to the window. It's happening in the house next door: it's a fight between the Barnes', the Barnes brothers, his neighbors.

The oldest, Freddy, weighs a hundred kilos of muscle and is the pride of the neighborhood. One year his team won the national youth rugby championship; he can drink seventeen pints of beer in a row. Furthermore, he can flip a car with his own hands, he alone, and every time he does it, turns over a car parked poorly on his street, all the neighbors clap and cheer as only the English can clap and cheer: by leaning their heads far forward, secreting a little more unswallowed saliva as their English eyes smile subtly, and emitting an indistinct sound from their mouths. Freddy's brother, Teddy, is considerably more alcoholic. He is a cow of more than 120 kilos, crippled by a double hip fracture, which was caused by a traffic accident that was caused, in turn, by his perpetual drunkenness. The accident also left him with a useless eye, a slowness of movement and speech, and a constant drool which his brother Freddy diligently cleans up.

Pierre hears how Freddy Barnes shouts blasphemies that echo off the walls as Teddy moans. The two are in their room of broken sofas and photos of naked women, visible from the street. Pierre hears Freddy smash a chair against the wall, hears him break something that sounds like a plate. He hears poor Teddy, with a voice that sounds like he's been chewing on grass for a thousand years, lost in a wetter time, a less clear time, who defends himself the best he can, repeating senseless words. The silences grow longer, constricting the air before every explosion. After half an hour, Pierre understands: a complete sentence leaves Freddy Barnes's wet mouth and explains it all. Freddy wants to wreck every last piece of furniture in the house and scream out his goddamn lungs and, if necessary, kill once and for all this lump of useless flesh that is Teddy Barnes, because a roll of bills has disappeared—a roll that had been growing thicker for a long time in a covered cookie tin on top of the fridge. Pierre hears how Teddy moans, hears him crawl across the room, chased by Freddy's insults, hears him snivel and fall with all his weight on the yellow sofa. Now Teddy keeps talking, but louder. Now he assembles longer strings of words, meaningless phrases that have lain in his big, wet, cow's brain since the time his mother was alive. From those depths he says things like *No no no no you shouldn't drink so much tonight, Freddy, go back to Dorham what would your father do Freddy don't drink so much.*

Ad infinitum. Pierre, my friend, listens to the brothers through the wall, paralyzed by his poor dog's curiosity, by that morbid fear which makes him smile. Suddenly he remembers his new gadget, a technological wonder that's been resting in its box in his apartment for a week. He takes out a minuscule microphone and proceeds to hang it from a nail stuck next to the Barnes' window. Five meters of cable connect the microphone to a recorder, whose laser will burn a little disc and register clearly each one of the rips and cries and blows of the beasts in the house next door. Two miniature speakers will allow Pierre to hear everything better. He looks at the ensemble with a smile, presses the appropriate button, and returns to the window.

Freddy is very drunk. The twenty lost bills amounted to two thousand pounds, all the capital the family had to buy a new fridge, a damn motorcycle, to live off the rest of the month. Now there's only an empty tin that smells like oranges on top of the fridge. Freddy knows that if Teddy didn't take the money, he at least saw who took it. He knows very well that his brother is hiding something. If he hasn't responded from the start, if he moans and sways and stares at the floor like a child, like a madman, it's because he knows something. And if it's not Teddy, someone else in the neighborhood has the damn roll of hundred-pound bills, and Freddy Barnes is going to find out who, even if he has to beat Teddy and drag his body through all the rooms of the goddamn house.

Every few minutes Freddy's voice's can be heard, like a portal out of the black recording box, as it rises and lunges and screams big words, very drunk. (He must have a bottle in his hand, he must be circling Teddy, staring into his eyes, screaming at his face, practically spitting on him.) Then, there are long lapses of silence. Maybe Freddy sits in a corner, stares at the red walls and at his brother's body. He sees all the days of the month will be the same, now that they'll have to live without a single pound. Pierre imagines Freddy found out about the cookie tin much earlier, that he searched the whole house and found nothing. That he questioned Teddy until he started to scream, that Teddy kept his mouth closed and crawled into his drawer of autism. He imagines that Freddy then went to the pub, sat alone at the bar, grunted, and drank all the gin he could until closing time, still unable to fathom the loss of his savings. That because of this he's now turned into a beast, that because of this he's going to find all his money or kill his brother Teddy Barnes, once and for all.

Freddy Barnes's words stab desperately as he shrieks about the past, about the accident that left Teddy crippled, God, his goddamn drinking habit, money. The goddamn money that has to appear before dawn, for the good health of Christ. He talks, alone, practically sobbing, for more than half an hour, until weariness starts to defeat him. Through the tiny speakers he sounds exhausted, impotent, ready to cry. He sounds ready to pass out on the carpet from drunkenness. Pierre imagines the two brothers waking up the next day: more tired and just as poor, fat, and abandoned. Hungry, alone. It seems all finally is coming to an end.

Pierre imagines Freddy in a corner, sitting, completely drunk, crying like he's never cried before, defeated by his shitty life, by his shitty house, by his brother who's turned into an idiot, who bellows to himself with words that aren't his, with the words of their dead mother, buried in a cemetery between two highways under the fog, and he imagines that the twenty hundred-pound bills will never appear in the orange-scented cookie tin. What Pierre does not expect is for Freddy to suddenly rise from his silence. He crosses the wood floor of his room with giant steps. He topples a table covered with plates as he passes. Wordlessly, without preamble, he lifts, with his big rugby champion arms, the TV, a monstrosity from the early 80s. With this stone box on top of his head he crosses the room, concentrating, a serious drunk, and he throws it through the window, and Pierre does not expect what happens next: the stone box turns back into a TV when it smashes on the ground with an explosion of glass, circuits, cables, red and green bits, contacts, crystals, fuses.

Once again there's silence. My friend Pierre grows more frightened. Through his window, he could see the glass of the house next door break, and now he looks at the television fragments growing wetter on the sidewalk. A minute of silence. Pierre imagines Teddy understanding, slowly, very slowly, that there will be no more television, that the television has left. There is a continuous cry, long, low. Suddenly there is a desperate scream, like that of a bear pierced by a lance, like the headless monster that is Teddy Barnes, practically a whale when he stands up on his two little legs, which have not walked for the last ten years. Teddy lurches across the room and throws himself down the stairs.

Then Freddy starts to scream, *Damned Irish dog Ted Barnes don't even think about running you cowardly rat because I'll make your brains fly you big son of a thousand bitches damned idiot, you've caused me enough harm.* Freddy continues his litany as he goes after his brother's noise, down the stairs, very slowly, barely staying up on his drunken feet. Pierre knows the house next door—it's identical to his—so he knows that Teddy is going to the kitchen. Through the bathroom window, standing on the toilet, Pierre can see Teddy open all the cabinets, desperate, breaking everything, knocking everything over before his brother makes it down the stairs, preceded by every insult he knows. Pierre sees Teddy manage to open a drawer, sees his trembling hands take out something black that weighs between his fingers, sees him go back the way he came in, toward the hallway. An instant of silence.

Then Freddy Barnes's battle cry can be heard as it spreads through the garden and sounds in the black speakers. Pierre hears a chair smash. Suddenly, a detonation. Heavy, huge, resounding through the neighborhood. Pierre feels his knees buckle. He puts a hand on the edge of the sink. More than five seconds of silence. A huge detonation, another, makes him grip the sink more tightly, and he loses himself in the empty streets. Then, total silence. Pierre stays quiet, lost. Afterward, slowly, with blurred vision and balance as unsteady as a drunk's, he returns to his room. On the way he imagines, without knowing why, the city's empty sidewalks, the stoplights flickering yellow under the rain. Smoke leaving a chimney. Below, in the Barnes' door, the lock turns. Pierre slowly moves from his desk and approaches the window. A huge man opens the door. Pierre can see his round, blonde, balding head. The man moans, stumbles. He staggers toward the street. His body seems ready to fall on its face; a dirty, white T-shirt covers his huge belly. The man has a revolver in his hand.

He is the younger of the Barnes. From above, his body seems bigger, fatter, balder, whiter. He trembles; he totters. He reaches the edge of the sidewalk and lets himself fall on his ass, with his feet to the street. He takes the weapon in both hands between his legs. He rocks back and forth, back and forth, the weapon squeezed between his hands, between his bent legs. He looks straight ahead and rocks, his back to Pierre. He looks at the posters, the trash, the wall of the school. He understands nothing. No one has come out to see what happened; no one wants to know. It will take the police more than an hour to arrive. From his window, Pierre keeps watching this man who rocks and moans loudly, who cries, growing wet under the drizzle, lost to everything.

2.

For half an hour Teddy Barnes sits on the sidewalk under the drizzle, observed by Pierre from his closed window. Perhaps a neighbor has appeared; perhaps someone has called the police. But the police must be very busy tonight, because Teddy keeps rocking from his waist, back and forth, under the drizzle. And Pierre keeps watching him.

Pierre has had time to think of many things. Without noticing, watching this man on the sidewalk, he has thought about himself. He has realized, sitting there, that he is alone in the world. And he has realized that he is free. He always has been free. And he can do what he wants. He can leave this fucking city and become someone real, alive. If he wanted. Someone real. He thinks he's going to get up from this desk, for once and for all, right now. He's going to pack a rucksack with all his clothes. He's going to take all his money out of the bank and start walking, now. He's going to walk past this bilious body that's still crying on the sidewalk. He's going to walk to the train station and once and for all get out of here. He'll dedicate his life to what he always dreamed of doing.

He'll live by stealing; he'll live in the parks. Maybe it would be best to buy a revolver. Use it to hold up a store, to survive. Or go to Australia, where every meter he treads will be unknown territory. He'll dedicate himself to theft. And wandering. Until they kill him. He'll make love to a dark woman, maybe, in an abandoned hut in the desert. He'll get drunk with truck drivers at a gas station. He'll bet all his money on cards, and he'll lose it. He'll spend a night with an Aborigine in an Australian jail.

Pierre hears the sound of sirens outside. The immense man, lost, rocks more slowly, soaked by the drizzle. His neck is rigid and the pistol remains between his legs. He keeps crying. A policeman stops ten meters away; he knows thirty rifles are aimed at the man's head. He spreads his legs and screams, *Throw down your weapon and put your hands behind your neck.* When he's a meter away he points the barrel of the gun at Teddy's temple. He stares him down. He starts to kneel at his side; he puts his free hand under the giant's bent legs. He clutches the weapon between his fingers. The giant does not let it go. The policeman pulls his thick fingers from the homicidal weapon. He slides it across the pavement, far from the assassin.

Teddy Barnes looks the policeman in the eyes, slowly, knowing nothing. Who he himself is. What he is. What he's doing here. He turns, stares straight ahead. A van approaches, rattling down the street. Ten armed agents jog behind it. Pierre sees how they hoist Teddy's dead weight, how they turn his neck, how they prop him up in the back of the van. Two policemen get in.

3.

Now, a month later, in the dining room of a mutual friend, Pierre sits with a plate of fish and a tall glass of white wine. He smiles. He has, in his right hand, his girlfriend's hand. His girlfriend is not pretty. He looks into her eyes for a minute, gets up, clears his throat, and asks for everyone's attention. He wants to share the big news of the night. The big news of the night is that the previous week he'd been promised two more years of work at the mediocre magazine for which he writes. They will continue to pay him the same salary for the same commentaries on film. He and his girlfriend are going to rent an apartment in Mainstream, close to the house where his bachelor pad is now. He's thinking of becoming an English citizen.

When Pierre finishes speaking, he looks at all of us, radiant. He raises a toast. To his girlfriend. To us. We stand up and look into his small eyes, eyes like those of a happy dog, into his smiling mouth, at the gleam of saliva that illuminates his lower lip. We toast. When he sits down, his little hands detach from the cup and from his girlfriend's skin. They pick up the silverware and skewer another piece of fish. He carries the bite to his lips, and while he chews, he passes a low, horizontal gaze over the table, never ceasing to smile. His gaze stops at me. He looks across the table, as if he were asking something. I can only incline my head and congratulate him, raising my cup, rehearsing the finest of my smiles.

THE LAST CORRIDO BY JUAN GABRIEL VÁSQUEZ (COLOMBIA)

I took the job because the pay was good, but more so because I'd gotten the notion—probably absurd—that a week-long bus trip would prove at last whether I could live in Spain, or whether I'd mistaken my fate once more, and I'd have to pack my bags for the fourth time and seek another place to settle down. The plan was to follow a Mexican corrido band on tour through the peninsula, write a story about them, and publish it in Mexico as part of an homage to the band, or rather, to their thirty-five years of existence. So on July 17, 2001, I met with one of their managers, a man with an enormous double chin and a shirt that was much too small. I got a laminated card to hang around my neck (with my name, misspelled, and my title: companion). That same night, a little before nine, I got to the Razzmatazz Room in Barcelona. There was a poster by the door, next to a cage where a girl waved her hands to show the tickets were sold out. The poster read: THE MÁRQUEZ BROTHERS, and underlined, ONE NIGHT ONLY.

Outside the day was still bright. I had been told this was one of the worst summers in recent years. Inside, though, the world was black, and the temperature dropped brutally. The concert had already begun in that windowless room, whose walls absorbed the light, whose air conditioning tried its best to confuse or neutralize the dense odor of sweat. I leaned against the bar, at a prudent distance from the audience, with their jumping and their Mexican flags the size of bed sheets, and I waited. When the last corrido ended, a woman got on stage, took her bra off, and gave it to the singer. The singer, a young man with a sparse mustache but a tough voice, took it, hung it carefully from the microphone (under the black lights the white lace turned an intense violet), and then disappeared behind the dressing room door. I followed him. I made my way through a group of bikers; I saw "Hell's Angels" written on their backs and smelled their belched beer breath, and I asked myself what a group like that could be doing at a concert like this. As I walked down the narrow hallway, lit poorly by a solitary neon bulb, I was greeted, or rather intercepted, by the same man who'd given me the card. "Let them change," he said. "You're not going to catch them in their underpants." I saw the musicians in the back, through a half-open door. I noticed that they didn't look at each other; they didn't talk. They moved as if each one were alone in front of the mirror, changing their shirts, running combs through their hair. And the thing that happened, happened afterward, when the audience had left.

The floor was still littered with plastic cups and trampled beer cans. On the bar, near the corner where I'd leaned when I arrived, there was a cheap paper tablecloth and an array of pitchers of water and soda and sandwiches and tortillas wrapped in aluminum foil. While we ate, the manager (Alonso was his name) told me that the band was formed in 1968, that they were all brothers, except Ricardo. I asked who Ricardo was. "Ricardo is our vocalist," Alonso said. "He's as old as the Márquez Brothers' first record. See him over there? He's the son of the guy next to him." The guy next to him was one of the musicians, the only one who didn't have a moustache. They told me his name, but I didn't remember it then. I saw them, compared them, and the truth is, they seemed to be the same age, not father and son. Then I asked an innocent question, a question with merely informative intentions, a question which—it seemed to me—diverged from the direct manner in which we'd been talking on our way over. "And who sang before?" Just at that moment, one of the bikers came over, forced a disposable camera on me, and went to stand next to the band. I took his picture and watched him take out a wrinkled piece of paper to ask for autographs. I heard him explain, while he fidgeted with a studded bracelet on his wrist, that he started listening to the band in San Francisco and had all of their records, from the time Ernesto was in the band.

"Who's Ernesto?" I asked.

"The oldest brother," Alonso said. "The one who created the group."

"And he's not here?"

"His father was paralyzed in the sixties. Ernesto put the band together purely to survive. You were asking who sung before? It was him, Ernesto. This group was his life."

"The greatest of all time," the biker said.

"Yes," Alonso said. "The greatest." He asked the biker to leave, putting a hand on his jacket's insignia and pushing him away diplomatically. Then he said to me: "But we're tired now. We're going to sleep."

We went out into the Barcelona night around eleven, into the hot wind, and Alonso told me where I should show up at ten the next morning to leave for Valencia. I walked home. Feeling strangely excited, I poured myself a gin and tonic and opened all the windows, the ones that opened to the courtyard as well as those that opened to the plaza and its palm trees, and then I began to read the press kit. That's how I learned that five years earlier, the Márquez brothers had gone on another tour through Spain, a tour identical—in its cities, set lists, practically in dates—to the one that just began with me on board. Five years ago the tour began in Barcelona, too; five years ago they went on to Valencia; five years ago they stopped in three cities and ended the tour in Cartagena, at an international festival of music which was broadcast live to all of Latin America, as would happen this time, too, no doubt. The only difference between the tours then and now was the presence of Ernesto Márquez. I looked in the press kit for a photo of Ernesto Márquez, the band's founder, the man who, because of his father's paralysis, recruited his brothers (guitar aficionados, weekend accordionists) to save the family from hunger. But I found nothing. The man who was no longer there, I thought. Ernesto Márquez, the missing.

On the evening in Valencia, in 1996, Ricardo Márquez was talking with the sound engineers before the concert, checking on the speakers and the equipment, when he saw Ernesto walking alone among the trees in the park. The idea of an outdoor concert had been his, so it seemed natural that Ernesto would want to take a walk around the stage, perhaps trying to anticipate where the groupies, who they never lacked, would enter. But he wasn't paying attention; rather, he walked with his head down. Every once in a while he lifted a hand to his throat, and once Ricardo saw him lift his face and look to the treetops as if a leaf had fallen on his graying head, and Ricardo knew that he was making a tremendous effort to spit. He recognized that movement, since he'd seen it before (after the Barcelona concert, for instance). He stepped down from the platform where the sound equipment was and thought that they'd need to light those stairs better, to keep someone from tripping on a cable and sending the whole show to hell. It was already dark, and all through the grounds the crickets' racket exploded almost simultaneously. Ricardo looked at his watch: there were just a few hours left until the concert, and Ernesto had started to spit.

Ricardo got to the two old trailers where the organizers set up the dressing rooms, where all the Márquez brothers, except Ernesto, were doing their warm-ups, all of them pacing their rooms like caged animals, from one side to the other, all of their ears covered with yellow headphones. They moved their heads, they stuck out their tongues, they screamed those warm-ups that Ricardo knew by heart, because, among other reasons, he could sing the warm-ups better than they. He looked for his father through the windows and rapped his knuckles on the metal wall of the trailer. His father took off his headphones, annoyed at the interruption. "I'm looking for Uncle Ernesto," he said.

"He's in his dressing room," his father said.

"He's not there."

"He should be there. It's almost time."

"He's not there," Ricardo said. "I just looked."

His father left the Walkman on a plastic table and left, and Ricardo saw he was already dressed up for the concert, in a jacket and blue leather pants with sequins that spit out gobs of light when he walked past a spotlight. They walked up to the corner of the trailers, where they could see the park without being seen by the audience that had already filled the grounds. Ricardo saw that his father was beginning to worry (his hands nervously caressing his embroidered flanks, his epaulettes) when his uncle Ernesto appeared. "What are you doing?" Ricardo's father said. "Aren't you warming up?" And Ernesto answered in a perfect octosyllable, like the ones he wrote in his corridos: "He who's a rooster always sings." Ricardo took a couple steps backward and saw the two exchange three phrases he knew perfectly. His father asked Ernesto if he felt well. His uncle said yes, why shouldn't he, and then somehow protested the vigilance he'd been subjected to since the last concert. And then his father would say something like *it hasn't been since only the last concert* and then *what's happening with you began a while ago* and then *you've been like this too long* and then *one day your throat is going to give out.* They must have said all that, because there, standing in front of his brother, Ernesto put his headphones on, and with a movement of his finger on the Walkman, he obliterated the entire world, with its demands, its worries, its threats. Ricardo's father stayed there, talking, watching Ernesto's efforts cause him evident pain (to his vocal chords, his larynx), but the quality of his voice didn't reflect that pain, and so the pain served to prove nothing. Ernesto Márquez went into his dressing room (you couldn't hear the warm-ups anymore), and he only came out when it was time to take the stage.

Ricardo watched the concert from the wings. He liked to do this, and during outdoor concerts he liked to get down in the middle of a song and walk behind the stage, where the world, perhaps through its violent contrast with the lights and the music, seemed unusually dark and secret, almost peaceful. He walked from one end to the other, and during these journeys he thought his destiny was on stage, in front of the microphone, in that space that Ernesto Márquez's voice filled during these moments. As he was growing up, Ricardo had admired that throat, which now seemed to beat a retreat, which had begun to betray the thirty years of forced labor, which had maintained his family and to which everyone owed gratitude, but which every day was growing less able to bear the demands of a tour. From the wings, Ricardo watched how Ernesto Márquez went up to the third level of the stage and then lowered himself, enveloped in artificial smoke, singing "The Powerful," even though Ernesto knew, just like everyone, that breathing that smoke wasn't good for his throat. Ricardo thought he would tell him when the concert was over, because much more than the vocalist's prestige depended on the health of that voice, and Ricardo, like any other Márquez, had a right to protect his family.

So afterward, while the technicians picked up the equipment and the makeup artists packed their makeup, when the Márquez brothers had sat down to rest (to enjoy the night's cool air, without the leather suits that made them sweat like donkeys), Ricardo made a seemingly casual remark about what he'd observed earlier. He didn't say it in so many words, but the image that floated through the night was that of a gray-haired man who lifted his hand to his throat and walked a little stooped, perhaps through the effect of the accordion's weight; a man who lifted his face to spit, without feeling any pain; a man respected by everyone, but who put the band's reputation at risk every year. With every concert, the moment drew closer when his voice, simply through the years of wear and tear, through the appearance of nodules or polyps or other, more serious enemies, would shut off like a light in the middle of a storm. Ernesto Márquez didn't answer. Instead, he stood up and walked slowly around the big plastic table. He got to where his nephew sat and gave him a violent slap in the face, and then another, until his brothers grabbed his arms. And in the silence that followed, before the gazes of the whole group, Ernesto Márquez raised his voice. "I still have songs inside me," he said. Then he addressed Ricardo: "And you, let me tell you: it's going to cost you much more to get me off the stage."

Everyone got on the bus.

During the six hour journey from Valencia to Madrid, I didn't stop thinking for a moment that the bus on which I traveled was repeating or tracing, with certain small differences in dates, the same route the other bus had covered five years earlier. (With two particularities: a passenger then was absent now; a passenger that didn't exist then was now present.) It was our third day together, and my spontaneous, almost involuntary inquisitions from the first night at the Razzmatazz hadn't left me in good standing. The Márquez brothers didn't seem the least bit eager to facilitate the writing of my story, neither through their answers to my questions—which were absent-minded, spare, more given to closing doors than opening them—nor through the simple fact of their company, which they withheld from me, no doubt from a certain fear that I would end up asking about Ernesto Márquez. When I got one of them to talk, it was to discuss inanities, and that's how I learned that Alonso had a dog, Chiquita, that he'd picked up off the street, and that he didn't plan to crossbreed her, because her body was too small and it wasn't designed to have more than two puppies. Alonso didn't want a larger breed to impregnate her and cause complications in birth. "You have to take care of God's creatures," he told me. "Or perhaps you haven't heard 'Dogs and Children'?" I told him no, I hadn't heard "Dogs and Children." Sitting in the back, Alonso wasn't too surprised. He even tolerated, with some paternalism, that I asked if he was talking about a corrido.

That evening, on the Madrid stage, the Márquez brothers had to perform in suit and tie—since our arrival they'd been filming a few scenes for a DVD of the tour—in spite of the fact that the temperature never dropped below ninety degrees. But to say suit and tie is a euphemism, since the Márquez brothers wore starched collars and double-breasted jackets and gold cufflinks and flared pants that Hugo, the drummer, fastened with adhesive tape so the hem wouldn't catch in the pedals (the same tape the musicians used to stick the set list to the stage.) That night I confirmed my first impression: watching them set up for the concert on the black stage, it was impossible not to feel an emptiness between them, a misplaced piece. As Ricardo and his father went over the lyrics on a laptop they'd set on the floorboards, Ricardo put a hand on his father's shoulder to keep his balance as he crouched or stood after confirming a change in rhythm or a modified line, with his finger on the screen. Those gestures, in any other situation, would have seemed caring or intimate to me. But they were contaminated by something imprecise, and it was impossible not to notice.

It was also impossible not to notice that my story was falling apart every minute I spent with the band. Suddenly I saw myself walking without a fixed path toward the concert grounds, like a guest who's not welcome at a party. The grounds were a kind of paved, walled courtyard, more like a nineteenth-century wall designed for use by a firing squad than an atmosphere conducive to the Márquez brothers' kitschy lines (their hymns to the immigrant, their stories of ruined love in Tijuana.) At any rate, the musicians' dressing rooms were in a trailer, practically leaning against the wall, like a sad animal. On the other side of the courtyard, some twenty meters away, a few Mexicans had set up a truck with food brought directly from Guadalajara, according to what they said. It was a kind of model stagecoach from which they sold soda, chips, tortillas, Corona. The truck had an inscription, which I crouched to read better:

The owner is out
He went to go beat up
A freeloading lout

I was doing this when Ricardo Márquez came over. He was wearing a blue leather suit, and a pair of headphones hung around his neck like jewelry. I stood up and said hello. I saw him ask for a bottle of water, though he kept three liters in his dressing room at all times. I suppose that what he wanted just then wasn't the bottle of water. "Was it like this five years ago?" I asked him. "Was the truck here, too?"

Ricardo smiled. "No, the truck wasn't."

"How about the rest?"

"The rest was exactly the same," he said. "You're Colombian, right?"

"Right."

"Once we played in Cali. But I wasn't singing yet."

"Ernesto was singing."

"Yes. Ernesto was singing."

We weren't able to talk more, because right then Ricardo's father let out a scream from the trailer door. "Ricardo!" he yelled, and we thought something had happened. And then: "Do you have a marker?" Ricardo nodded; he said something about his jacket and a pocket, and after a little while his father came out to us. "What's your father's name?" I whispered to Ricardo. "Aurelio," he said. Aurelio walked as if he were in a hurry, carrying an accordion in his arms.

"It's a fan's," he said. "He wants everyone's autographs."

Aurelio pulled up a chair, rested the accordion on his lap like a baby, and scribbled a dedication on the white keys, saying to no one, "Let's see if it has any music." And then, while he opened and closed the bellows, he explained to me (he explained to no one, but it was clear that his explanation was meant for me) that he knew some Colombian *vallenatos*, but he'd left his *vallenato* accordion at home, because it was too heavy to carry on long trips. "It purrs like a kitten," he said about the autographed accordion, passing the marker to Ricardo.

"Where should I sign?" Ricardo asked.

"Wait, let's go over there, so everyone can sign."

"Let me sign, and you can bring it over," Ricardo said.

Aurelio said no, they needed to go to the dressing rooms, it was time to warm up, everyone was there, didn't Ricardo like to spend time with his family anymore, and then he let out a laugh that echoed through the stone courtyard. "Well, see you later," Ricardo said, and

I said, later. And then I thought a singer never drinks cold water before a concert. He wants to talk to me, I thought. He wants to tell me something.

Ricardo entered one of the empty boxes on the second floor. He sat on the velvet chair and looked at the inscription on the ceiling: HONOR TO THE BELLES ARTES floated between the clouds and angels with trumpets, near a chandelier that threatened to break loose and fall on the mezzanine. That afternoon, while all his uncles were taking tours of Málaga, Ricardo decided to stay at the hotel. Then, nervous, as if Ernesto Márquez's slaps in the face still hurt and kept him from lying in his bed, he went down to the lobby, asked questions, got a map, and walked, through the afternoon's murderous heat, to the opera house where the concert would take place that night. He was sweating when he got there (his last name written on a plastic card was enough for the doorman to let him in the back), and now the sweat made his pants stick to his skin. Even worse was the sensation that his skin was sticking to the velvet. Ricardo put up with it: he didn't stand up, he didn't go back downstairs, though now he began to hear noise behind the stage, the metal creaking of a door, three meters tall, the motor of a truck that backed up to unload the lights and sound equipment, the engineers' directions—that goes here, put that there. Today he didn't feel like lending them a hand. Today he would stay at the margins.

He stayed at the margins while the technicians set everything up. He stayed at the margins while he watched the band arrive little by little, pace the wood floor, and tune their instruments. He stayed at the margins through the rehearsal, listening, practically hidden in the box, never sure whether the Márquez brothers noticed his presence, since they never looked up and the lights shone in their faces. Ricardo didn't take his gaze off of Ernesto Márquez, who dressed in thin pants, a short-sleeved shirt and the worn-out moccasins of a penniless tourist. Ricardo noticed he'd begun to despise him, and the more he watched him the more he despised him. A couple times he closed his eyes, only to search the singer's voice for the signs of wear and pain. He realized he liked to imagine that pain, the clearing of this throat that he heard (that everyone heard) the night before, the swelling his father detected (and then everyone detected) after the concert in Madrid. Yes, that's how it went: after the last lines of the last corrido in Madrid, after Ernesto sang, *The friends from your land / cause you problems and pain / You feel like a stranger / Life hurts you again*, Ricardo noticed what all the others noticed: the reflex of the hand that moved toward his throat, that repented halfway and slipped back under the accordion strap. Afterward, in the trailer, his father had gone up to Ernesto and put an affectionate hand on his throat. "You're swollen," he'd said.

And all through the Málaga concert, all through the sad show of mummies who went to hear corridos in their velvet chairs, paralyzed below the waist, Ricardo heard the songs in his uncle Ernesto's voice and entertained himself by imagining the qualities of this inflammation and asking himself if there was pain, how much pain. Ernesto, like the best of his kind, knew every trick there was to manipulate his voice, to dodge the most difficult notes in a way that didn't seem obvious or coarse, but this wasn't the important thing: what was important, as Ricardo had told his father on the bus from Madrid to Málaga, was that little by little, Ernesto was renouncing certain traits that years before (months before) defined him. Little by little, he stopped being the Márquez Brothers' vocalist. He was losing his identity, and the group's identity was starting to go with him. "Don't be insolent," his father had told him. "He started the group. He is its identity." "Do you really believe that?" Ricardo said. His father didn't answer, which, to Ricardo, was no doubt the best answer. As Ricardo remembered that conversation, reliving those words in his distracted head, he felt a kind of curious emptiness next to him in the concert hall that he hadn't felt before, something like a shift in the air, and it took him a couple of seconds to notice that Ernesto Márquez had missed a note, or rather, that his throat had refused to give it to him.

Ernesto Márquez stepped away from the microphone. Ricardo thought: He's going to cough. He's going to cough and the world is going to end.

But Ernesto took a deep breath and grimaced with effort; his eyes watered. The band came out in his defense, singing the rest of the corrido in chorus and saying goodbye at the end (doing what they had never done: ending a concert one song short.) The mummies, of course, didn't notice a thing, or it seemed that they hadn't, since just a few minutes later they thronged the steps at the theater's main entrance, and when the Márquez brothers came out they were mobbed by hands holding out CDs and waiting for autographs, and where there weren't CDs there were old photos or tape recorders hoping for one or two statements for a radio station in the province. Afterward the band was invited with their companions to the Restaurante Juan y Mariano: down a steep hill on a narrow little street, a glass door, a place with little light and too much noise. But Ernesto excused himself: he was tired, he said, so that everyone could hear him. He preferred to go back early to the hotel and rest for the remainder of the tour. The Márquezes saw him walk alone to the next corner, suddenly an old man, lost in the middle of a traveling party of the young, a graying head that stood out under the yellow of the Málaga street-lamps.

"This can't happen again," Hugo said.

"No," Ricardo's father said. "It can't happen again."

"But I wonder who will tell him."

"I wonder who," Ricardo's father said. "I wonder how."

When we arrived in Cartagena at noon, the thermometer read 107 degrees. The international music festival was being held at the highest point in the city, a kind of Athenian amphitheater constructed on top of a mountain that looked out over the Mediterranean. There, with the winds blowing over the stone steps, the temperature was three or four degrees below what it was at sea level, and I can say I felt the difference as I went up—walking, because I'd decided to have lunch on my own and go to the concert on my own instead of taking advantage of the tour bus—and as I climbed up the bumpy asphalt, I felt I was peeling off one layer of skin after another. I remember the temptation not to go to this last concert, the resignation I felt at having lost a week traveling with people to whom I was visibly a nuisance and a pest in the best of cases, and an intruder (almost a paparazzo, a literary paparazzo) in the worst. But it was the last concert of the tour, just like it was five years before. Something drew me to be there, to witness it, as if my week with the Márquez brothers were a house, and only I had the keys to lock it after everyone had left. I entered the amphitheater through a brass door that I found half-open. I continued inside, and for a while I stood in front of the empty stage. The Márquez brothers weren't there. I waited a while longer. The Márquez brothers were missing.

I climbed up to the stage on the little side stairs and saw all the signs of a suspended rehearsal: they had been there, but they'd left. Their instruments were on the black wooden floor, the guitars, a saxophone, the abandoned accordion, its bellows soaked with Aurelio's sweat, a water stain that took on the color of blood on the red fabric. Just then Alonso entered the amphitheater, accompanied by one of the festival's local organizers. One of the sound engineers, a man with Indian features who wore the name of a rapper on his boots, came out to see them. They were talking to each other, explaining things. I went up to them and asked where everyone was, and Alonso explained that there had been a change in schedule: they'd been asked to push back the time of the concert, planned for nine, to eleven at night. "Eleven?" I said. Yes, eleven: the TV people wanted the concert finale to coincide with the fireworks, and the time for the fireworks, for reasons related to the live Latin American broadcast, had changed this year and was unmovable. "We'll have to stay here until later," Alonso said.

"And so?" I said.

"So what?"

"Where is everyone?"

"At the hotel," Alonso said, "resting from the heat." And then: "Everyone except Ricardo, who's waiting for you."

He moved his head like an uncomfortable horse. I followed the movement and saw him: Ricardo was sitting in the last row of the amphitheater, in the shadow of a colonnade that a pair of young men was beginning to decorate with Latin American flags. He's waiting for you, Alonso said, and I hid my surprise and avoided asking why and for how long. Going up the stairs, I felt the weight of the mountain I had just climbed in my muscles and lungs, the violent heat, the weariness. But when I reached Ricardo, my weariness evaporated, and the shade of the colonnade was the sweetest I had known for a long time. "It's nicer up here," Ricardo said. I sat down next to him, stretched my legs out like his, and like him, I kept my gaze fixed on the stage where the technicians moved and where the instruments seemed to vibrate in the afternoon sun. Neither of us had to initiate dialogue, like actors in bad plays; neither had to break the ice or execute those complicated steps with which two people approach a conversation that both want to have but neither knows how to begin.

None of that happened. One minute we sat in total silence, like two old friends who no longer need to fill their silence with banalities. A minute later, without any transition, Ricardo started to talk.

"It wasn't as hot as it is today," he said. "But it was hot. Really hot. We all felt uncomfortable; we were all sweating. We felt dirty—yes, that's it. We felt dirty." They'd arrived late the night before, from Málaga. On the bus, the Márquez brothers had behaved like they were in a troubled marriage (in a marriage of four people): all of them pretended to sleep so they wouldn't have to face what had happened in the theater, what happened to Ernesto Márquez's throat at the end of the concert. "No one's going to say anything?" Ricardo said to his father that night, in the dark room of the hotel. And his father—lying a few feet from him, in the other bed, his silhouette traced by the line of light that filtered beneath the door—had also pretended to sleep. Ricardo imagined his Uncle Ernesto standing in front of the bathroom mirror, bringing a hand to his neck, thinking of words like polyps, nodules. So he went to sleep, and the next day he woke before his father did. He went down to the dining room at the hour when only bitter waiters and old insomniacs occupy hotel dining rooms, that hour when all of the newspapers still lie on the table at the doorway, patient and virgin, since no one has touched them. And there was Ernesto, of course, nibbling a croissant like a mouse. "There was nothing else on his plate," Ricardo told me. "And he held it with two hands. He had the croissant in both hands. Croissants are small. It's hard to use both hands to bring one to your mouth. But that's what my uncle was doing. He was putting it in his mouth with one of those mouse bites when I told him." Since the family didn't dare, Ricardo thought, it was up to him to tell his uncle what everyone was thinking. "The family thinks it's time for you to retire," Ricardo blurted out. "The family wants you to go."

"How dare you," Ernesto said.

"You're finished, uncle," Ricardo said. "It's that simple. We don't want you to keep singing."

"How dare you," Ernesto Márquez repeated.

Ricardo spent the day apart from the band and even the technicians, hiding and running away without admitting to himself that he was running and hiding, ultimately preventing his family from reacting. The reproaches would come, his father's disavowal, the accusations. They would call him insolent (he was already used to it). They would talk about hierarchies and lines and who had the right to cross them. Ricardo walked without direction through the burning city, taking refuge from the heat in supermarkets—pausing for long minutes in front of the refrigerators, looking at the cheese and juice and milk as if it were a small, private show—and spending the last minutes before the concert at the port, counting the boats, distracting himself. The sky turned purple and then grey, and then the outlines of things disappeared, and the light of the streetlamps turned everything yellow, and on lifting his head Ricardo saw a distant gleam, above, on the mountain. Ricardo focused. He tried to hear the music, to detect the tremor of the bass; he believed, without too much conviction, that he had. He counted out the songs before the black hole of the sea: "The Wild One." "The Powerful." "Shadows of the Soul." He sang the next one, "The Virgin of the Poor," from the first verse to the last. And then he sang three more, calculating not only their exact times, which was no longer hard for him, but also the time between the songs, the routines of silences and pauses in the concert he had been hearing since he was born—it had been impressed on his consciousness as clearly as his name. And then, walking as slowly as he could, he began to make his way up.

It didn't surprise him that his calculations (that's to say: his hearing) yielded perfect results. Ricardo skirted the wall of the amphitheater just as they finished the last bars of the last corrido—*You feel like a stranger*, the audience sang, *Life hurts you again*—and he showed his plastic card to the doorman at the same time that the Márquez brothers walked off the stage. Ricardo mingled with the members of the audience who were standing between the stage and the first row, moving with difficulty toward the middle of the crowd, jostled by their elbows and hips. Then the Márquezes came back on the stage, this time without their instruments. They raised their hands and greeted the audience, all of them except Ernesto, and then the sky lit up.

Fireworks? Ricardo thought. He didn't know that they'd been planned, but how would he have known, if he'd been gone the whole afternoon, if that afternoon he'd stopped being a Márquez. Flashes of color burst through the pitch black sky—at this height, the city lights didn't interfere; they didn't cut the perfect darkness; it was as if the lights remained below—and Ricardo thought of the art projects he did as a child in school, when the teacher had him cover a piece of paper with colored crayons and then cover it all with a layer of black, so that afterward, on scratching the surface with a pin, the colors came out from the paper like the red and blue and green lights that now emerged from the back of the sky. Ricardo would never know how to explain why, at that moment, he stopped looking up and looked for his uncles on stage; why, upon noticing Ernesto wasn't there, he felt uncomfortable, attacked, and why, a second later, he was shoving his way through the audience, looking for the stairs that went down to the dressing rooms.

"It was my turn," Ricardo told me that afternoon, a little before the concert in Cartagena. From our distance, he pointed to the space where he had moved five years before; he pointed to the entrance to the stairs. "It took me several minutes to cross; it was crowded. I ran down the stairs in a hurry, as if someone were waiting for me. Have you seen the dressing rooms yet? They're horrible. I haven't wanted to go in this year, you know? I asked them to let me change on the bus and warm up there. No one said anything. They all understand." He told me that the bottom of the walls and the floors were covered with ceramic tiles, like a locker room: everything was lit with bright neon lights, all white, everything so clean and bright that Ricardo, coming in from the darkness of the night, had to squint when he entered. Then his eyes got used to the brightness, and Ricardo stopped a couple steps from the mirrors and the sink. "I think I saw him in the mirror first," he said. In the mirror he saw the half-open door of one of the bathroom stalls, and the half-silhouette of a man sitting, not firm and concentrating like someone who's taking a shit, but limp like a rag doll. The door hid the man's head, but Ricardo understood who it was even before he pushed the door open with his fingers and found Ernesto Márquez. He had covered his head with a trash bag, one of those blue bags with orange ties. He had closed the opening for air with the same silver tape that he used to stick the set list to the black wooden floor of the stage, and he'd asphyxiated himself. The orange ties stuck out from under the silver tape, and they hung over his lifeless neck.

Ricardo told me all of that there, in the last row of the amphitheater, a little before the last concert of the tour. The heat had let up some, but you could still feel the weight of the day's sun between your head and shoulders. "You understand, right?" he said. "You understand that you can't write this. I haven't told you all this for you to write about it." I told him yes, I understood. He asked me if I understood why he had told me this, and I said yes again. But that time I wasn't totally sure. I couldn't understand that burden, because I'd never felt anything similar (empathy has its limits). I couldn't understand how the image of Ernest Márquez, sitting on the toilet, had overwhelmed the family's life these five years, nor could I understand what they must have felt—all of them, not just Ricardo—on repeating the steps, the songs, the sets of the terrible year of 1996. Ricardo stood up; we walked together toward the stage, and then he told me he was going to change and put his headphones on and warm up a little before the others arrived. We separated, and Ricardo had already crossed the door and walked out to the street before I started to go down toward the dressing rooms, just like he had done five years before. When I arrived below I ran into one of the engineers, who was pulling up his zipper as he left. The white ceramic walls weren't as clean as Ricardo described them. I went up to the sinks and tried to imagine which of those mirrors (there were three) had reflected the figure of Ernesto Márquez. I took two steps back; I moved left and right trying to find the position, the right angle, but it was impossible to know for sure. I opened the tap and let the cool water wet my hands, and then I wet my face. Then I took two steps back, moved again, and looked again for the position, the right angle.

HURRICANE
BY ENA LUCÍA PORTELA (CUBA)

It's my choice. It's mine, only mine. I don't plan to discuss it with anyone. That's my right, isn't it? I made my decision toward the end of the nineties, when I was twenty-two or twenty-three years old, I don't remember exactly. What I do know is that I made the decision in full possession of my mental faculties. I wasn't drunk or under the influence of any drug. Of course, you might doubt the mental faculties of anyone who makes that kind of decision "cold," and without any apparent motive. But that's exactly why I don't want to discuss it. I'm tired of people calling me crazy.

The first chance came with Hurricane Michelle, in October 2001. My mother had already died (her heart, her heartache), and thanks to the negotiations of I don't know what international human rights organization, my father was finally released from prison . . . directly to the airport. Now he lives in Los Angeles. My older brother Nene was shot through the neck. Why Nene, I don't know. He had nothing to do with anything. Not politics, not drugs, not his neighbor's wife. He was just a little clueless and absent-minded, just like our mother. He liked to read a lot. Poetry, mostly. He loved W. H. Auden. Nene was a nice guy. I suppose they killed him for being in the wrong place at the wrong time, as they say. Or maybe they thought he was someone else. I really don't know. It was just me and my little brother Bebo now, living in our faded but still solid house in El Vedado.

It was a little after three in the morning, near the beginning of that October. Bebo was sleeping in his room, and I was curled up on the sofa in the living room watching TV. At that time of night they almost never show anything except the Olympics or the World Series, which always happen in distant countries, or else it's news about a terrible hurricane that's passing through a nearby country. And there it was. Michelle. Like the Beatles song. Michelle, my belle . . . A glamorous name for a monster. A category five on the Saffir-Simpson scale, which means sustained winds of over 250 kilometers per hour, with even stronger gusts. The worst you could imagine, as far as hurricanes go.

So now Havana, the west and central parts of the big island, plus the Isle of Pinos and a few nearby cays were under hurricane warning. In a few hours, the hurricane was going to hit the Cuban archipelago. But no one knew where. It would hit. Period. Neither the weather station in Miami nor the one in Casablanca would dare to predict its precise path. On the TV, the director of the Meterological Institute wouldn't stop talking. He was standing next to weather maps and satellite images (mysterious, like always: I've never understood them) saying current location, so many degrees north and west. Moving slowly. Oh, this looks bad! He wiped the sweat off his brow with his sleeve. Precipitation, so many millimeters. Atmospheric pressure, so many hectopascals. These are hurricane winds, really strong, incredibly strong! We haven't seen anything like this in decades. But stay calm, please? He wiped his sweat again. You must stay calm, ladies and gentlemen, and follow the instructions of the Civil Defense in case of e . . . e . . . emergency. Poor guy. He was clearly afraid and obviously wanted to send the damn Civil Defense to hell with all their damn instructions and run like the devil was after him. Running made no sense, of course. He would have gotten nowhere.

Then images from CNN en Español came on the screen. Michelle had traveled with a chilling slowness along the Caribbean coast of Central America, and journalists had followed it (or followed her, no?) with their cameras and microphones. At a prudent distance, of course. The images were frightening. Teeming rivers, fallen houses, uprooted trees, dead people and animals floating in brown water. All the misery and suffering of the world could be seen in the eyes of the survivors. Who, to top it off, were poor, and whose governments, as some of them said, never paid attention to them and wouldn't help them rebuild, etc. Some indigenous people, who might not have spoken Spanish, remained silent, serious, with furrowed brows. Though there weren't really that many interviews. A lot of areas ended up isolated by floods and were inaccessible by land, so the images (of utter devastation) were shot from a helicopter. A dramatic off-screen voice narrated: "This is Nicaragua . . . this is in Honduras . . . this, Guatemala . . . northern Belize." The voice continued: "This powerful hurricane is headed back to the Caribbean, where it will gain in size and intensity. It's now heading toward Cuba . . ."

And right at that instant, just as the voice said, "Cuba," bam! The power cut off.

I imagined how the ladies and gentlemen, probably in the millions, must have felt facing that darkness a little after three in the morning. I think I heard screams in the distance. I don't know. Not even Stephen King could have come up with something more terrifying.

As for me, I wasn't afraid at all. It's not that I'm very brave. I'm not. When I was a child, I suffered all kinds of terrors. Way too many. So many that I lived in perpetual anxiety, biting my fingernails, with a knot in my throat . . . But when I made my decision, at the end of the nineties, all my fears disappeared like magic. Poof! It was like an exorcism. I didn't even have nightmares after that. Now, with the power out, I only worried whether the heat would wake up my little brother. It was a hot, humid, and sticky night, and without a fan . . .

Bebo wasn't a little boy. Not at all. He was only three years younger than me; he had the strength to ruin my plans. And he would try, of course. He always did. I don't mean to say that he was violent, that he abused me or something like that, no. But he had an Alyosha Karamazov streak that was frankly intolerable. When he got started with all his God-loves-everyone and we-should-seek-the-salvation-of-our-souls and I don't know what else, there was no way to stop him. I told him, Oh, Bebo, please, leave me alone . . . And he'd say: But Mercy, what are you saying? Leave you alone! Let the Lord enter your heart . . . And so on. It was better that he didn't wake up.

In the dark, I went to sit on the ledge of the window that opened to the front porch. Total silence. Not even the crickets chirped in the yard. Maybe they'd run off with their music. I've heard that animals perceive the approach of natural disasters much better than we do, we who perceive nothing without satellites and radar. Who knows. The fact is not even the slightest breeze blew. The night was clear, cloudless, with a moon and stars and everything. If it weren't for the TV, no one would have suspected that a hurricane was coming, not to mention such an apocalyptic one. My eyes ("like a cat's," Nene used to say) quickly adapted to the darkness. I lit a cigarette. It wasn't time yet. There was no hurry. I sat there for a few hours, smoking, contemplating the darkness. I thought of nothing. I had nothing to think about. Bebo, luckily, didn't wake up.

At the break of dawn I got down from the ledge. I stretched my legs. According to my calculations, it was time to act. Stealthily, careful not to trip over anything, I walked to my brother's bedroom at the back of the house. There he was on his bed, wrapped up in the sheets, his window open. He slept like a rock, a stranger to the heat, Michelle's imminent visit, and my plans. He must be having a wonderful dream, I thought.

Neither Bebo or I worked. With our records, no one would have given us a job except in agriculture or construction. They weren't criminal records. We hadn't committed crimes. Or maybe we had. It depends on your point of view. There are actions, or omissions, that are legal in some countries but not in others, according to the system of government. So we survived, more or less, thanks to the remittances a friend of Papa's sent us from the United States. It was assumed that at some point we would go into exile to reunite with our family, or what was left of it. But we needed an exit visa from Immigration, which hadn't arrived yet. (It still hasn't.) Bebo, with his back problem, wasn't fit for military service. That was good, because if it were otherwise, he would have declared himself a conscientious objector, and God knows what would have happened. As for me . . . let's say I barely existed, that I barely exist. Really, I don't even weigh a hundred pounds. According to the men in this country, addicted as they are to volume and weight, I'm green eyes, long hair, and nothing else. What interest could someone have in keeping me in one place or another? None. And I don't understand the delay with the visa. But I don't care. Oh, no. I haven't cared since then. There are so many things I just don't understand in life.

Bebo didn't understand, either. But he took it to heart. For a while he was really, I mean really, anxious, unable to concentrate on anything, going fucking crazy for us to finally get away once and for all. To anywhere, he said, even Timbuktu. Because he felt that they were watching us, that they tapped our phone to listen to private conversations, and that they prowled outside the house (dressed as civilians, of course, so they wouldn't look like police, as if they could fool anyone!). In other words, that they sought to annihilate us. I asked him who, and he answered, them. Who else could it be? Them. The dogs. The sons of bitches. The same ones as always. I asked him if he was sure, if they weren't figments of his imagination, because in the final analysis it seemed a little absurd . . . He looked at me with an expression of horror. He said: A little what? Oh, María de las Mercedes Maldonado! You're in the clouds, like always. You're in the hanging gardens of Babylon! You're the crazy one . . . Between that and Nene's inexplicable death, my brother was on the verge of a nervous breakdown.

Then one day he saw the light. That is, he decided he'd had enough of being a Catholic, which to him meant being reasonable in excess, lacking in passion and authentic religious fervor. So he joined the Protestants. He became an evangelical, I think. Though I'm not sure. Maybe he was Lutheran, or Anabaptist, or Pentecostal . . . Really, I don't know. It was a sect whose followers spent their time jumping and shrieking. Sometimes they fell into a trance and writhed on the floor, their eyes rolled back in their heads, they foamed at the mouth, really, like they were having a seizure. And they considered it all terribly spiritual. I respect other people's beliefs, I really do. But those loud, spastic believers made my hair stand on end. I couldn't respect them. I locked myself in my room when they came over, really. It was so they wouldn't tell me that I had an instrument of torture hanging around my neck. My God, an instrument of torture! These very abnormal people were referring to a little gold cross of the most inoffensive variety. And if they started with their howling and hollering, I left and went to the park at the corner to sit and read on my favorite bench, under a flame tree. By the way, I don't remember what that book was about or who wrote it, but I liked it a lot at the time. I don't know why. I think it was called *Iceland's Bell.* Isn't that a nice title? But getting back to the evangelicals, or whoever they were. The thing is that, despite their howling, they helped my little brother in a certain way. That has to be acknowledged. They kept him entertained with their antics, safe from misery, alcoholism, and nights of insomnia. It's true he grew annoying with all that God-loves-everyone stuff, but at least he slept peacefully sometimes. Like that morning, on the eve of hurricane Michelle, when I snuck into his room.

I took the flashlight and the keychain, which were on top of his nightstand. The wind had begun to blow already with some force, but there was still a suffocating heat due to the low atmospheric pressure. It would cool down later, once it started to rain. For a second I wondered whether to close the window. I preferred to leave it open. I didn't want Bebo to wake up yet. Why? He'd wake up soon enough, when things got ugly. I also asked myself whether I should leave him a note. People who make the decision I made tend to leave notes before going through with it. They write something like, "Don't blame anyone . . ." or the opposite, "So-and-so is to blame . . ." or whatever. All this just seemed pathetic to me. Really, it's like they want to give supreme importance to an act that doesn't really matter at all, if you consider it a little objectively. I know other opinions exist, but anyway. Whatever the issue, there are always other opinions. If people have too much of something, it's opinions. In any case, I wouldn't have known what to write in my note without it sounding ridiculous or like a lie. Nene always said I had a talent for literature, but I don't know. I don't believe it. All my works (ha, ha, my works!) can be reduced to five or six stories, of which I've published only one, in a Mexican magazine. So I didn't leave Bebo a note. Now I ask myself, if I'd left one, would it have changed the course of events? Who knows. It seems to me it wouldn't have.

In my mind, I gave my brother a kiss. And a hug. And more kisses. Though I'm not that emotional or passionate, I'm not a rock, either. I wanted to touch him. But I couldn't take the risk. So I said goodbye in my mind. I told him I loved him lots and lots, despite the evangelical pests. (It was true.) I told him I hoped he wouldn't miss me too much. I wished him luck with the exit visa, that it would come soon so he could reunite with Papa. And I left, before the winds began to strengthen and the windowpanes rattled. We never saw each other again.

As I walked away it was already dawn, though it was barely light. The sky was so cobbled, so gray, that anyone would have felt depressed. The humidity smelled strong. Any moment now, the first big drops would fall. And then, almost immediately, the flood. From the weather it was clear that Michelle had already hit the big island. Where was she headed? Who knew? If the eye of the hurricane hit Havana, which already was in ruins, it would be the biggest catastrophe of the last fifty years. For a moment I felt something like patriotism. I hated Michelle.

From the porch I walked down the path that led to the garage. The side windows on the house next door were all closed. Good, I thought. I didn't want anyone to see me.

I opened the garage door. There, inside the garage, it was as dark as the mouth of a wolf. It smelled like rust, mold, and gasoline. I got into the Ford pickup with the flashlight and tried to start it. It wasn't easy. I got it going on the third try. I didn't check the gas, since I had filled the tank the afternoon before. The pickup was a real antique, a true museum piece. Every time a tourist saw the truck, he immediately wanted to buy it. Or if not, take a picture with it. Or take a video of the truck in motion. It's true that truck moved purely by miracle, not having had a single part replaced in more than four decades. If that's not a Guinness record, it must be close

Once in the street, I looked in the rear-view mirror. The garage door was still open. But I wasn't going to get out and close it. No way. There was nothing in the garage that could be stolen, and most likely it would serve as a shelter for somebody. There were always bums, beggars, drunks, and crazy old men who run away from home and have nowhere to go when hurricanes come. Street dogs and street cats, too. Anyway, all I wanted was to get away as quickly as possible. It had started to rain, and the wind shook the treetops, trying to destroy them. So I picked up speed, more or less, praying that the Ford dinosaur wouldn't give me hell now.

I think I drove aimlessly for a few miles. I got turned around. I drove some more. I got to the iron bridge at Almendares, and then I went back, along a different route. I didn't feel like going anywhere in particular. I just drove and drove. The rain kept getting stronger. The wind shifted, now one way, then the other. It made whirlwinds, whorls, a downpour. I drove a little slower, but without stopping. I still had some visibility. I vaguely remember the streets of El Vedado: somber, deserted, without vehicles or pedestrians. The streetlamps went out. My headlights, too. I was like a ghost moving through a ghost town. I felt happy for the first time in years.

The landscape was blurring behind a curtain of rain. It was to be expected. Windshield wipers, half a century old, can do nothing against a torrential rain. The last thing I could distinguish was a human silhouette. I drove my holy piece of junk onto Calle 23, and someone, I don't know if it was a man or a woman, was walking down the narrow street of Montero Sánchez. Or down Crecherie. I don't know. They were walking down a narrow street perpendicular to Calle 23. They staggered. They fell on their knees. They got up, with what seemed like tremendous effort, and took a few steps. Then they fell again, flat on their face. They got back up. They walked again, with a limp . . . until the curtain of water became a wall, and I couldn't see anything. What became of them? I never found out.

I kept driving blindly, a little faster now. Something had to happen to me, right? I was sure of it. And in fact, something did.

The truck stopped suddenly. Of course I wasn't wearing a seatbelt. I just missed crashing through the windshield. In fact, I smashed my forehead against the steering wheel, or something; I don't know. What the hell happened? The engine kept running, but the truck wouldn't move. I tried to put it in reverse, but nothing. I couldn't go backward. Never has there been a more immobile truck. Not even a mule would resist so much! I muttered a few other words besides "hell," worse ones. I don't usually have a dirty mouth. If you swear too often, it loses its effect. Better save it for important occasions.

Meanwhile, a warm liquid ran down my face. I touched it. It was blood. I looked at myself in the rear-view mirror. The cut on my forehead didn't look so good. Strange how it didn't hurt. Though that didn't matter much. I tried to drive forward again, and nothing. The motor turned off. I think I would have had more luck if I'd gotten out and walked at that point. But I didn't. I stayed there, inside the truck. There was water all around me. The rain drummed on the windshield diabolically. I wouldn't be surprised if the rain shattered it, I thought, and this idea restored my calm.

What's for sure is that I'd gotten stuck in a pothole. Nothing extraordinary, after all. Everyone knows that the streets of El Vedado, just like most in Havana, are full of potholes, some very large and dangerous for any vehicle. I had fallen into one of those. Only a tow truck could have pulled me out. And the problem with those holes, apart from the flat tires and getting you stuck, is that they flood every time it rains. A mere tropical storm causes them to overflow, let alone a hurricane. The water level rose until it reached the motor, and naturally, the motor turned off.

But I didn't know this until much later. At the time, I didn't know shit. Shut up in the truck, I was bothered by the smell of blood, so much like copper, and the heat. Because there was a lot of blood, and it was really hot. At least that's how I remember it. I asked myself whether I should roll down the windows, to let out the bad air and let in all this crazy rain and the wind that howled like a thousand demons . . . That's when I felt another blow. That one hurt. A lot. But only for a second, maybe less. After the pain came calm. A strange sense of fullness, well-being. I could hear the rain and the wind, yes, but muffled, as if they were thousands of miles from there. Then sleep overcame me. Little by little, I was enveloped in darkness.

I wasn't lucky. I woke up in the Farjado Hospital emergency room. They had given me a blood transfusion, an IV, an oxygen mask, a bandage around my head, and I don't know what else. They even changed my dress for a gray hospital gown! What an outrage. My first impulse was to rip all that junk off of me, even the gown. But I couldn't lift a finger. I felt weak, dizzy, and had a splitting headache.

As soon as the nurse saw that I had woken up, she took off running. A doctor appeared immediately. A fat man in his fifties with a childish grin. The first thing he said was: Aha! So we have green eyes! And he rushed to study them with a little flashlight. Then he took off the oxygen mask and asked how I felt and also asked for my name, address, telephone number, close relatives, etc. I didn't answer any of his questions. I didn't feel like talking. He accepted that silence as if it were the most natural thing in the world. He asked if I could hear him. I assented with my eyes. (Pretending to be deaf is much harder than pretending to be mute, at least for me.) So he put the mask back on me and talked. I don't remember everything he said, only a few things. What had fallen on the truck was a poplar. Of course the thick part of the trunk hadn't hit me, since if it had, I would have been crushed to pulp. Really, anyone who's seen poplars knows they can be taller than a two-story house. This tree, in its fall, first crushed a fence, a few shrubs, a car, and finally hit the truck with one of its branches. I was unconscious for three days. Apart from the cut on my forehead, which needed stitches, there were no other visible wounds. They'd taken some X-rays and done a few tests, and nothing. Everything seemed to be fine. But you couldn't be sure. The shock had been strong. I should stay under observation a few more days. As for talking, he smiled at me and said there wasn't any hurry. I would talk soon enough. For the time being it was better to maintain complete rest.

When the fat man left, I glanced around. There were other beds and other patients in the emergency room, the patients' friends and families, nurses and the nurses' boyfriends, the woman who cleaned the floor, the one who made the coffee, the man who sold lollypops . . . It looked like a Marx Brothers scene. Everyone talked, argued, had opinions, interrupted each other. A TV was at the top of a wall in front of the row of beds. Playing at full volume, of course. Some "complete rest," hmm?

I started to watch TV. Michelle's adventures still monopolized its attention. After leaving Cuba, she continued her way up through the Gulf of Mexico and into Louisiana or Florida, I don't remember exactly. As for Cuba, the eye of the hurricane had passed through the center of the island. Only the outer rings of the hurricane reached the capital—in other words, the "weakest" part of the phenomenon. What I saw on my wrecked drive, all that fury of water and wind, was nothing compared to what happened in the center of the island, which UNESCO would later declare an official "disaster zone." That's where much of the national and international press was directed. The pictures taken from the air, now appearing on screen, were as terrible as one could imagine. Utter devastation, just like the Caribbean coast of Central America.

Then they broadcast a story about a little town named Jícara in the central region. It was one of those villages that doesn't appear on the map. If I remember its name it's because it made me laugh that the townspeople called themselves "Jicarenses." In truth, Michelle had showed no mercy on that place. Not even a hut was left standing, not a palm tree, nothing. The Jicarenses' situation was very much like the condemned Central Americans'. There were no indigenous among them. Only blacks and mulattos. Still, you could see their misery, hunger, and helplessness just by looking at them. And now, on top of everything, they'd been crushed by a hurricane. But when a journalist asked them how they felt, they answered, very good. Oh, yes. Just wonderful. Anyone would have thought they were being ironic, since the question was a little idiotic. But really. The Jicarenses were serious. They felt really good! They had survived the hurricane, yes! And they'd survive whatever they had to for their country and for the revolution! And they would fight against Yankee imperialism, yes! To the last drop of blood! And may the immortal Commander in Chief live forever! They shouted all this at the top of their lungs, shaking their fists frenetically, as if to erase even the slightest doubt about how they felt. So help me God, I thought, and they say that I'm crazy . . . In the emergency room, you could hear a few laughs. Look at that, on your life! They're in hell, those stupid hicks! Ho, ho, ho! I don't think anyone held back their laughter. You know that city people tend to make fun of country people.

If that fat man really thought I'd talk about myself, he was wrong. I told him nothing, not even my name. Why not? It wasn't his business. I kept silent for a few days, quieter than an oyster at the bottom of the sea. He tried to coax it out of me, growing increasingly more nervous. He told me that anonymous patients weren't allowed, that he wasn't my nanny, and he didn't have to put up with my whims. He even threatened to send me to the psychiatrist. I gave him nothing. As soon as I could, I ran away from the hospital. It was only then that I learned.

As you know, Michelle's outer bands caused immeasurable damage in Havana. Buildings destroyed, ocean flooding, most of the electric wires on the ground, along with the phone wires, trees, and all kinds of objects that don't fly normally but that the winds made fly. The hurricane also left behind it about a dozen dead. That isn't many for a city with more than three million people, so it wasn't a humanitarian catastrophe. It's just that one of these victims was my little brother, Bebo. They found his body thrown onto the street, a few blocks from the house. He was severely bruised, with multiple fractures, one at the base of his skull. What happened exactly, I don't know. I don't think I'll ever know. Given the circumstances, I'm afraid it would be difficult, perhaps impossible, to find out. And why speculate, why, I ask myself, if he's not coming back anyway . . .

Now I'm alone in our house in El Vedado. I don't know why I say "our." It must be out of habit. The exit visa still hasn't arrived. Papa's friend keeps sending me a little money, month after month, and I get by on that. As you might imagine, the Ford pickup is in a better place now, after the pothole and the poplar. I have an ugly scar across my forehead, but I don't care. If I hide it behind bangs, it's to deflect attention on the street; I can't stand strangers staring as they walk by. I've always liked to go unnoticed. I wouldn't go see a plastic surgeon, supposing it was within my reach, for the same reason that I won't get a dog, or keep myself busy fixing up the yard, or write a novel . . . Nothing like that makes sense to me. Because I'm resolute in my decision. Oh, yes, I'm resolute. Every year, from the first of June to the thirtieth of November, I devote myself to watching the TV news. That's how I learn about the evil in the world and how good everything is in my country. But what interests me most is the weather report. Oh, yes. I don't ever miss one. Just like Penelope waiting for Odysseus, I'm waiting for a hurricane.

FAMILY TREE
BY ANDREA JEFTANOVIC (CHILE)

What is forbidden? "Society expressly forbids only that which society brings about."
—Lévi-Strauss

I don't know when children's asses first began to interest me. Ever since the priests, the senators, and businessmen all started appearing on TV with their evasive looks. I'd thought about the curves of their asses ever since children's diaries had become valid evidence in courts of law. I'd never before felt a throbbing for these incomplete bodies, but then there was the media's constant bombardment with "the 0.7 centimeter abrasions in the area below the anus." Or the sentence in the newspaper, "In repeatedly violated children, the transverse folds of the rectum disappear." The brigade against sexual offenders advising the public to watch for changes of behavior in their children and to conduct a periodic examination of their genitals. The forensic specialists verifying accusations after physical examinations. The suspicion that there was a twisted silence, a wayward desire.

My daughter Teresa would catch these news stories from the corner of her eye and stop what she was doing, uncomfortable. We'd been living alone for five years, since her mother left. My daughter never said or asked anything about the episode. I never knew whether the two had talked the night before. No one who packs a suitcase and closes the door with such determination comes back. She closed it slowly, the latch just caught, and her stealthy feet brushed the pavement across the front yard. I didn't want to look out the window. I didn't want to know whether a car was waiting for her, or a taxi, or if she walked alone down the sidewalk. Teresa was nine years old. She took all her mother's photos down, and without my asking she assumed the role of lady of the house. "We need this, we need that, we've already eaten too much meat." The rest went on just like before: her friends, school, the things she liked. A studious girl, shy, who drew trees while she gazed past the mountains.

For a while Teresa had spied my tired gaze with a special gleam in her eyes. She was doing her best with the food and had decided that her nanny couldn't spend the night anymore.

"Why did you tell her to leave?" I inquired, irritated.

"I'm big now, I don't need anyone to watch me at night."

"I disagree. Sometimes I come home late."

"I like to be alone," she replied bluntly.

"It can be dangerous."

"There's a watchman in the hall, and we have a dog."

"Fine."

Things continued to be strange. Now if I invited a woman over for coffee, Teresa prowled around the house and made strange noises through the walls. Just when I began to feel the desire to meet other women. Once I timidly kissed someone from work on the sofa. She was a sweet young thing. When I pulled my lips away from hers, I saw my daughter's eye through a hole in the wall. It was the eye of a Cyclops, ruling over the scene with hate. I contained my scream and invented an excuse to take my guest back to her house.

Teresa dressed differently; she wore heavy makeup. If she came home in her school uniform and I was there, she ran down the hall to change clothes. She reappeared in the living room dressed up. Her childish figure looked somehow grotesque in this adult costume. She rubbed up against me; she sat on my knees when I read the newspaper and placed her hips between mine. I didn't know how to handle the situation. She was a girl; she was my daughter.

"What do you want?" I said to her one day, bothered.

"Nothing, to look pretty, to look pretty for you."

"I don't like it when you wear so much makeup."

"Whatever you say." She walked indifferently to her bedroom.

That night I came home late; I was trying to revive the romance with my coworker, and we had gone out for a drink. It had been a beautiful night. I sat on the bed, a little nauseous, and there was Teresa, in a thin nightshirt, her hair combed, her face clean and perfumed.

"I missed you."

"I missed you, too. But it's late. Go to your room," I said, with my head between my hands.

"I can't sleep."

"Yes, you can. Go read a book."

"I can't."

"What do you want?"

"To sleep with you."

"Daughters don't sleep with their fathers. You have your own room and your own bed."

"I don't want to be alone."

"Fine. Stay just this once."

I moved over to the edge of the bed, careful not to touch her. I turned my back to her and fell asleep. When I woke, I rolled over, and there were her open eyes, fatigued, fixed on me. I got the impression that she hadn't closed her eyes all night. I shaved, mulling a few things over. She observed me from the doorway, still in her night shirt, playing with a lock of hair.

"What's going on?"

"Nothing, I like watching you shave."

"It's very boring."

"No, it's not. I like to watch how you stretch your neck, how you turn your face and run the razor over your skin."

"You're going to school today, right?" I asked.

"No, we're on break. I don't have class until March."

"And what are you thinking of doing with your time? Do you want to take a class, maybe? Tell me, and I'll go with you. We can go to the coast for a few weeks in February."

It was absurd, but I felt cornered, harassed by my own daughter. I imagined her like an animal in heat that couldn't distinguish its prey. She slunk along the walls with her hair on end, her muzzle wet, her ears fallen. How could I tell her to go look for a boy instead, a boyfriend? She lifted her skirt and bent over to throw out the trash, showing off her skimpy underwear. Now she wore bras, and she adjusted them in front of me. She was a female animal, scattering her hormones around the house. Marking her territory and fencing me inside it. I don't know whether this was good or bad, but Teresa didn't look anything like my ex-wife. Instead, she had a feminine version of my angular face. The next day she waited for me to come home, dressed in her mother's clothes. The image disturbed me so much, I now realize with shame, that I slapped her. She stood there, astonished, with her cheek bruised and her eyes open wide. I went out for fresh air, and I returned after she'd fallen asleep on the bed, evidently following a crying spell.

The summer went by stiflingly as she embarked on a mysterious investigation. She surfed the internet for hours, printing documents, clicking from one site to another. The news channels showed the courts dismissing the cases of the senator, the businessman, the priest. All asking to go free on bail, letting the summer inertia protect their cases. All appealing to their innocence. The politician who defended children, the priest consecrated to the care of the little ones, and the charitable businessman who had done so much for at-risk youth. So how to explain the children with disfigured genitals. One night we were watching an interview with one of the pedophiles. On being asked whether he'd had sex with a list of minors given by their ages and initials, the accused said indifferently, "Yes, with every one you've mentioned." And he added: "I was someone who was tremendously alone at that time, and in a certain sense, I paid for the service of having a companion." Teresa muttered a sentence between clenched teeth that I'll never forget:

"Let's go, before these guys get here."

It wasn't easy to get away. At work I kept covering for people who were on vacation, and I wasn't able to make any extra money. When my turn came, a coworker helped out by lending me a cabin on a certain beach that didn't get many visitors. Despite my insistence, I couldn't get Teresa to invite a friend. We arrived at a modest little house in the middle of a pine forest. Inside, there was a chair in the corner, a bed dividing the room in two, a wooden wardrobe with its doors half open, and a big mirror hanging from the wall. The first day, Teresa arranged everything to her liking, stuffing the drawers with poorly-folded turtlenecks and winter clothes. She had come to stay. As she did this, I walked around the bedroom, looking for an exit, but it was too late.

Once, Teresa handed me a drawing: a green tree with a wide brown trunk and thick brown bark. I thought this was one of the last vestiges of her childhood. But when I put on my glasses and examined the details, I understood what she was plotting. It was a lush tree, with a single trunk that emanated many branches, from which more branches came. There was a square on each branch with a man's name inside and a circle with a woman's name. The geometric figures multiplied exponentially across the four sketched generations.

"What does this mean?"

"It's our clan. We're at the base."

I saw her name and mine on the drawing. Then I listened, astonished. Teresa gave me a sermon, citing the Bible, affirming that in the beginning there was incest. Humanity begins with a founding couple that procreates. To allow a society to emerge, one must break a prohibition. At a certain point, filial love should turn into sexual love. The father or the mother, depending on whether they have a son or a daughter, should sleep with their offspring to breed a new son or daughter. This is a necessary act for a new society to be born.

"A new society," I muttered, incredulous.

"Yes. A new species, coming from us. You will be the father and grandfather of our child. It's the curse of origin, but it's for a better future."

"And afterward?" I asked, half-confused and half-absorbed in the drawing.

"Another child, until we come up with the daughter or son that we need to multiply this new network of people. You have to break the triangle and form a quartet that keeps fracturing in new geometric figures. Two original siblings will give way to new children who will multiply without distinguishing between aunts and uncles, cousins, brothers and sisters, nieces and nephews."

"Be quiet, you're only fifteen."

"But I've read too much," she gravely replied.

The argumentative sequence that linked her ideas gave me goose bumps. She had studied all of the factors. The consistency of her plan left me mute as I traced the white line of her scalp.

"They'll all be born sick, deformed, retarded. Is this the new society you want to create?" I managed to say, somewhat stunned.

Furious, she looked into my eyes and asserted: "Inbreeding isn't necessarily harmful. That's a myth. Sharing a genetic inheritance sometimes strengthens positive characteristics." She took the drawing and said more, paying no heed to my ignorant judgment. "Every time we have a child, we'll add a branch to the tree, and the tree will grow bigger and bigger."

The night came when I couldn't avoid her seduction. We collapsed on the mattress, feeling the warmth of the sheets. I opened myself to the flame of her long-held desire. I connected with the memory of a lost appetite. On top of her, looking into those gray eyes, which were my gray eyes. I was kissing myself. I was caressing my own marked bones, I ran against my own aquiline nose, I traced my narrow forehead. In the distance, the sound of the rattling gate. With every caress, I envied her youth and tenderness. Her palms, softer than mine, her taut muscles, a smell of violets that emanated from her nape. I was afraid and I wasn't: I was more afraid than I believed I was. She said, "Come closer, closer." We stumbled over the furniture. My skin against hers, the blow softened by the same essence. Suddenly I saw the amorphous mass of our bodies in the mirror on the wall. I saw myself with empty sockets for eyes. I threw a shoe to destroy the image, but not our embrace. The glass fragmented in a thousand shards. Irregular pieces, ground glass spread on the floor where we urgently caressed each other. No more witnesses. The secret had yet to be written in the mirror.

When I lay down with Teresa, she was no longer my daughter, she was another person. I wasn't her father; I was a man who desired that young and docile body. A man doomed to the task of making her ambiguous body mature. A sculptor dedicated to chiseling her imperfect figure, her half-formed members, her crude extremities. I did my best to narrow her waist, to darken her pubis, to stylize the curve of her neck, to draw the contour of her calves. I wanted to draw the woman out of the budding adolescent. No, she wasn't my daughter, she was the mission of shaping her pointed breasts, of doting on the sensuality of her narrow hips, her ungainly movements. To leave behind all the horror of childhood and inaugurate sophisticated movements and thoughts. I ignored what she thought, perhaps to smooth the creases around my eyes, to revitalize my tired skin, to reduce my bulging abdomen.

From time to time I was conscious of my daughter locked in this cabin, surrounded by wooden walls. I tried to decipher the message of her lips. She wasn't a girl to wait for her knight in shining armor. She brought her forehead, covered with sweat, close to mine; her nostrils flared. She mounted me, she forced my legs while she kept saying, "More sap for the new shoots, more." Her thirsty tongue called up names: Sebastians, Carolinas, Ximenas, Claudios, a family tree with last names that annulled each other because they were all Espinoza Espinoza. I, born a thousand times in my children, in my grandchildren, nieces, nephews, cousins. Her young uterus would send out a fetus every nine months. Days simmering in the wait for more children. And during that time, the man three times your age, twice your body, blood of your blood, it didn't bother him anymore that he gazed at you at length, that he paused at your mouth and descended to your sex. He yearned for the moment when we would lay together with our languid heads too close, with the sensation that we had each other, each other.

We didn't return to Santiago; we pitched our world here. One day, I observed Teresa and saw that the cause of her weight gain, the curve of her belly was logical. We waited for the baby in peace, walking between the cypresses and pines, lifting our heads toward their crowns. She sunbathed on an improvised terrace while the diameter of her figure increased; her breasts grew; and the first stretch marks wounded her fresh skin. I went into town once a week to look for provisions. Sometimes I bought the newspaper and caught up on the cases of the politicians, the senators, the priests. I breathed a sigh of relief to be away from all that. But I don't deny it. "Where's the city?" This is the question I'm afraid my daughter will utter like a blast of air. Yes, a buzz of syllables: "Papa, where's the city?" and the curtain of the horizon will open wide. The clarity of what the sun reaches. For now, I think of the foliage, of this life under the trees, counting their perennial leaves, caressing their ancient roots, cutting wood for the winter. Foretelling the time when the branches that reinforce this trunk will allow it to split in two.

RAZOR BLADES
BY LINA MERUANE
(CHILE)

It was what men did to their faces, with shaving cream and thick brushes with soft bristles, pressing closely to the mirror so as not to cut themselves. But we girls, too, looked at ourselves in the trembling mirror of astonishment, shaving each other during the first recess on Mondays and the last on Thursdays. We waited until we felt stubble to repeat the slow ritual by which we removed this scratchy hair. We never left a trace of soap in each other's armpits, and each time we did it, our excitement became more intense. Soon we were running the razor blade down our arms and up our calves and thighs. We shaved each other punctually, as punctually as we arrived every morning at the spiked iron fence, and as precisely as the matron rang the bell with her hard, insistent finger. Shaving was as mathematical a procedure as copying each other's algebra exams, the equations solved and the solutions whispered, unheard by the deaf ears of the old hag who taught us. But not all the teachers were so old or deaf. We always had to proceed with signs and whispers, so we could keep our secret.

Gradually, our bodies were beginning to swell, filling out with surprising bulges. Our breasts grew simultaneously and our nipples rose, with hairs encircling them, hair that we also carefully removed. Our pubes had become dark tangles that spilled blood at the same time without warning, and the blood had a metallic taste that excited us like the murmur of our hoarse voices, and like the labyrinth that we were penetrating passionately. We began our task eagerly with the little hairs on our toes. The razor rose up our naked insteps like a sharpened sock, sliding over our thighs like pantyhose, leaving a path of pale skin through the foamy bathroom soap. The sharp caress crept around our groins, up to our navels, and then descended under the elastic, under the soft fabric of the underwear that we finally removed; spread your legs, open up a little more, idiot, keep still, and then laughter would overtake us when we saw the tongue sticking out from the pubis, a loud, nervous laugh that made us tremble as we watched the razor blade kiss those lips.

One of us kept watch at the bathroom entrance, a black door at the end of a long walkway, past a thorny rose bed. Our lookout covered up our murmurs, singing "God Save the Queen" over and over like a litany until she saw the matron at the end of the hallway, at which point she began singing our national anthem, to warn us and distract the thin matron whose chest swelled when she heard this patriotic harangue and who thrust her lips forward, emphasizing the dark line of hair that we dreamed of someday shaving by force. And then our lookout would say, "Good morning, ma'am," while inside we hid the razor blades. The matron responded, "Good morning, young lady," and then commended her, "Don't stop, keep singing," and remained there a moment longer, enjoying the song with her eyes closed. The matron then left the scene like a watchman sleepwalking through his rounds; the danger always passed, and we got down from the toilets, retrieved the blades hidden and warmed in our underwear, lifted our uniforms again, and each girl kept shaving the other. Behind us, white-tiled walls.

Our other classmates didn't suspect anything either, or maybe they did but pretended not to. None of them ever came near us; none of them dared to venture into our bathroom. It was as though they sensed that the territory was marked, fenced, as if our gazes emanated a dirty warning. We let them admire our evident physical superiority out of the corner of their eyes and admire our knee socks and our lustrous knees; from a distance they observed how we obsessively peeled quinces in the corner of the concrete schoolyard. Because that's what we did when we weren't in the bathroom, peel quince after quince with our small pocketknives. We practiced our dexterity skinning this acidic fruit; we competed to see who could make the longest peel without it tearing first, though the thick, opaque coil always tore. We consoled ourselves for this failure by licking the pulp that left our tongues stinging as we roared with laughter. We still would be laughing when the bell rang and we had to put our pocketknives away to go back to class. We kept the torn peels in a plastic bag; they were an excellent disinfectant for accidental cuts.

It was Wednesday, and already we were restless. Sitting side by side in the last row, we scratched each other. It felt itchy when the hair began to grow, and since we'd first started shaving, it kept growing back faster and thicker. Our fingernails left white marks on our skin, though we avoided showing any expression of pleasure or pain, not for an instant taking our eyes off the blackboard where the old hag who taught Spanish explained subordinate clauses. We had new razor blades, but there were still fifteen minutes until recess, and a whole day remained until Thursday. Our impatience to return to the bathroom began to weaken us: our will was wearing thin. At that moment, in the middle of a copulative sentence, when the itching reached its peak, the door opened, and the principal entered with the new student. The whole class stood up and recited a greeting in English in unison, and then we heard her name. We didn't notice Pilar's hard features or her penetrating eyes at all at that point; the newcomer's surprising height did not attract our attention, nor did her scrawny body, hidden like death in her dark polyester uniform. We were disconcerted only by her calves, which were covered with hair. We saw nothing but this exciting tangle: a whole virgin mop of hair that made us bristle with disgust and joy.

A cold breeze seeped through the wintry windows, our last winter at the school, and there was Pilar, defiant like a bonfire in the wind. Only one seat was left, in a corner at the end of the first row, and that was where she took her place, at the wooden desk: she took off her navy jacket, her blue vest, and she rolled up her sleeves shamelessly, showing the thick hair on her arms. Before she sat down, she turned toward the back of the room, and from under her bushy eyebrows, her gaze moved slowly back and forth between us, as if she were surrendering to us, letting us lick her with our eyes. She loosened her ponytail and began to write while we hurried our pencils under the desks. "She doesn't seem like a woman," read the first line of the notebook page we circulated. "It's true, she's hairy, she's too skinny to have so much hair," another of us wrote. Someone was torturing herself, pulling at a fingernail, when the hands of the clock finally moved and the matron sunk her stiff finger into the bell. We all ran together down the hallway, crossed the rose bed, and entered the bathroom without leaving a guard. Frantically, heedlessly, letting ourselves get carried away by our ecstasy, we used our new blades in a futile carnage. Each against the other. Trying to free ourselves from Pilar's burning hair, from her infinite mop of hair that enveloped us more and more, entangling us.

Pilar walked past us in the schoolyard while we peeled quinces. We let the juice run down our hands; we sucked our fingers, imagining her spread-eagled on the bathroom tiles. Her insidious gaze that afternoon took our breath away. Then we saw her venture slowly down the hall, stopping by the black door to shake her long hair. We followed her. We heard her lock herself in a stall, the endless flush. Did she want it or didn't she? She was washing her hands when we surrounded her and told her how good she would look when we were finished. She didn't move when we took out the razor blades, but she grew pale: we knew she would scream, and we had to grab her hands and feet, hold her firmly to the floor, and stuff a handkerchief in her mouth to silence her. She resisted, but we lifted her uniform, pulled off her socks, and took off her black shoes. She even had hair on her insteps, and this inflamed our passion for her even more: she would be so naked when we finished. So soft, so pale. But she kept writhing with her eyes wide open, and I kept whispering, razor in hand, that she should keep still for her own good, so she wouldn't get hurt. I began to shave her, cutting her every time she moved. Instead of scaring us, her blood incited us, urging us to continue. Our saliva would anesthetize the pain.

The floor was covered with hair and blood. All that remained was her pubis, and Pilar had stopped moving, finally. For a moment we thought she was being suffocated by the handkerchief or bleeding to death, and we had no choice but to take the handkerchief out of her mouth. If you move, idiot, you're going to lose your eyes. Pilar was sweating, her eyelids pressed shut, but she was breathing softly, and we sighed because we feared having to fulfill our promise to kill her. The razor sliced down the sides of her panties, and without exposing her completely yet, the blade began shaving the skin carefully above the elastic and then below, delaying the appearance of Pilar's precious pubis, which we yearned for. Her black, swollen pubis. She smiled ambiguously when we removed the fabric and saw an enormous tongue appear between her lips, a dark tongue that, when it swelled, left us with our mouths hanging open, wordless, astounded for a moment as it began to rise. Then we threw our razor blades onto the floor and kissed that mouth and then each other with our tongues, crazed by the ecstasy of our discovery.

34
BY ALEJANDRO ZAMBRA (CHILE)

The teachers called us all by our numbers on the roll, so we only knew the names of our closest friends. I offer this as an apology: I don't even know my character's name. But I remember number 34 clearly, and I think he would remember me, too. At the time, I was number 45. Thanks to the first initial of my last name, I enjoyed a firmer identity than the rest. I still feel a certain affinity with that number. It was good to be last, number 45. It was much better than being, for example, 15 or 27.

The first thing I remember about 34 is that sometimes he ate carrots at recess. His mother peeled them and placed them harmoniously in a little Tupperware that he opened by carefully dismantling the top corners. He measured the exact amount of strength it took to open it, as if he were practicing an extremely difficult art. But more important than his taste for carrots was that he was repeating the grade, the only one in our class.

Repeating a grade was shameful to us. In our short lives, we had never come so close to that kind of failure. We were eleven or twelve years old; we had just entered the National Institute, the most prestigious secondary school in Chile, and our records were, as such, impeccable. But then there was 34: his presence proved that failure was possible, that it was even tolerable, because he wore his stigma naturally, as if deep down, he were content to review the same subjects. You have a familiar face, the teachers sometimes told him, ironically, and 34 responded kindly: Yes, sir, I'm a repeater, the only repeater in the class. But I'm sure this year will go better for me.

Those first months at the National Institute were hellish. The teachers took it upon themselves to tell us over and over how difficult the school was. They urged us to repent, to go back to the schools on our corners, as they disparagingly called them, with a gargle that terrorized us instead of making us laugh.

I don't know if I need to clarify that these teachers were real assholes. They had first and last names, of course: Mr. Bernardo Aguayo, for example, the math teacher, a total asshole. Or the shop teacher, Mr. Eduardo Venegas. A motherfucking cunt. Time hasn't lessened my rancor. These people were cruel and mediocre. Frustrated, stupid. Fawning fans of Pinochet. Pieces of shit.

But I was talking about 34, and not about those bastards we had for teachers.

34's behavior completely went against the natural conduct of repeaters. It's assumed that they are bad-tempered and blend into their new class late and with bad feelings, but 34 always proved himself disposed to share our condition equally. He didn't cling to the past like unhappy or melancholy repeaters; he didn't suffer a perpetual attachment to his classmates from the year before or an incessant battle against those who were supposedly to blame for his situation.

This was definitely the strangest thing about 34: he didn't seem angry at all. Sometimes we saw him talking with teachers we didn't know. Their conversations were happy, with gestures and pats on the back. He liked to maintain cordial relations with the teachers that had reproached him.

We trembled every time 34 showed signs of his undeniable intelligence in class. He wasn't a show-off, however: on the contrary, he raised his hand only to suggest new points of view or signal his opinion on complex subjects. He said things that weren't in our books, and we admired him for that, but admiring him was a way of digging your own grave: if someone that smart had failed, it was all the more likely that we would fail, too. Behind his back, we surmised the true reason he had to repeat: we invented tangled family conflicts, or a long, painful illness, but deep down we knew that 34's problem was strictly academic. We knew that tomorrow his failure would be ours.

One time, he suddenly approached me. He looked at once alarmed and happy. He took a while to speak, as if he'd thought for a long time about what he wanted to say. You shouldn't worry, he finally got out: I've been observing you, and I'm sure you're going to pass.

It was comforting to hear that. It made me very happy. It made me happy in an almost irrational way. As they say, 34 was the voice of experience, and that he'd think this of me was a relief.

Soon I learned this scene had been repeated with other classmates, and then word spread that 34 was making fun of all of us. But then we thought that this was his way of giving us confidence. Without a doubt, we needed confidence. The teachers tormented us daily, and everyone's report cards were disastrous. There were almost no exceptions. We were headed straight to the slaughterhouse.

The key was to know whether 34 had transmitted this message to everyone or only the supposedly elect. Those who hadn't been notified started to panic. 38—or 37, I don't remember his number exactly—was one of the most worried. He couldn't stand the uncertainty. One day, defying the nominations' logic, he went to ask 34 directly whether he'd pass. 34 seemed uncomfortable with the question. Let me study you, he proposed. I haven't been able to observe everyone; there are a lot of you. I'm sorry, but until now, I haven't paid a lot of attention to you.

Let no one think that 34 was putting on airs. Not at all. There was always an undertone of honesty in his speech. It was hard to doubt what he said. His frank look also helped: he was careful to look straight at you, and he spaced out his sentences with almost an imperceptible amount of suspense. His words beat with a rhythm that was slow and mature. "I haven't been able to observe everyone; there are a lot of you," he'd just told 38 (or 37), and no one doubted he was speaking in all seriousness. 34 spoke strangely and seriously. Although perhaps we believed that in order to speak seriously, you had to speak strangely.

The next day 38—or 37—asked for his verdict, but 34 answered evasively, as if he wanted—we thought—to hide a painful truth. Give me more time, he asked, I'm not sure. Now we all believed our classmate to be lost, but at the end of a week, after completing the period of observation, the psychic came up to 37-38 and told him, to everyone's surprise: Yes, you're going to pass the grade. It's definite.

We were happy, of course. But there was still an important matter to resolve: now every student had been blessed by 34. It wasn't normal for the whole class to pass. We investigated: never, in the century of the school's history, had it turned out that each of the 45 students in seventh basic passed.

During the months that followed, the decisive ones, 34 noticed that we didn't trust his judgments. But he didn't acknowledge our mistrust: he kept eating his carrots faithfully, and he participated regularly in class with his valiant and attractive theories. Perhaps his social life had lost a little of its intensity. He knew that we saw this, that he was on the sidelines, but he greeted us with the same warmth as always.

The final exams came, and we confirmed that 34's predictions had been right. Four classmates had jumped ship first, including 37 (or 38), and of the 41 who remained, 40 passed the grade. The only repeater was, precisely, 34 again.

The last day of class we went up to him to console him and talk. He was sad, of course, but he didn't seem too put out. I was expecting it, he said. I have a really hard time studying, and maybe I'll do better at another school. They say that sometimes it's good to step away from a problem. I believe that it's the moment for me to step away.

It hurt us all to lose 34. His abrupt departure was an injustice for us. But we saw him again the next year, standing in the seventh grade line, the first day of class. The school didn't allow students to repeat the same grade twice, but 34 had gotten—who knows how—an exception. What surprised us most was that he wanted to relive the experience.

I went up to him that day. I tried to be friendly, and he was cordial, too. He seemed skinnier, and the age difference between him and his new classmates was too obvious. I'm not 34 anymore, he finally said, with the solemn tone that I knew well. I appreciate your concern for me, but 34 no longer exists, he said. Now I'm 29, and I should get used to my new reality. Really, I prefer to blend in with my grade and make new friends. It's not healthy to remain in the past.

I suppose he was right. Every once in a while we saw him from a distance, socializing with his new classmates or talking with the teachers who'd reproached him the year before. I believe that this time he was finally able to pass, but I don't know if he stayed at the school much longer. Little by little, we lost track of him.

ANY OLD STORY
BY RONALD FLORES
(GUATEMALA)

She went to the capital a few months after she got her first period. She left town to improve herself, to become somebody. The men were closing in on her already. It was only a question of days before one of them would bring a bundle of firewood to the door of her hut, and she wasn't ready to marry yet. She knew that if she stayed any longer, her fate would be next to the fire, making tortillas, bearing children until her body dried up, keeping vigil through her husband's drunken nights, and enduring his beatings. Her parents didn't want to let her go, but from the time she was a child, she'd been indomitable. Besides, other girls had already done what she longed to do. It wasn't as though she were breaking new ground. Her family didn't give her permission, but she didn't run away from them, either. They knew that she would leave, and she knew that they would try to stop her. Anyway, she left.

Her cousin lived in the city and worked as a maid in a rich family's house. When she got there, she visited her cousin to ask for work, but there wasn't any. Find something on your own, her cousin advised her. Find something fast so you don't go broke; she'd be happy to, her cousin said, but there was nowhere for her to sleep.

Her cousin recommended a house where they rented rooms; she herself had lived there for a time. She found it by asking around. The house was situated next to the railroad, near the center of the city, in a dangerous area. A few blocks away were the customs office and the street famous for its prostitutes, who sold their services to construction workers, drunks, and petty thieves. They rented her a small room with adobe walls and a zinc roof. She shared the kitchen and a single bathroom with more than thirty people who lived as renters in that pigeon loft's dozen rooms. She paid 150 a month, plus water and light, a bill they all divided equally, without taking individual consumption into account. She settled in and went to look for work. For a couple of weeks she left early every morning and came back late, with empty hands and swollen feet, eating once a day to save the few cents she had, which were running out.

She got them to take her at a factory that was urgently hiring inexperienced workers. They offered her minimum wage and the protection of the law. The shift ran from seven in the morning until six at night, if they made the quota.

She showed up her first day of work a few minutes before the designated time. Some men made them form a line with the other employees. The foreman assigned her a place and a job. She was to glue metal eyelets on shoes where the laces passed through. Four eyelets per "piece," sixty pairs of shoes a day: the quota. There was no room for error. If she wasted a single eyelet she would have to pay for it. If she attached it wrong and wasted the piece, she would have to pay for the whole shoe. That's how it was. Better to do the job carefully, patiently, with accuracy and precision.

The foreman said she had twenty-five minutes at noon to eat lunch and use the bathroom, that she wouldn't have a break, and the day wouldn't end until she finished the quota. The foreman explained what the work entailed to each of the new employees. When he finished talking, he left the building and locked the doors. He warned that he wouldn't come back until lunchtime and that if someone felt the need to use the bathroom, she would have to hold it.

She worked carefully for the next five hours, never taking her attention away from her work, never moving from the machine she operated. Her job essentially consisted of jamming the eyelet properly onto a sort of nail, placing the piece where this nail fell on the table, holding the piece tense so it wouldn't move on impact and the hole would turn out, and then aiming and stepping on a pedal so that the machine would work and the nail would punch through the piece. As quickly as possible. The pedal stuck; maybe it needed oil.

She was about to collapse when lunchtime arrived and she separated herself from her workbench. Her legs were asleep and her shoulder muscles stiff. She had twenty pairs of shoes done, forty pairs left for the afternoon. At the end of the shift, she hadn't finished more than thirty, half the quota. The foreman told them that was fine for the first day, but they would pay half the daily wage since she'd only done half the work, understood? She agreed; she didn't have any other choice. She struggled to walk. Her legs were swollen from slamming the pedal for the eyelet, first because she needed to, then out of rage, and finally weariness.

She showed up the next morning in spite of the fact that her legs were swollen and a pain pierced her lower back whenever she bent forward, as if she might break like a dry branch. She worked with great care and dedication; she tried to work quickly, to make the quota. It was useless. She didn't make more than thirty pairs again.

For the first seven days, the same thing happened with all the new hires. The next week, the foreman warned them that they had to try harder, since if they didn't, he'd have to fire them. If they didn't make the quota by the end of the shift, they'd have to stay until they did, because there was no other way to complete the company's order. He reminded them further that they needed to show up in the morning at seven sharp, or they would be fired, regardless of the time they went home the night before.

That shift ended a little after two in the morning. She walked the distance home from the factory alone, fearing every shadow, suspicious of every noise. The next morning she showed up right on time, yawning, and the lack of sleep brought tears to her eyes. She felt she would fall down from weariness. She finished her quota a few minutes earlier than she had the night before.

That was her schedule all week. The next week, thanks to all the practice, she managed to go home a little earlier, around midnight. To motivate the workers, the foreman played music, the Broncos or the Bukis, after "closing time," and at eleven o'clock he served each one a mug of porridge. He also announced an excursion scheduled for the end of the month, paid for by the company.

It once seemed an impossible dream and then a nightmare, but she completed her first month of work. She got her first paycheck and used it to pay rent and the debts she'd built up, especially with her cousin, whom she saw every Sunday.

The day of the excursion arrived. They loaded the workers on two buses and took them to the beach. She'd never been to the sea, and seeing it brought her enormous joy. She was excited. She entered the water as she did in the river by her town, in her bra and underwear, almost naked. Her brown skin shone, her legs were hardened by work; her round breasts spilled out of her tight bra. She wasn't pretty, but she had a certain grace. Moreover, she was young. The foreman liked her. He saw her from a distance, from the shack where he was drinking.

She didn't ride either of the buses on the way back. The foreman asked his second-in-command to tell her to come with them in the company car. She agreed, naïve, fearful, not knowing why. Her coworkers, men and women both, had left. She was putting on her dress in a little shack when the foreman came over. He pushed her down. He tore off her bra; he took off her panties. He grabbed her wrists. He forced her. She had never known a man before, and she was scared. She shook. When the foreman mounted her she clenched her teeth. She felt a strong, indescribable pain. She knew nothing more than yes, and if he did it, she preferred not to remember.

Back in the city, back to the routine: when her shift ended, the foreman or the second-in-command offered to take her home in the car. There was no way to finish the quota before ten. Though she wanted to leave on time, they wouldn't let her; the doors were chained. They made her stay until she finished. If she didn't take the ride, they followed her through the desolate, deserted streets. Then in a dark corner, they forced her in the car; they did as they pleased with her. They threatened: if she complained, if she quit, if she said anything. There were more excursions. Months passed. She got pregnant. They fired her.

"For being a whore," the foreman told her and slammed the factory door in her face.

She didn't want to return to the town. She wasn't yet fifteen; she was already pregnant and didn't know by whom, the foreman or his second-in-command. Her family wouldn't take her back like this. She had to face it alone. There was no other way. She grew sad. She stopped eating. She was unemployed, and with that belly, they told her, no one would hire her anywhere. She had a little money saved. It would pay for a couple months' food and rent, nothing more.

She shut herself up in her room. She spent the day lying in bed. Sometimes, out of rage, out of guilt, out of the dirtiness she felt, she beat her belly with her fists; she threw herself against the wall. Until she spent one whole morning in the bathroom, bleeding. She fainted. One of the tenants brought her to the emergency room at the General

Hospital. They admitted her. After a few hours, they told her she had suffered a miscarriage. This meant joy to her, not suffering.

On Sunday, the day of rest, her cousin came to see her. They cried. Her cousin told her she had gotten married and would return to the town. As they said goodbye, she asked her cousin one last favor:

"If they ask for me, tell them that you haven't seen me; the city swallowed me up. Make up any old story."

VARIATION ON THEMES BY MURAKAMI AND TSAO HSUEH-CHIN

BY TRYNO MALDONADO (MEXICO)

The Emperor's only daughter was born in the Year of the Rat. Her name was composed of the beautiful character *Hui* for *brilliance*, with symmetrical strokes, and the complex and inharmonious character *Ying*, for *intelligence*. Hui Ying's prophetic abilities had been known throughout the Empire since her childhood, when, as with those omens which deserve to be buried without a scruple, she dreamed of her father's death the same night it took place.

The middle of the night had passed when the stubborn pecking of a bird on the windowsill interrupted her sleep. Steered by the enthusiasm which the noble art of contemplating birds always awoke in her, little Hui Ying tried to spy it from the corner of her eye, sleepily, from her bed. The bird had disappeared. Though the girl was filled with disappointment, she had little trouble recovering her sleep. Minutes later, when the pecking started to resound again, she opened her eyes like sieves, her reflexes spurred by the reappearance of that monophonic sound. This time she was luckier: she finally saw the bird with the help of a summer moon that cut a perfect square as it burst through the window. She got up, trying not to frighten that rare-colored bird, and walked barefoot in search of an illustrated book of birds, a gift from her father. She was sure that with its help she would learn her visitor's identity. Nevertheless, when Hui Ying returned, hugging the heavy volume exultantly, the bird launched into flight and came to rest on the branch of a nearby oak tree. Leaning on the windowsill, aided by a bench, completely focused on the business of spying the bird, the girl noticed two men approaching, sheathed in black, who stealthily fled from the moon as they advanced between the trees of the majestic garden. What Hui Ying wanted least was to be caught awake in the middle of the night. She relinquished her plan, abandoned the book of birds, and prepared to reconquer her sleep. Soon she was halted by a new sound proceeding from the garden. It was the crackle of a spade repeatedly thrust into the earth, as she was able to verify by climbing up to the window discreetly. One of the two men was digging a hole in an area defined by the roots of the oak tree where the strangely-colored bird went to hide. The other man, a little stouter, scanned the surroundings with a dun-colored shape between his hands. Nothing conceived at this hour, and in this clandestine manner, could be good, Hui Ying thought; there was something undoubtedly sinister behind all this. When the man with the shovel considered the pit sufficiently deep, the second introduced the bundle he held with almost religious devotion, and then, between the two of them, they filled the trench with greater hurry and carelessness than when they began. The girl knew she shouldn't have been part of that that scene, since the simple fact of witnessing it, even unseen, covered her with the same cloak of complicity that swathed the two shadows at the foot of the tree.

After the impromptu gravediggers fled, Hui Ying felt that her heart might burst into particles at any moment, particles that would obstruct her veins until they cut her circulation. Part of her found herself immobile and begged her to lie down and reconcile herself to sleep, to forget all that happened; the other part, however, urged her to run to the garden and unearth the mysterious bundle before someone else, perhaps a hypothetical, nocturnal thief who had observed everything from the beginning and had embarked on a treasure hunt, left her with nothing but empty hands. Imprisoned by these kinds of ruminations, Hui Ying passed minutes in astonishment. Finally, as the night advanced further, she decided to slip out with the oak tree as her goal, concentrating on each step through the total solitude of this part of the garden. A tickle of gnats ran up from her toes, and a terrible new sensation seized her tiny body: she believed that she was shedding the real world, as if an *inside* and an *outside* existed, much like what one experienced diving into a pond to see *reality* from there. Hui Ying was attacked by a carnivorous horror that didn't compare even to the wildest animal's, a horror that not even damned souls could bear had they seen what the girl saw that night. She felt out of touch with herself. After digging into the earth in the shallow pit, making the most of her tiny hands, she opened the kerchief, tinted crimson, which until that point had covered the recently-severed head of her father, the Emperor.

Without understanding the meaning of what she found, Hui-Ying threw the head as if it were the inanimate object it had become and quickly retraced her steps, shrouded by a ruthless terror. She was overwhelmed by a vehement desire to sleep. She placed her hope in an invincible logic that showed her that only thus, by returning to a primeval sleep, could she liberate herself from the nightmare to which she'd been bound. But when Hui Ying returned to her bed, she found it occupied. To her surprise, a girl of her stature, perhaps her age, peacefully slept on top of it. She walked around her, preserving her silence, and when she had the girl in front of her, she observed the stranger's face for a moment: round, jaundiced, like her own. The person sleeping in her bed was *herself.* With a cry of rage at the flagrant intrusion, Hui Ying began to shove the stranger until she almost sent her to the cold floor. The mere thought that her identity had fallen victim to larceny bewildered her exceedingly, as when someone hears an extraordinary revelation without knowing oneself to be the subject of it. Soon she understood that she herself was no more than a dream, only a dream of the real Hui Ying, the one who slept, as in the old fable of the mirror and the hare. She had shed her body in some scene of the terrible masquerade, and so she knew that she needed to return to her original vessel as soon as possible. But how? And if she could never return to her body?

When the sun lit the air, the people woke to the tragic news of the Emperor's murder at the hands of two hired assassins. The assassins had been caught in their escape and would be immolated publicly that evening, as custom dictated. Once they confessed their methods, under torture by one of the guards, the oak was torn out by the roots. However, they never found the Emperor's head.

Hours later, in the din that fed off the Empire's disorder and uncertainty, someone noticed the absence of the Emperor's only daughter. Her name was composed of the beautiful character *Hui* for *brilliance*, with symmetrical strokes, and the complex and inharmonious character *Ying*, for *intelligence*. Hui Ying's prophetic abilities had been known throughout the Empire since her childhood, when, as with those omens that deserve to be buried without a scruple, she dreamed of her father's death the same night it took place.

The middle of the night had passed when the stubborn pecking of a bird on the windowsill interrupted her sleep. Steered by the enthusiasm which the noble art of contemplating birds always awoke in her, little Hui Ying tried to spy it from the corner of her eye, sleepily, from her bed. The bird had disappeared. Though the girl was filled with disappointment, she had little trouble recovering her sleep. Minutes later, when the pecking started to resound again, she opened her eyes like sieves, her reflexes spurred by the reappearance of that monophonic sound. This time she was luckier: she finally saw the bird with the help of a summer moon that cut a perfect square as it burst through the window. She got up, trying not to frighten that rare-colored bird, and walked barefoot in search of an illustrated book of birds, a gift from her father. She was sure that with its help she would learn her visitor's identity. Nevertheless, when Hui Ying returned, hugging the heavy volume exultantly, the bird launched into flight and came to rest on the branch of a nearby oak tree. Leaning on the windowsill, aided by a bench, completely focused on the business of spying the bird, the girl noticed two men approaching, sheathed in black, who stealthily fled from the moon as they advanced between the trees of the majestic garden. What Hui Ying wanted least was to be caught awake in the middle of the night. She relinquished her plan, abandoned the book of birds, and prepared to reconquer her sleep. It was then that she saw herself trapped in a nightmare: from her bed she saw a girl of her stature enter, dressed in her nightgown, but her feet were covered with clay and her hands marked with blood and earth. The person who entered her chamber was herself, out of breath, as if she had just run a long race. Hui Ying could feel the intruder start to hook her with her gaze, in a fit of ire made clear through tears and a sulky face, only to push her out of her own bed later, with violence and outrage. Hui Ying burned with the need to scream, to ask for help: she fervently desired it, but she had turned into a log, an anchored anvil. When *the other* Hui Ying recovered her calm, as a natural result of her fatigue, she approached her stiff body and whispered in her ear:

"Tonight my father died. You knew it would occur. In your hands was the power to avoid it, and instead you have chosen silence."

Then she lay down on the half of the bed that she had managed to clear and kissed her icy lips. Both went back to sleep, forgetting any trace of anxiety, as if in an agreement validated only by the restoration of silence.

When the sun lit the air, the people woke to the tragic news of the Emperor's murder at the hands of two hired assassins. The assassins had been caught in their escape and would be immolated publicly that evening, as custom dictated. Once they confessed their methods, under torture by one of the guards, the oak was torn out by the roots. However, they never found the Emperor's head.

Hours later, in the din that fed off the Empire's disorder and uncertainty, someone noticed the absence of the Emperor's only daughter. Her name was composed of the beautiful character *Hui* for *brilliance*, with symmetrical strokes, and the complex and inharmonious character *Ying*, for *intelligence*. Hui Ying's prophetic abilities had been known throughout the Empire since her childhood, when, as with those omens which deserve to be buried without a scruple, she dreamed of her father's death the same night it took place, only to later unearth his head, driven by the madness of her augury, and run with it, directionless, for whole days.

PSEUDOEPHEDRINE
BY ANTONIO ORTUÑO
(MEXICO)

The first to get sick was Miranda, the oldest. We were upset because it meant we couldn't go to the movies on Friday, the only day my father-in-law could watch the girls. Despite Miranda's sneezing, Dina, my wife, insisted that we go to the kindergarten *posada*. "It's the last day of class. We'll take care of her flu over the weekend, and on Monday we'll go to the beach." We'd decided to spend Christmas by the sea so as not to face another year of the same debate: whose family to have dinner with, hers or mine.

There were more parents than students at the posada and more liquor and pork rind tostadas than candy and pop. "A lot of kids are coming down with the flu," the principal explained. "But since the parents already bought their tickets, well, they came." "Miranda's also getting sick," we confessed. "That's why the baby's all bundled up." Marta, just seven months old, poked part of her nose and a cheek through the tangle of her wool blanket.

After getting in line for food, I discovered that some of the mothers had preserved their tits and asses in good condition. And I discovered that one of the fathers, for his part, had noticed that my wife's weren't bad either. He was chatting with her, taking advantage of my distance. The two smiled. The subject in question was short, with his feminine gestures and black curls. I struck up a conversation with Ronaldo's mother, a woman around thirty years old with a look of contained bitterness that my wife called "the face of a woman who needs a good fuck." Claudia was her name, one of those deceptively thin women who, beneath a brittle neck and above scrawny calves, exhibit breasts and a behind more voluminous than one might expect. She had pierced her nose and dyed her bangs purple since our last encounter. She didn't have a boyfriend or a husband, so the other kindergarten mothers tracked her movements, and more than one observed with some concern how I offered to light her cigarette and how she laughed at the entire repertoire of jokes I use to hit on women.

We went home in a bad mood. Miranda started to cry: she had a fever of 102 degrees. We called the pediatrician, who recommended that we give her a drop of Tylenol and let her sleep. He also let us know that that Friday was his last day of work: he was going to spend Christmas on the beach. "Like us," I told him. "Okay, but if Miranda's fever keeps up, you shouldn't travel," he said before hanging up. "Leave a message on my voicemail if it gets bad, and I'll find a way to call you." I didn't repeat this to Dina, as I didn't want to induce hysteria.

Medicated and without an appetite, Miranda spent the night in our bed watching TV. Marta, who had slept in her own bedroom since she was three months old, was meticulously wrapped in four blankets. I took the space heater down from the top of the closet and plugged it in next to her door. Miranda's presence kept Dina and I from making love or even trying. In any case, even the girls' tiniest sneeze would have scared away my wife's sexual appetite. I fell asleep thinking of Claudia's nose and her purple bangs.

We expected to spend Saturday morning buying beach clothes

and paying bills to travel worry-free, but Miranda woke up with a fever of 102.5 degrees, despite the Tylenol. Mechanically, I dialed the pediatrician's number. His voicemail picked up: "Hello, this is Doctor Pardo. If you have an emergency, please call the hospital. Otherwise, leave a message." I left a message.

We agreed that my wife would take care of the girls and I would go out to pay the bills and buy beach toys for Miranda, baby sunscreen for Marta, some flip-flops for Dina and a baseball cap for me. I had thought about talking Dina into buying herself a bikini, but I decided not to mention it. I would buy it myself and give it to her at the beach. Before leaving I thought I heard sounds from Marta's bedroom. I poked my head in. It was an oven, thanks to the space heater. I turned it off. Marta sneezed. I took off one of the blankets and opened the window. I left without telling Dina. I didn't want to induce hysteria.

Barely anyone was at the store. I ate a muffin in the cafeteria for breakfast and paid the bills in less than ten minutes. I took a cart and went to the clothing section. On the way, I picked up a bag of beach toys for Miranda and the baby sunscreen. Also anti-flu medicine, an enormous colored box that I included on my list so that my wife and I wouldn't end up being the sick ones. Then I picked out a cap and a plain white T-shirt for me. For Dina, some closed-toe sandals like the kind I use, the kind she says she hates but always ends up stealing.

I remembered the plan with the bikini. Morosely, I approached the women's section. Dina had a slightly inharmonious body. Like many women who've had kids but haven't nursed them, her hips and butt were wide, but her breasts remained small, adolescent. So I found myself ransacking two different bikinis to make one her size.

"Do you buy women's clothes often?" Claudia appeared next to my cart, smiling, her hands full of leopard-print lingerie. "Honestly, no." "That's too small for Dina. She won't want to wear it." It was true, but I only smiled, as if to make her understand that my wife was accustomed to using whips and rubber toys every Friday. I accompanied Claudia to the dressing room to watch her cart. She wasn't going to try on the lingerie—it was prohibited by the store's hygiene rules—but a pair of jeans instead. While I waited for her to come out, I pretended to be very interested in the label on the anti-flu medicine. The active ingredient was pseudoephedrine, and the label warned that it could cause nausea, dizziness, dry mouth or excessive drooling, drowsiness or insomnia, severe allergic reactions, and in extreme cases, death. I felt satisfied. "How do they look?" She came out so I could admire her ass in the jeans. They looked good, just like all tight clothes do on women who are excessively gifted in the ass. Claudia smiled again. She didn't look like she needed a good fuck any more.

At the checkout we ran into the kindergarten principal. She greeted us warmly, until her cerebellum advised her that the Father at cart one didn't match up with the Mother at cart two. She said goodbye with a simple tilt of her head. While we waited to pay, Claudia started paging through a women's magazine, and I went back to exploring the mysteries of the medicine label. Pseudoephedrine, the good stuff. "It says here that women in Africa have their clitorises removed," she remarked without lifting her gaze. "And that anal sex is common there, and that's why AIDS is uncontrollable." I raised my eyebrows, and she let out a laugh that she muffled with her hand and said, "Better no one hears us talking about clitorises and anal sex, or the gossip is going to get even worse."

Since the gossip couldn't get any worse at that point, I carried her bags to the car and helped her put them in. She seemed interested in talking more, but I dodged her under the pretext of Miranda's flu. "Ronaldito's sick, too." "What doctor do you take him to? Ours went on vacation and isn't taking calls." She put her hands on her hips. "I don't take him to the doctor. I know homeopathy. If you want, I can give you medicine for your daughter." I didn't accept, but she insisted on putting a card with her phone number in my pocket. "Call me anytime you need."

There was a car in my spot in the garage, next to Dina's. I entered with the bags in one hand and the keys in the other. I didn't hear any noise, except for Marta's sporadic sneezing. Miranda was asleep, apparently without a fever. I imagined that the principal had driven home a hundred miles an hour to call Dina and tell her that I was at the checkout, talking about African clitorises and rectums with Claudia. I imagined Dina armed with a knife, ready to slit my throat as soon as I walked in.

In reality, she was in the kitchen, drinking coffee with the curly-haired guy who'd admired her at the posada. His was the usurping car. "I didn't hear you come in." "Some idiot parked in my spot." The guy looked at me resentfully. "He's not an idiot: he's Walter, Igor's dad, Miranda's little classmate. He's a homeopathic doctor, and I called him to check on the girls since the pediatrician isn't answering."

Walter stood up and offered me his hand. I shook it with hypocritical joviality. "Walter thinks Miranda doesn't have the flu. She's just tired, and Marta's teeth are coming in." The homeopath nodded a couple times, supporting the diagnosis.

I don't tend to be distrustful, but I noted the flush on my wife's face. And her scent. She smelled like she did when she consented to make love my way, which is less neurotic than hers. Walter's fly was open, which could mean nothing. Or something. I looked at the homeopath, opened the bottle of pseudoephedrine, poured myself a glass of water, and swallowed two pills. "I don't believe in homeopathy, Walter." He gave me another belligerent look. Dina twisted her mouth. "And please take your car out of my spot. I don't like to leave my car on the street. That's why I'm renting a house with a garage." Walter said goodbye to Dina with a kiss on the back of her hand and left silently, shaking his curls. I left the kitchen before she could unleash her revenge.

There was a handwritten note in the dining room, with a painstaking script that wasn't my wife's. The homeopathic prescription. I memorized the compounds and the doses. I called Claudia's number, holding her card in front of my eyes. Her writing was ungainly, just like she was. "Yes?" "Hi. That was quick. You were waiting for my call." Her clear laugh over the speaker put me in a good mood. She listened skeptically to Walter's prescription and snorted. "The flu is the flu. No one sneezes because they're teething or they're tired. Listen, what you're going to do is buy what I tell you to and trick your wife into thinking that you're giving the girls her medicines." "You're asking me to trick my wife?" Claudia's bell-like laugh filled my ears.

"Who were you talking with?" "The pediatrician." "And what did he say?" "Nothing. He didn't answer. I left a message on his voicemail." Dina was standing in the hallway with her arms crossed. She looked like she needed a good fuck. "You acted like a brute with Walter." I acknowledged it with my head down. My strategy consisted of admitting she was right and using my nerves about the girls' sickness as a pretext. Dina looked at me with an intensity that boded a fight or a quick, violent screw when Miranda started to cry. She had a fever of 103 degrees. We put her in the bathtub and gave her Tylenol.

Dina didn't cook, and we didn't feel like ordering food, so each of us attacked the fridge when we were hungry. I made myself a bowl of cereal with milk and a mayonnaise sandwich, like I did when I was eleven years old and my mother didn't come home for dinner. After drinking a big gulp of milk, I felt like my throat was melting. I coughed. Dina stuck her head through the door and looked at me, horrified. Another cough answered in the distance. It was Marta.

She had a fever of 101.5 degrees. Two chills ran through my shoulder blades and deltoids. We didn't know how much Tylenol to give the baby. The pediatrician didn't answer. Dina ran to call Walter. I hid and called Claudia from my cell phone. "My daughters have a fever." "Have you given them the medicines yet?" "No." "Well, it would be a good idea to start." "You don't know how much Tylenol to give a child?" "I don't give children Tylenol. It has horrible side effects. They end up born with two heads." "My daughters have already been born, I'm afraid."

Dina left the house, slamming the door. She came back after half an hour with a bag full of homeopathic medicine and a diet soda. "You drink diet soda?" "Sometimes." "Walter must not like fat girls." I took advantage of her confusion to leave the house. I didn't know where to find a homeopathic pharmacy, so I called Claudia again. "I have what you need at home. Come over." What I needed was to leave the girls asleep in their cradles and sit in a jacuzzi with Dina at a hotel by the sea and take off the bikini I had bought her. It took a while to find the address. She opened the door, without makeup and her hair uncombed, wearing a sweater and glasses. She already had a bag in her hand with little bottles and a list of doses and schedules. I asked her about Ronaldo. "He's upstairs, watching TV." The house was huge and ugly, like all inherited houses. "My father wanted to live near the fire station. He was obsessed with fires. That's why we live here." My charisma depends on my jokes, and I didn't have the presence of mind to tell one at that moment. I made a face and left looking nervous, which tends to flatter women more than any joke.

Dina was crying. Miranda's fever was more than 103 degrees and Marta's, 102.5. Dina wasn't crying because of that. "The principal called." I imagined a languid conversation, full of understandings. "What were you doing at the store with that whore, Claudia?" "The same thing you were doing with your dear Walter: seeking medical advice." "That whore is a doctor?" "Homeopathic," I said, raising the little bag full of bottles.

I made a final attempt to dial the pediatrician's number before administering the first homeopathic dose. The voice mail answered. I muttered an obscenity and hung up. We flipped a coin for the first turn. I lost. My throat burned, and my back muttered its list of complaints. Dina struggled with Marta to give her the drops. She had a coughing fit. Dina threatened to make Miranda swallow her pills. I opted to lie down on the sofa and take a nap. I thought about how bad Claudia looked with glasses, about how badly Walter's pants fit, about Dina with clothes and without them. I woke up stiff with cold. The house was dark and silent. I stood up, attacked by an intense desire to piss. Just when I felt relieved, a wave of nausea overcame me. I cursed the mayonnaise sandwich. Then Dina started screaming and picked up the phone. Miranda was crying. She must have had a fever. Marta sneezed with the persistence of a motor. It was hot, and sweat ran to the corners of my mouth. I dragged myself out of the bathroom. I asked for water in a fading voice. I was helped. I drank. I reached a carpet. I let myself fall.

The next thing was Walter, his long hands on my temples. "You fainted. You're sick. Did you take any medicine?" "Pseudoephedrine, Walter, the very best." "You must be allergic." Dina poked her head through the homeopath's curls. Maybe she was waiting for my death. Maybe not. Maybe Walter made her his, quickly and uncomfortably, in front of my closed eyelids. I swallowed the solution that was offered to me in the minuscule glass of a professional homeopath. It tasted like brandy or something like it, thank goodness. I managed to stand up and walk to the bed. The nausea returned, accompanied by shaking and chills. I didn't want Walter to leave my side; I wanted, even, to caress those little curls, provided that he stayed. But Miranda's temperature was 103.5 degrees and Marta's 103, so he went off to check on them. Dina followed him and he closed my bedroom door behind them, without even coming near me. The female selects the strongest male to ensure the fittest offspring. But our daughters had already been born.

I dialed Claudia's number. Through the window I could see a dark sky that could signify any time of day. It took her two, three rings to answer. Now I felt so hot that if I were to close my eyes, they would shoot out of their sockets and explode against the wall. "Yes?" "I fainted. It appears that I'm allergic to pseudoephedrine." A long silence. "Do you want me to come over? Are you alone?" "Dina's here. With Walter. I don't want to bother them." "Walter?" Another long silence. "Come over tomorrow at three. I'll make sure that I'm alone." "Okay. I'll bring medicine." "Bring yourself, nothing else." "Whatever you want."

I hadn't cried since I was eleven years old, when my mother didn't come home one night. I did it quietly, into the pillow. At 2:24 in the morning I awoke to the red numbers of the digital clock and Miranda's screams. The girl either had a nightmare or had broken her arm: a simple fever didn't merit such a fuss. 103. Either Dina had forgotten to give her Tylenol, or Walter had ordered her to stop. But Walter wasn't the pater familias. I gave Miranda her medicine, which she took with an admirable resignation, and I put her to sleep, cradled in my arms, despite her five years, murmuring nonsense about kittens and bunnies. I got up, still nauseous. Pseudoephedrine. I felt sweaty, hot, my heart pounding in my feet, my stomach, my teeth. I stopped by Marta's room. 101.5. They hadn't given her Tylenol, either. I interrupted her sleep to do so and kissed her on her head and ears until she smiled. I set her softly in her cradle.

Dina was sleeping in the living room, worn out, her skirt hiked halfway up her thighs, which were damp from the heat or something worse. Next to her hand rested one of those useful little glasses of a professional homeopath. I smelled its contents. It had to be some kind of supreme sedative. I started to caress her legs. She didn't react. I slid a finger under her panties and over her ass. She drooled. A band of twenty musicians could have mounted her before she woke up. Walter must have given her the medicine to hurry the process of adultery. Bitch. The worst is that he made her forget to give the girls their Tylenol or even prohibited her from doing so; he, a new lover before a slave who was too timid to disobey. I poked my head through the curtain. His car was no longer there. Asshole.

I got up, cotton-mouthed, my heart beating in my fingers, my eyelashes, my ankle. The girls breathed slowly. It was 5:02. I threw myself on the bed and slept maybe an hour; the sky was still black when I opened my eyes. It was hot. I stretched and discovered that I wanted Dina. Miranda slept with her fingers in her mouth. 99. Marta snored lightly. 98.8. I had to take off my shirt to go out to the hallway. Too hot. Pseudoephedrine or Walter's antidote. A slightly higher dose would have driven me to the kitchen for a knife, but what I wanted was to take Dina's clothes off, bite her, scratch her. She barely moved when I slid into the chair. I thought: When the court judges me, I'll say it was the pseudoephedrine, or I'll blame Walter for giving me an irresistible aphrodisiac. I lifted her skirt and inhaled. I tore her clothes off. Her body. 104. I separated her legs and began to kiss her obstinately. I grunted and howled, although part of my brain tried to muffle my effusions so as not to wake up the girls. Dina opened her drunken eyes and started to swear at me. 104.5. We howled and insulted each other; I told her that Claudia's butt sagged, even in jeans as tight as sausage casings, and she reflected on Walter's very possible impotence. I bit her breasts and she brutally clawed at my back. We were woken by a roar and an evil laugh. It was Miranda, now standing up, who had managed to knock over her mother's magazine pile. Dina and I got dressed without looking at each other and went upstairs. Miranda was jumping on my illustrated book about the Crusades. I chased her to her bedroom and ordered her to pack her suitcase. I looked at myself in the mirror in the hall. I wasn't sweating and my appearance looked normal, my hair barely ruffled. I went to get water and felt a pang of hunger. Dina came downstairs with Marta in her arms. The baby was chewing on the neck of a stuffed giraffe with a vampire's glee. "Her bottle ran out," my wife informed me, perplexed. We ate eggs and tortillas for breakfast, and I drank my first coffee of the day. Claudia was scheduled for three. Dina confessed that Walter would come by at 2:30. We decided to move up the trip to the beach. The hotel was able to advance our reservation and changing the plane tickets took five minutes.

Dina looked at the table. "Let's go, then?" She said it with disappointment and hope. At the airport I confessed my purchase of the bikini and gave it to her. "It's too small; it'll make me look obese." I spent the flight reading a medical magazine. There was an article about pseudoephedrine, but I preferred to skip it and focus on one about the clitoral circumcision in African women and existing reconstructive surgeries. Dina and our daughters sang.

At the beach we asked for umbrellas and set them up to protect the girls from the sun. Marta was lathered with baby sunscreen, and Miranda was topped with a little straw hat. There weren't any tourists, just two old people riding horses, going off into the distance to the south. The sky was clear and splendid. I heard my phone ring and reached out a lazy hand, letting it first brush Dina's ass, which hardened at the tribute.

It was the pediatrician.

I let it go to voicemail.

WITHOUT ARTIFICIAL LIGHT BY MARÍA DEL CARMEN PÉREZ CUADRA (NICARAGUA)

From the kitchen sink, you can watch the street without being seen. The window is made of mirrored glass; he always thought that *Vanidades* magazine had good ideas. The heliotropes had wilted and the girl who sold flowers had not appeared for nearly a week. Muriel is a mature man but his skin is firm and soft, like an adolescent's buttocks. He has shaved his chest to look more seductive, and he goes riding on his horse half-naked; his hair, bleached blonde, looks natural against his copper skin. I see him from here, standing at my wall of dirty plates. Out to conquer new women, believing, perhaps, that no one can see him. He doesn't know; he's never come into my kitchen. Muriel lives in the house in front. Sometimes his lovers fix their hair and makeup before my mirrored window, as if taking part in a furtive ritual. I measure their breasts with respect to mine; I judge whether they would fall perfectly into Muriel's warm hands. Slowly, I observe the curve of their necks, sometimes I feel the warm tremble of his kisses. He's like a perverse god who loves them and litters them like orange peels.

Secretly, from behind the china cabinet, which shields me with the veined gleam of its precious wood, I hear my husband speak with

Muriel without my intending to hear them. My husband is proud of me, a perfect woman. Muriel complains about my permanent silence. My husband claims that it's part of my perfection, "the wisdom of silence," he says. But Muriel doesn't know what silence is; every conquest is related to his circle of friends with full details of height and weight. I don't hear them, but I can read their lips from the kitchen. The tree between his house and mine, almost in the middle of the street, is witness to Muriel's desire for public display. I prefer silence instead, my privacy.

The girl with the flowers returned with her tin smile to tell me that she's going to school now in the afternoons. That's why she hasn't come lately. She shows me a poem she has written:

Rose blood of Christ, running in my veins
Madonna lilies to erase my pains,
Mint for forgetting, though it stings
To go on, walking in rings
Around the heart, while my grandmother sings.

She asks me if I like it. She's nearly a woman now; it's good for her to express her thoughts. One can only hope she keeps studying and makes something of herself. My husband says we women don't think; we float only to smash against the blade of ideas; we express our intelligence through our hands and feelings when we cook, embroider, or provide tactful consolation. He says women are made of love and tears, the good ones, and the bad ones of envy and tears. "What can you women know, save philosophies of the kitchen." I give the girl the advice my husband always gives me:

"Read books of poetry, if you think that's what you like."

The days pass and no one discovers that I am neither good nor bad, neither sweet nor salty, I am only myself, the compass of my heart, the shine of my skin, the fading color of my hair. If she finds a way, if she learns what path to follow, the flower girl will go far. She will teach her own mother a lesson.

Heat in the lunar dawn. I awoke from thirst; insomnia from thirst is recommended for no one. Naked, since tonight I fulfilled my marital duties; no one sees me, no one realizes that I exist here in this nouveau-riche house in this poor neighborhood. My cactus and my violets need water, too. The moonlight streams through window, so I don't need artificial lights. Perhaps this is the most important moment of freedom in my life.

Before my eyes, Muriel leans, as always, against the mango tree. He has no idea I see him; this time he's squeezing the flower girl's skinny ass. Her little rosebud breasts and her scapular don't seem defenseless in his hands, they seem perverse, young, enviable. Muriel's grotesque, almost bestial caresses have ripped off her skirt, and they reveal the soft curve of her virgin hips, the opening of her bottom, the warm throbbing of her sex. A nocturnal migraine flogs my temples. My glass of water falls to the floor and smashes to bits. The noise startles the couple. They look up on hearing the noise. I try to pick up the broken glass and see only my blood flowing from the wounds. I want to cry and can't. I clean, sweep up, put things in order, like I always do with everything. I stand up to see what is happening outside. It's the girl's father. The three argue, nearly silent, but tense. Her father happened to be walking by at this late hour, piss-drunk. He tries to fight with Muriel but Muriel knocks him down, almost without effort. The father goes away; a cloud draws over the spectacle I see from my window. I chose this window; my husband doesn't see that it's like the mirror from *Law and Order*, since he doesn't watch television. I feel like a judge, since from here I can dictate the verdict no one will ever hear. So I test the salt of my blood and the hard tips of my breasts. I see him. He comes walking, slowly, surely. They must have seen him—the cloud disappeared—but they are too lost in each other to notice. Then the girl's boyfriend drags her off from Muriel by force, pulling her by her limp black hair, now tangled.

The girl tries to intercede but her boyfriend throws her back. He pulls a gun from his jacket and points it at Muriel. But what could I do? Tell my husband? Run out to the street screaming, as if Muriel mattered to me? Let Muriel at last receive his punishment? I reflected awhile. The young man has shot the flower girl in the chest. November dawn. Who would have known, Muriel, that your adventures would end with one shot to the forehead and another to the crotch?

My husband comes to ask me for something; he says that we should go to bed, it's cold. I ask him if he heard the shots; he says no, he was taking a shower. "Figments of your imagination." He goes back to bed.

In the crepuscular darkness a neighbor woman enters through the patio gate I always leave open. She turns on the lights. Call the police, there's a dead person in the street.

I answer, "There's two. You call, because I'm naked."

The truth is that my hands are stained with blood.

BOXER

BY CARLOS WYNTER MELO (PANAMA)

We don't know that Martínez is a bad person. But neither can we say that he's a kind soul, exactly. Absent, if any word defines him, it's that: absent. And no one knows what he feels, and no one understands why he's happy with such a simple life of boxing and shadow puppets.

Martínez didn't know Orlando the Nica Mojica: no, sir. They'd said hello to each other once, that's all. They didn't have a reason to hate each other, as a few newspapers had insinuated. The Shadow Martínez—as I've told reporters—is incapable of hating anyone.

There are those who might think, seeing Martínez's distracted appearance, that he's stupid. That's not the case, either. You can't call someone stupid who projects figures onto the wall with such mastery. If they ask me, I tell them that Martínez is simply a blank book. Nothing more and nothing less. And no one knows what will appear on his pages from one instant to the next. The guy lives behind his eyes, and at the right moment, bam!, he comes up to the surface. So he's a genius, as he proves through his mathematical boxing. Even now, with the years on him, the way that he plans and develops a fight is brilliant.

On the eve of the fight with the Nica, the Shadow told me about a dream he had. More than a dream, it was a nightmare. Suffice it to remember the life Martínez led before being a champion: poor, dying of hunger in every sense of the word. When he was six years old—and he never forgot this—a guy stole all the gum he was selling. He told him: "Little beggar, I'm going to buy all of your gum, all of it, but you have to give it to me and wait here just a minute. I'll come right back with your money." Of course, the guy never returned. That day, Martínez swore by all the saints that no one would ever take advantage of him again. He told me once: "As a boy, I was stupid. But after that, I changed and became a man."

In the dream, the Shadow got a beating, an all-out trouncing. He dreamed the same thing several times: he looked at himself in the mirror, and in the dark glass a face sprung up, one that wasn't quite defined, and one fist came out after another, and Martínez didn't even know where the punches came from. While they thrashed him, a voice said: "You're too old now, boxer; you're an old man, you've gotten weak." He'd wake up soaked in sweat, his arms tense. While he dreamed, fear kept him from breathing. Afterward he remarked, a little scared: "Man, I haven't felt like that for years. I was defenseless. I don't want to sleep anymore, so I don't feel that way again."

Maybe that hidden fear made him work extraordinarily hard. He never accepted his age. According to him, Martínez would be around for a while. And no one would doubt that anymore after his fight with the Nica. People would respect him again.

The Shadow had won a thousand bets making figures on the walls. It comes to him as naturally as breathing. Someone tells him, "Make a panther," and quickly, he contorts the fingers on one hand, adjusts them on the other, and the panther appears. His favorite figure is a boy walking, his profile very-well defined, his arms moving to the beat of his march and his legs flexing back and forth. One night, someone who was astounded by this talent said that it might very well be that the shadows project Martínez. I've observed him often, and, by God, to the naked eye, it seems like it.

For his part, the Nica was—God forgive me—a loudmouth. He was one of those guys who repeat, over and over, that no one can last more than a round with him, that he will beat his opponents to a pulp. Martínez kept his cool under this verbal assault. He didn't waste gunpowder on a vulture; he focused on training. He was obsessive. And it hurt me to see him like that; I told him more than once it wasn't normal.

Anyway, the day of the fight came, and we all know what happened: the Shadow killed the Nica. It was a historic bout! We can't detract from the Nica's merits (may he rest in peace); he was at his peak. But the Shadow was relentless. He took punches like an animal, and even then, he kept on the offensive. When the Nica gave in to the heat, the Shadow applied his winning strategy: he worked him from the left, and then immediately delivered a hard right hook. By that point, both of their faces were already covered with blood. And the Nica fell. His body began to convulse on the canvas. The doctor came in, and that was it. The Shadow kept jumping on his tiptoes, though you couldn't tell if he was happy or contrite.

We took Martínez out, covered in his silk robe. A lot of people booed him, and some journalists followed him. Cans and leftover food rained on us. Well, that's what everyone knows. Now I'm going to tell what only I know: I, who went to visit the Shadow during his convalescence and listened to him as only those who truly love can listen.

I know, for instance, the reasons why the champion left his boxing career. And I also know what changed him so drastically, what made him another person, precisely.

I remember that he greeted me with a wide and playful smile and that he was the first to speak: "The Nica died on us."

I only agreed.

"I haven't stopped thinking about him. The nightmares went on after his death, you know? I thought that they'd stop once I beat him."

"Well, champ, what do the nightmares have to do with the Nica?"

"I got it in my head that the Nica was the face in the mirror. I thought the Nica was my destiny, and I was damn afraid of my destiny, you get me?"

We sat in silence. It was the first time the Shadow had spoken to me from his heart. He added, as if he were talking to himself:

"The nightmares went on after he died, because defeating the Nica didn't resolve anything. I had focused on overcoming my destiny, but really, I overcame nothing."

We were quiet again.

"Do you remember what the guy said about my shadows? That he didn't know if it was the shadows that projected me? Well, I don't know either. I don't know if hate moved me against the Nica. I don't know if I hit him too hard. I don't know."

"Don't think about that now," I said to calm him down.

"Don't worry. I'm not speaking out of anguish. From now on, I'm free, for better or for worse. Nothing matters too much to me now. I discovered the identity of the face in the dream! It's all very obvious, my friend: When you look in the mirror, whose face do you see?"

LIMA, PERU, JULY 28, 1979

BY DANIEL ALARCÓN (PERU)

There were ten of us and we shared a single name: compañero. Except me. They called me Pintor. Together we formed an uncertain circle around a dead dog, under the dim lights just off the plaza. Everything was cloaked in fog. Our first revolutionary act, announcing ourselves to the nation. We strung up dogs from all the street lamps, covered them with terse and angry slogans, *Die Capitalist Dogs* and such; leaving the beasts there for the people to see how fanatical we could be. It is clear now that we didn't scare anyone so much as we disturbed them and convinced them of our peculiar mania, our worship of frivolous violence. Fear would come later. Killing street dogs in the bleak gray hours before sunrise, the morning of Independence Day, July 28, 1979. Decent people slept, but we made war, fashioned it with our hands, our knives and our sweat. Everything was going well until we ran out of black dogs.

One of the compañeros had directed that all the dogs were to be black, and we were in no position to question these things. An aesthetic decision, not a practical one. Lima has a nearly infinite supply of mutts, but not all of them are black. By two o'clock, we were slopping black paint on beige, brown, and white mutts, all squirming away the last of their breaths, fur tinged with red.

Given my erstwhile talents with the brush, I was charged with painting the not-quite-black ones. We had one there: dead, split open, its viscera slipping onto the pavement. We were tired, trying to decide if this mutt's particular shade of brown was dark enough to pass for black. I don't recall many strong opinions on the matter. The narcotic effects of action were drifting away, leaving us with a bleeding animal, dead, a shade too light.

I didn't care what color the dog was.

Just as we were coming to a consensus that we would paint the dead mutt we had at our feet—just then I saw it: from the corner of my eye, darting down an alleyway, a black dog. It was spectacularly black, completely black, and before I knew it, I found myself racing down the cobblestones after it. I dropped the paintbrush one of my compañeros had handed me. They called after me, "Pintor!" but I was gone.

Enraged, I chased after the black animal, hoping to kill it, bring it back, string it up. That night, the way things were going, I wanted, more than anything, for my actions to make sense. I was tired of painting.

You should know the homeless dogs of Lima inhabit a higher plane of ruthlessness. They own the alleys, they are thieves of the colonial city, undressing trash heaps, urinating in cobblestone corners, always with an eye open. They're witnesses to murders, robberies, shakedowns; they hustle through the streets with self-assurance, with a confidence that comes from knowing they don't have to eat every day to live. That night we ran all over the plaza, butchering them, in awe of their treachery, raw and golden.

I knew how many cigarettes I smoked each day, and I knew how little I ran except when chasing a soccer ball now and then if a game came up, and I knew that there was little chance of catching it and—I'll admit—it angered me to know that a dog might outdo me and so I resolved that it would not. We ran. It surged ahead. I followed along the narrows of central Lima, beneath her ragged and decaying balconies, past her boarded buildings, her cloistered doorways, her shadows. I wanted the mutt dead. I ran with cruelty in my chest, like a drug pushing me faster. My leg buckled and I sputtered to a stop. I was blocks away from the plaza, in the grassy median of a broad silent avenue lined with anemic palm trees, dizzy, lungs gasping for air. The poor dog slowed on the far sidewalk and turned to look at me, standing only a few feet away, panting, its head turned quizzically to one side, a look I've seen before, from family, from friends, or even from women unfortunate enough to love me, the look of those who wonder at me, who expect things and are eventually disappointed.

You should know that I felt nothing for the dog other than steely blue-black hatred. I was cold and angry. Hurt by too many German philosophers in translation. Wounded by watching my father go blind beneath great swaths of leather, bending and manipulating each until, like magic, a belt, or a saddle, or a soccer ball appeared. Frustrated by an absurd evening spent killing and painting for the revolution. I hated the dog. In the Arequipa of my youth, a street mutt had slept in our doorway once in awhile, and mostly I had ignored it, had not petted it, but had watched it scratch itself or lick its own testicles and had never been stirred. I have loved many things, many people, but I felt no warmth toward this beast. Instead I envisioned there were stages of death, degrees of it, a descending staircase, and I wanted with all my heart to see this mutt, with its matted black fur, resting at the bottom. I called it and held my hand out. I sucked my teeth and coaxed it to me.

And it came. With a pit-pat of paws on the concrete, it crossed the avenue, as if it were coming home, as if it were somewhere else entirely, not in the midst of war. It was a beautiful dog, an innocent dog. It had a shiny black coat. It had been playing a game. Still, I felt anger toward it—for making me run, for each drop of sweat, for the heavy beating of my heart. I petted it for a moment, then grasped it by the nape of its neck, plunged the knife through its black fur, and twisted.

At that last moment, the dog struggled mightily, growling, lunging, but I held on and it did not bite me, but fell to the ground in a heap, blood gathering in a pool beneath its wound.

It groaned sadly, helplessly. I admired it as it bled: its strong white teeth, its muscular hind legs. It panted and heaved. I might have stayed there all night if not for a flash of light and gruff voice that called out. It was a police officer and he had a gun.

In Arequipa, I chiseled decorations on the saddles my father crafted each year for the parades. I helped him dye the leathers, and took the hammer and the small wedge and banged and hit and bled until each was beautiful. This is how I was raised: my father and I in the workshop, the intoxicating smell of the cured leather, the tools each with their purpose and their mythology. He taught me the meticulous process as his eyesight abandoned him. By the time I had mastered the process, he was too blind to see my work. My mother would tell him, "the boy is learning," and he glowed.

I dressed impeccably in my gray and white school uniform, and always did more than was expected of me. I placed first in my class, and took the University entrance exam at age seventeen. I was accepted to the University in Lima. My head was shaved, my father danced happily, and my mother cried, knowing I would soon leave her. Lima was known then for swallowing lives, drawing people from their ancestral homes, enveloped us in her concrete and noise. I became one of those people. I saw the city and felt its chaos and its energy; I couldn't go home.

I have lived through Lima's turbulent adolescence and her unbounded growth. She is mine now. I am not afraid of her, even as I am no longer in love with her. At the University I studied Philosophy, and then transferred to Fine Arts to study painting. I made angry canvasses of red and black, with terrorized faces hidden beneath swaths of bold color. I painted in Rimac, just across the dirty river, in a small room with a window that looked out at the graceful contour of the colonial city. It was often cloudy, and my elderly landlady, Doña Alejandra, liked to let herself into my room to look at my work. I came upon her there, wrapped in my threadbare blanket, asleep in my chair, her chest rising in shallow breaths, on one of the handful of sunny days that I remember. Her own room had no windows.

I caught the eye of some people with a painting I exhibited at the University: a portrait of a man, eyes averted, his mouth squeezed in a tight grimace, gripping a hammer in his right hand, poised to nail a stake square into the flat of his left palm. He was blue and brown geometry against a red background. He was my father.

In the cafeteria, students stood on tables to denounce the dictator and his cronies. Slogans appeared on brick walls and were whitewashed by timid workers, only to appear again. We knew the struggle would come. It was the same all over the country. Many left school to prepare for the coming war.

My father's blindness had hurt me. I longed to show him what I had accomplished. On my last visit home, in our small anteroom, I repainted my canvasses with words, slowly, and only for him. He gazed blankly at the walls. I talked him through years of my canvasses, but never cracked the austere dark of his blindness. He nodded, told me he understood, but I knew I had failed him.

I returned from Arequipa and made my decision. I left the University for the last time, only three months before I was to receive my degree in the Fine Arts. Instead I traveled to the countryside to study explosives with my compañeros.

If I were still a painter, I could show you some truths about this place: the children, cold and hungry, lining up each morning at the well, carrying water back to their families. Five kilometers. Seven kilometers. Nine. The endless bus rides across the city, when a young man in an ill-fitting suit steps aboard to recite poetry and sell Chiclets. "It's not charity I am asking for," he shouts over the rattle of a dying bus, "I am selling a poem to ease your commute!" The passengers look down and away.

In 1970, a town disappeared beneath the Andes. An earthquake. Then a landslide. Not a village, but a town. Yungay. It was a Sunday afternoon; my father and I listened to the World Cup live from Mexico City, Peru playing Argentina to a respectable draw, when the room shook, vaguely. And then the news came slowly; filtered, like all things in Peru, from the provinces to Lima, and then back out again to all the far-flung corners of our make-believe nation. We were aware that something unspeakable had occurred, but could not name it just yet. The earth had spilled upon itself, an angry sea of mud and rock, drowning thousands. Only some of the children were spared. A traveling circus had set up camp at the higher end of the valley. There were clowns in colorful hats and children laughing as their parents were buried.

In Arequipa, to the south, we had scarcely felt the earthquake at all: a vase slipping off a windowsill, a picture hanging askew, a dog barking.

If I were still a painter, I would set up a canvas on that barren spot where that town once stood, select my truest colors, and show you that life can disappear just like that. "And what is this, Pintor?" you might ask, pointing to the ochre, purple, orange, and gray.

Ten thousand graves; can't you see them?

When I was a painter, I would stroll through the city, eyes wide open. On my way home each afternoon, I passed the roadside mechanics standing along the avenue at the end of a days work. Stained oily black from head to toe, they were the fiercest angels, the city's living dead. Lima was full of those worn down by living. I rushed home, reeling, sketching on napkins, papers, on my skin, all that I had seen so it would not go unrecorded. Everything meant something, hinted at an as-yet-unasked, un-dreamed-of question. There were no answers that convinced me. I painted toward those questions—a cinder block resting in an abandoned parking lot, a dented fender reflecting the streets—sometimes for a day or two or even three, catnapping in the corner of my room just as my landlady Doña Alejandra had once. I awoke well before dawn, awash in the metallic odors of paint and sweat and hunger. I forgot my body almost completely.

I have found that sensation a few times since: lost in the tangle of vines, in the jungles of northern Peru, running from an ambush; setting a bomb in the bitter cold of the sierra beneath a concrete bridge. But like a drug, each time the adrenaline rush is less powerful, and each culminating boom means less and less.

I have not painted since that night of the dogs. Not a stroke of black or red, not animal or canvas.

And I will not paint again.

Only the walls of my cell—if they catch me—a shade recalling sky, so my dreary last days can be spent in grace.

What I recall of him: a thin and shadowy moustache and the gun. I remember the diminutive length of the barrel and its otherworldly gleam, backlit as it was by his flashlight. There was something drunken about the way he swayed, the unsteady manner in which he held his pistol, arm outstretched and wavering. I imagine he stumbled upon me after a few drinks with friends. "Hey you there!" he called. "Stop! Police!" Picture this: a man in this light shouting, gun held unsteadily, as if by a puppeteer. I looked back toward him and said meekly, drawing on an innocence I could not have possessed, "Yes?"

"The hell are you doing?" he shouted from behind the blinding light.

I scoured my mind for explanations, but found none. The truth sounded implausible; especially the truth. The silence was punctuated by the dog's pained cry. "This mutt bit my little brother," I said.

He kept the barrel trained on me, skeptical, but stepped closer. "Is he rabid?"

"I'm not sure, Officer."

Bent over the dog, he examined its dying body. Blood ran in thin streams through the grass, fanning out toward the edge of the street. It reminded me of the maps I studied in grade school, of the Amazon Basin with its web of crooked streams flowing to the sea.

"Where's your brother? Has he been seen by a doctor?"

I nodded. "He's with my mother at home," I said, and waved my arm to indicate a place not far away in no particular direction. There was a glint of kindness in him, though I knew he didn't exactly believe me. I was not as accustomed to lying as you might think. I was afraid that he might see through me. So I continued. I told of my brother, the terrible bite, the awful scream I had heard, the red fleshy face of the wound. His innocence, his shining eyes, his smile, his grace. I gave my brother all the qualities I lacked, made him beautiful and funny, as perfect as the blond puppets they use to sell soap on television. I was sweating, my heart racing, telling him of the jokes he told, the grades he got. A smart one, my brother! And then I gave him a name: "Manuel, but we call him Manolo, Manolito," I said, and the officer, gun in hand, softened.

"That's my name."

I looked up, not quite sure what he meant.

"I'm Manolo too," he said delicately, almost laughing. I chuckled nervously. The dog whimpered again. We faced each other in the still of the broad avenue and shared a smile.

The officer put his gun in the holster and moved to shake my hand. I wiped the blade of my knife on my thigh and put it down. We shook hands firmly, like men. "Manuel Carrión," he said.

And I said a name as well, though of course not mine and not Pintor.

He was a *cholo* like me, I knew it by the way he spoke. His father worked with his hands, as surely as he had cousins or brothers or friends who worked with their fists. He said he was pleased to meet me. "But what are you doing exactly? Killing this mutt?" he asked. "What will that accomplish?"

"I chased it down to see if it was rabid. The little bitch struggled with me. I guess I got carried away."

Carrión nodded and leaned over the dog once again. With his nightstick he poked it in its belly, eliciting a muted, pathetic yelp. He peered into its eyes for a particular shade of yellow and into its gaping mouth for the frothy telltale saliva. "No rabies. I think Manolito is going to be fine."

I was relieved for a brother I didn't have, for a bite that never was. My heart swelled. I imagined Manolito and his long healthy days, running, playing among friends, his wound healed with not even a scar. I loved my fictitious brother.

But Carrión was drunk and kind. If things had gone differently that black morning this episode might have become one of his favorite stories, when asked by a friend or cousin over a drink, "Hey cholo, what's it like out there?" *Compa*, let me tell you about the night I helped a man kill a dog. No, that sounds too banal. *Hombre*, one time, I came upon a man decapitating a street mutt . . . Who knows how he would tell the story now? Or if he would tell it at all?

"I used to be just like your Manolito," he was saying, "always getting into something. I liked to fight the big guys, but I was small. Always coming home with a broken this or a bruised that." Carrión spoke warmly now. "Are you taking him anywhere? The mutt, I mean."

"The doctor wanted to examine it," I said, "just to make sure."

Carrión nodded. "Of course. Good luck." He stood up to leave, unfolding himself, clearing grass from his knees. "You should put it out of its misery, you know. No point in being cruel."

I liked him. How simple and mundane.

I thanked the officer and assured him I would. We were pulling away, our goodbyes restless on our tongues, when suddenly there was a noise, an abbreviated yelp. Looking up, I saw one of my compañeros, breathless, not thirty meters away, crouching savagely over a dog (white), holding it up by its muzzle, arm raised, knife in hand, poised to enter the fleshy underside of its neck. He had come down a side street and hadn't seen us until it was too late. Now he saw us and stopped. Confusion. Panic. Fearful, I reverted to form, abandoned my revolutionary training: I wanted to paint it: the brutal outline of a man at war with a mutt, caught in the act, frozen arms akimbo. I saw what I had looked like. Carrión looked my way, puzzled, then back at my compañero, and for a moment the three of us were caught in a triangle of wants, questions, and fears—a record skipping, a still life, a mutually-agreed-upon pause during which we each considered in silence the intricate and unfortunate relationships that connected us. An instant, nothing more.

Then Carrión drew his gun, just as I grasped my knife. My compañero let the dog drop unceremoniously to the sidewalk and took off running down the avenue away from the plaza. The white dog scampered off, still whimpering. And Carrión faced me, whatever shadow of friendship we had briefly cultivated lost in fog. My options ticked off before me like the outline of a brutal text: Point A) stab the cop, quickly; Point B) run, run fast, imbecile! Point C) die like a man. And that was all my mind produced. Despairing, only my last choice made any sense. Can it even be called a choice? I held my blade, true, but weakly and without conviction. I made as if to rise, perhaps even run, but there was nothing there. And while I dawdled with limp and half-formed thoughts, Carrión acted: forgave me, inexplicably spared me, struck me with the butt of his gun and ran off in pursuit of my comrade—sealing his own fate.

He died that night.

Reeling, I fell toward what I recognized as death. It was only sleep. Into the grass, clutching my jaw, eyes closed, my sight swelled into black. Half-dead dogs howled and whimpered. In the distance, I heard a gunshot.

A DESERT FULL OF WATER

BY SANTIAGO RONCAGLIOLO

(PERU)

Vania doesn't seem to be riding in the boat but to be floating on the ocean breeze. She's so light. But not too skinny. And she's careful not to be. Beneath her beach wrap, her thighs sketch soft farewells to adolescence. Now that her breasts have started to emerge, she chooses her bras less to protect her breasts than to show them off and push them forward defiantly, like a herald of her arrival, like the flag of her apathetic, languid gaze that passes over others when she remembers to look at them. Karen says that Vania is full of herself. Vania says she doesn't think she's anything she's not; she's just what Karen wants to be. Verónica swears that Vania has pectoral acne instead of a bust. Vania accepts their teasing, only because she knows that she's prettier and more of a woman than they are, to the point that she invites them to her house in Pucusana so they see how nice she is and that she shares. Verónica, for her part, has enough bust to share with the whole fourth year class, but she carries the weight of her pride alone.

Now Martín turns off the motor and starts rowing. Vania's house stretches from one end to the other of a small islet in Pucusana, and it isn't a good idea to approach it too quickly. Hernán's boat already has run aground five times on the surrounding rocks, though this might have something to do with the fact that Hernán drives at full speed, a Cuba libre in one hand, not taking his eyes off the girls on the beach. Vania thinks her brother crashes just to get attention, but still, her mother thinks that it's best to row up to the dock and not to take the risk. Mrs. Barandiarán could travel to the Pucusana house in an ocean liner, provided that she didn't take a risk or get her feet wet.

Martín knows this. So every time he takes them out, he follows the same routine. He stops rowing a few meters from the house, arriving by momentum, not even throwing the ropes to the small dock on the deck. He maneuvers so that the inner tube on the prow bounces softly against the dock's edge. Getting out of the boat, he takes care not to throw it off balance with his weight before tying it to firm ground. Then he extends his hand to Vania's mother, who never thanks him but still keeps hiring him to take them out in the boat and do the shopping by the resort. Vania has seen him out by himself, and he doesn't behave the same. He shoves the boat off the dock and uses the motor the whole time, turning it off only when he practically has landed on the dock in town, lashing the ropes like a whip to stop. Vania often thinks he'll capsize when he leaves the island standing in the boat, toying with the waves, or when he threatens to crash into the boats on shore. Sometimes when he takes Vania and her friends out, if her mom isn't there, he indulges in the pleasure of hitting the fishing boats just to insult them, making faces and teasing the fisherman. Once a grumpy fisherman came over to answer his jokes, his prow aimed at the motor, but Martín remembered who his passengers were, turned serious, and, happily, stopped the fisherman on time. Happily at least for Mrs. Barandiarán, or for how she thought things should be. If she found out, she'd never hire that reckless man again. Vania, however, was fascinated by the thought of capsizing and having to swim home. But it never happens. Vania always floats between the waves—rather, she glides, like a seagull—with total and boring security.

After helping Mrs. Barandiarán get out of the boat, Martín turns toward the girls, his hand outstretched. The guests want to prove that they can climb out by themselves, and Karen does so without any trouble; she doesn't even need her hands to step up to the dock. But it's not so easy for Verónica: her breasts sway like a trawler in Pucusana's peaceful sea, and she loses her balance and falls against the driver in an involuntary embrace. Vania notices that Martín doesn't bat an eye. Normally, boys salivate at Verónica's appearance, even without such a fuss, but Martín smiles politely and acts like a big feather pillow had fallen on top of him. Elephant feathers, Vania thinks. Verónica, for her part, who acts like a little whore every chance she gets, barely thanks him for his help and continues toward the deck with her indifferent swaying. Vania asks herself whether it's that fishermen don't know how to drool like men, or whether Verónica is so dim-witted that she isn't aware that the fishermen are men. Without answering herself, Vania holds out her hand for Martín to help her out.

The house is the same every summer. It never changes, and Vania appreciates it now more than ever, because she has fond memories of last year and the winter has been long. She hadn't been able to focus at school like before, and she only won two awards at the closing ceremony. Karen and Verónica, intolerable as they've become, have always been the most fun and frequent guests at the house, and this weekend, Vania only wants to have fun and forget her shame that the nerd, Manuela Rabínez, won more awards than she did. The scene on their arrival is the same as every year. Martín stays outside; Mom complains about the dust on the furniture that no one else can see—how awful, what a pigsty, she always says—Karen and Verónica run giggling to their rooms, and Hernán, who arrived on

Wednesday, isn't here, but he's thrown an empty six-pack on the living room table to make it clear that he's already taken over. He'll be back before long, at any rate. Vania can almost predict the exact moment when the motor will announce her brother's presence to the house and to everyone else within a thirty-mile radius. Last summer, tired of this sound, Vania wished with all her heart that Hernán's next crash would be irreparable. It was. Hernán spent three days in the hospital and totaled the boat. But he told their father that the boat was a piece of shit; its steering was off and it didn't brake fast enough. His father understood, took pity, and bought another boat that was sturdier, safer, noisier. So Vania learned that you should be careful what you wish for, since your wishes might come true. Now, as the motor's noise draws near, she begins to wish that her father might someday turn poor and not buy any more boats or have any more retarded sons like Hernán.

But of course Mom doesn't think that way. She runs out to the deck to greet her little Hernancito as soon as she hears him approach. Every year it's the same, of course, but this time there's something new. Mom's voice isn't the only one greeting Hernancito. Karen and Verónica toss out hellos, smiles, and little squeals from the rooms upstairs. They've been waiting, Vania thinks. Bitches. But they don't wait any longer; they run downstairs and practically drag their host to the deck. Hernán is with Lucho, whom he calls his best friend and whom Vania calls the retard's apprentice. Lucho does, in fact, act like a real man: he smiles and his pupils dilate when he sees Verónica, who's wearing a bikini skimpy enough to be a bracelet. Hernán warns Karen that she's pale and that she'll need someone to rub sunscreen on her back. By this point, Vania can't even comprehend why she's only been at the beach ten minutes and already is in such a terrible mood. She doesn't even notice Martín, who is standing there but seems to be dissolving into the salty air until he's invisible.

As was bound to happen, they all ended up going out in the boat in spite of Vania's annoyed face and Mrs. Barandiarán's warnings, all of you be careful, don't go too fast, Hernancito, there's five of you, make sure the tank is full so you don't get stranded, these boats should have seatbelts, blah, blah, blah. Hernán answers everything with, Yes, Mom, of course, Mom, and kisses her on the forehead and smiles from behind his sunglasses with his perfectly gorgeous white smile that neither wine nor cigarettes nor marijuana have ever stained, which Vania thinks is the only thing her brother has to offer. Lucho, on the other hand, doesn't even have that. But Verónica doesn't seem to care once they get into the boat, or when they speed between two moving trawlers, or when they almost capsize a fisherman's boat, or when they careen along the shore to scare the swimmers. She just keeps laughing harder. And Karen does, too. They drink beer straight from the bottle. They never do this at parties, but apparently they do in boats, as the salt water sprinkles them with a joy that seems louder than the motor.

When their prudishness abates a little, which takes hours, Hernán stops the boat so that they can swim away from the bay. Everyone jumps in the water, except Vania. Hernán teases her for being boring, but she doesn't care. She listens to the others play in the water, not knowing what she'd do there, the fifth side of a square she drew herself. Between their laughter and splashing in the distance, Vania resolves to invite Gerda, the girl with crooked teeth, next weekend, and Manuela, that nerd. She's sure that they'll appreciate her invitation more. They don't even have beach houses, you can tell, definitely not their own houses. Vania smiles on the inside, imagining them on the deck, sunbathing in their grandmother swimsuits, which probably reach their ankles. Dear brother, don't you want to take the girls out in the boat? Won't you have a beer with my new friends? You won't rub sunscreen on their backs? Mom, tell Hernán to take my new friends for a ride. Hernancito, dear, listen to your sister. On the inside, Vania's smile turns into silent laughter.

But her laughter isn't all that's silent. Suddenly, the giggles have stopped reaching her ears, and the occasional drops of water that Hernán sends flying with his horseplay have stopped raining on her skin. She looks everywhere, but nothing. Not the guys, not the girls, not on either side of the boat. The Pucusana current can't be dangerous; Vania hasn't ever heard of anyone drowning, but they've disappeared, and Vania realizes that she's never heard anything about anyone in Pucusana outside her own house. She calls out to them, first quietly, then screaming. There's not even an echo on the water to repeat their names. She waits a little while in case they answer. She's just realized how far they are from the beach; they couldn't have swum home. There's not even a buoy nearby for them to catch their breath. Vania's pulse accelerates. She's never wanted to hear her idiot brother's voice so much. He must have dared the others to swim, maybe to the old trawler grounded on the other side of the island. But from here? Besides, if that were the case, she still should be able to see them somewhere. Without any further thought, Vania takes off her sarong and her polo shirt and jumps in to find them. Maybe one of them got a cramp from all the cold beer they drank and can't swim up from the bottom; maybe the others are trying to help; but all her explanations seem incoherent, just ideas running through her head, trying to be answers.

The ocean water isn't like a pool's; it's denser, greener, impenetrable; still, it won't be the first time Vania has dived in. In fact, she dives better than her brother, who probably can't hold his breath for more than three seconds because of all the junk he puts in his lungs. But hopefully he can, Vania thinks. If something's happened, she hopes that he can get out of trouble. Hernán has never been so good at that; he's lucky to have a smile and a father who allows him to evade the police, hospitals, even the university. But wallets and white teeth mean nothing to the ocean. The ocean only splashes you with happiness when you stay on its surface.

So Vania dives until she has no more air in her lungs and then dives a little deeper. It's useless. She can't get near the bottom because of the pressure she feels in her ears. She sticks her head out above the water, her tears mingling with the ocean. She doesn't know what to do. She resolves to keep looking until she finds them, not knowing where to look. Then she glances toward the boat. She wants to believe that what she sees there is a mirage. Hernán and Karen are on board, waving goodbye with their respective bottles of beer in their hands. Lucho helps Verónica climb over the prow. Before Vania can react, the boat shoots off toward the shore. At least this time the motor's noise serves to cover up the boys' laughter.

Just fifteen minutes later, as dusk begins to fall, the boat comes back to pick her up. She's dying of cold, fear, and exhaustion. She's so mortified, her fury has subsided, but the others' laughter hasn't. Silently, she climbs into the boat. The whole way back Hernán doesn't stop repeating that she's boring and they did this just to make her see how nice the water was and learn to live a little; she should be grateful. Vania keeps her mouth shut. Relax, Karen tells her, we didn't mean to make you get like this. Vania wishes that her friend's tongue would catch on the motor, and this time, she's not afraid her wish will come true.

Back home Mrs. Barandiarán announces that her dinner is ready. The one who really cooks is Deolinda, but Mrs. Barandiarán always talks about *her* food, because she's its intellectual author. Vania eats the little that she does in silence, between the knowing smiles that the others exchange as if she were blind. Mrs. Barandiarán remarks that it's too bad your father couldn't come, he likes the beach so much, Hernancito, and Hernancito says, It's too bad, Mom, and thinks that since Mom takes sleeping pills, there won't be any problems tonight. Tonight there can't be any problems.

Karen and Verónica, however, have a hard time getting Vania to join them. They try to convince her after dinner that she takes things too seriously; she shouldn't make such a big deal out of a joke. Vania knows they're saying this just to spare themselves the guilt of having fun without their hostess and to spare themselves the risk of not being invited back. Vania knows that they have nothing to worry about; rather, they should feel certain that they'll never come back. Over her dead body, drowned, boat and all, in the deepest sea. Or better, over their dead bodies. Karen scolds her for acting childish. If her problem is that she doesn't have a boyfriend, well, she shouldn't worry, since nothing's going to happen; they're just friends with the boys. But Verónica doesn't exactly agree. She thinks things should happen spontaneously, and she's not going to limit her fun because of a girl who's not interested in either of these boys. Because you don't like Lucho, or do you? Of course Vania doesn't "like" the idiot's apprentice; she's known him as long as she can remember, and he still hasn't grown up. Verónica doesn't think he's that immature, not after everything: he's funny, and you can't take guys too seriously, just like jokes. She's known this since she lost her virginity, and maybe Vania could stand to lose hers, too; it would put her in a better mood, which she certainly could use. Vania tells Verónica not to confuse maturity with sluttiness, and Karen reminds them that they'll be there for two more days, so they'd better act like friends, because they are. Vania decides to go to the party, virginity and all, to get through the night in peace and deny them the satisfaction of talking about her behind her back.

It doesn't take her long to regret her decision once she's there. Hernán seems to pull beer out from under the rocks; the girls drink it like water. They laugh. While Vania, out of obligation, drinks her only can of the night, she worries that they'll wake up her mother, but Hernán reminds her that she takes enough sleeping pills to knock out a whole soccer team. After they drink a few beers and make a few jokes about Karen's shorts, very daring, how scandalous, ha, ha, Hernán asks them how daring they feel, and Vania's eyes widen like two plates. When Hernán takes out a joint, she doesn't know whether to be shocked or relieved. She chooses to remain silent. Two weeks ago, Karen told Vania that she'd never smoked pot, but as the boys light up, she remarks that it's been a while since she's smoked. Vania asks herself whether this is true, and whether it's a lie that Verónica lost her virginity. And she asks herself why they're not spending the night making fun of her brother and painting themselves with shoe polish, like last year.

After everyone takes a hit, they laugh more and talk more nonsense than usual. The worst comes when Lucho suggests they play spin the bottle. Vania doesn't know what to do: she can't kiss her friends or her brother, and she'd rather kiss an octopus than Lucho. The game is called off, and Vania has to come up with a new one, and she gets a deck of cards down from her room. Two hands of casino are enough for everyone to be bored out of their minds, and Vania won't agree to the game of strip poker that Lucho proposes, for the same reasons as spin the bottle, though this time Verónica and Karen acknowledge with little smiles that they don't want to play either, they don't play these games—as if sticking your tongue in a guy's mouth, Vania thinks, were somehow more decent than taking off your shirt. As if I cared whether or not these dumb bitches were decent, she corrects herself mentally. But the minutes tick by, and the climax of the party has passed. Little by little, the guys' yawns grow more obvious, and the girls' desperate efforts to have fun grow more pathetic. None of that laughter remains, and the boys announce that they're going to sleep, which is what Vania wanted and the others feared. Just then, Vania gets the idea that they could gossip, laugh;

after all, they're right, you don't need to take things so seriously; they even could look for some of Mrs. Barandiarán's shoe polish, which she brings to Pucusana along with a brush for the lint and dust. Do you remember when we cut up a dress to make three identical skirts? She wants to say, when you see me wearing the skirt, remember that you have the same one, but she doesn't know what happened to hers. She finally suggests that they stay up a little longer, but it's late, it doesn't make sense; the girls are tired, too; they've been running around all day and that wears you out, plus the trip to the island was long, and when they leave to go to sleep, neither of the girls has to say anything too venomous for Vania to feel that the end of the party has been revenge for the afternoon's joke. She wants to feel satisfied, she wants to feel she's gotten even. But, as with the rest of the day, she doesn't know what she feels, apart from the sensation that the winter hasn't really ended: it's only just begun.

At the beach, one always wakes up earlier than usual, effortlessly, lulled by the slow crashing of the waves and the salty air. But this Saturday, Vania doesn't want to open her eyes. Or she wants to open them and find herself at home in Lima on Friday, next to the phone in her bedroom, with Mom telling her to call her friends, we're leaving for Pucusana now, call Gerda and Manuela. But she can only call someone whose number she has. She's never asked them for their numbers. She lies like this for hours, half-asleep, letting her dreams grow out of her thoughts and her thoughts escape her conscious control. She dozes and imagines things for so long that it almost seems like a dream when she hears her mother scream to Deolinda, Make the grocery list, woman, you have to do the shopping. Do you think that no one eats here? And maybe it's a dream, the thought that occurs to her to flee for a while, to leave the house and to leave the fresh air that asphyxiates her. Mom thinks this is a strange idea, but she's distracted and forgets because Deolinda is so slow, goddamnit, when is she going to finish making the list. Vania gallops down the stairs and finds the others on the first floor, just as their laughter trails off. Want to go for a ride? Hernán asks. Vania completes this question mentally: Would you rather break a leg, by any chance, or catch tuberculosis? I'm going into town, she replies without hesitating. Deolinda finally finishes the list and gives it to Mrs. Barandiarán. Vania has already gotten in the boat—without help—by the time Martín takes the list from the deck, always from the deck.

Martín pushes off with the oars to leave, not because of the rocks now but because the motor's noise gives the lady a headache. In any case, after he's gone a few meters he pulls a faded cord called a starter rope, Vania asked him what it's called. The boat shakes as they move forward, and the motor bellows out a thick blue smoke. Vania practically has to scream to make the fisherman hear her: If you want to go faster, it won't bother me. Yes, Miss Vania. Martín smiles a little but does nothing; the motor has only one speed. It's better that way, she thinks. The wind and the water don't lash at her face, unlike yesterday; they caress it. She keeps moving forward, facing the sun, her eyes closed. No other boats come near them. But when it's time to tie up the boat, Martín acts quickly, with strength, as if Vania were invisible, as if now it were she who was dissolving into the air.

As they walk through resort town, she asks him if he's always lived in Pucusana. Yes. He fishes all year, but he wants to go to Lima this winter; he'd like to study computer science. He doesn't say any more. Vania wants to know if he doesn't like fishing anymore. He loves it, but it's time for a change. There's not much to do in Pucusana; all his friends are leaving. As they walk around the shops, Vania asks him to explain everything. She's never been to the market; she doesn't know the difference between a corvine and a sole; she doesn't even know what parsley is. Martín explains each item patiently. He's not a bad guy; he isn't anything like the others. Vania keeps asking questions, and at one point he answers, Radishes, Vania. He says Vania, not Miss, and he goes on as if nothing happened. She goes on as if nothing happened, too. They even laughed once, when she pulled the leaves off the chard, thinking that the stem was the important part. They had fun. She could remain like this forever, completely content. He could always be a good guy, and she could simply be Vania, listening to his explanations and sticking her foot in her mouth with the chard. In fact, they've almost finished shopping. Soon they'll head back, and he'll remain on the deck or go inside only to drop off the things, and then he'll leave, and Vania will watch TV while she waits for the others to return just so that she can ignore them. But Martín gains confidence and can't hold back a little laugh, which bothers her. Why are you laughing? she asks. Nothing, Miss, it's nothing. He doesn't call her Vania anymore. This seems strange, and his attitude intrigues her. You have to be laughing about something, tell me, you can tell me. Martín means well; he never has a bad word to say about anyone, though sometimes he annoys the other fishermen. But well, he is annoying, that's true. He says, How can you not know what you eat, Miss? And then she gets irritated, furious. Do you know English, by any chance? Huh? Can you do algebra? Literature? A deep, frigid silence falls around her, like the sea without a boat. Martín pales. No, Miss, I'm sorry. And he lowers his head, and Vania feels satisfied that she put him in his place; at least she can put someone in their place this shitty weekend. When she's about to let it go, she realizes that she screamed too loudly and the women in the shops are giving her dirty looks; that's not how you treat people, so what if he's an Indian; the nun at school says there's nothing wrong with being one, but Vania wants to explain to these women that it doesn't matter what he is; no one should laugh at her like that. But she doesn't have to, because no one scolds her; the women stare at her a while, and then they go back to work, and he's silent, buying the last few things, and he doesn't look at her anymore, either; she seeks his gaze but doesn't find it; she only hears his voice saying, That's it, let's go back. She sees herself reflected in Martín's back as if she were her mother, with her nightgowns and skirts and neuroses and pills, and she hates herself; she despises herself as much as if she had a son named Hernán and a stupid daughter who didn't know how to treat people.

Now Martín gets into the boat as if no one were with him, not even close by, and he almost hurls the bags into the back. He barely waits for Vania, and he loosens the ropes with a yank. He starts the motor with his back to her, and that's how he remains the whole way home, not saying a word. This time their backs are facing the sun, and in the distance, Vania can see her brother's boat clearly, and though it's far away, it seems closer to her than Martín does. It also seems that the boat is going faster than before, as if it were rushing to leave her on shore or throw her against the rocks. Martín, however, turns off the motor before reaching the dock and goes through the same ritual as always. He even holds his hand out to Vania, though this time his arm seems like one more joist on the dock. They cross the deck and stop at the screen. Vania imagines the screen like the force field in the cartoons Hernán watched when he was little, when he stole the remote from her. Only she can break the silence, and she does it with an order that sounds like a plea: Carry the groceries to the kitchen.

Vania only enters the kitchen of any of her houses to ask Deolinda for sandwiches, but now she goes in with Martín and tries to help him put away the groceries. Just leave it, he says, Deolinda and I can take care of it. We know what we're doing. His words hurt Vania more than any did the night before. The worst is that she doesn't know how to answer; she can't; she doesn't want to. What will she take out of the bag when they tell her, Put the celery here? How will she know what celery is? She pours herself a Coca-Cola and decides to go to her room and forget about it; it doesn't matter, after all; after all, she tried to be friendly. She's not going to lick Martín's boots. He doesn't even have boots, since he doesn't wear shoes. When she's about to leave the kitchen, before running into anyone, her mother comes in to check on the shopping. She analyzes the contents of each bag and finds something to criticize in each one. Oh, Martín, can't you tell a ripe avocado from a green one? And these mangos, they look like limes. Where's the oregano? Wasn't oregano on the list? Well, Martín, if you don't pay attention, I'll just have to hire someone else. Vania is outraged when she hears this, because Martín does know what avocados and radishes are, and of course he knows when they're ripe, and she wants to tell her mother to go shopping herself, that she must not know what she's eats, either, that she only pretends because she's the boss and she's supposed to know so that the servants don't cheat her. But Martín says he's sorry like always, docilely, with his chin practically glued to his chest; he takes his coins, and Vania thinks that maybe he'd like a thank you instead.

When Martín leaves, she sets her Coke down and goes out after him. With every passing moment she feels worse, but he doesn't even look at her; he crosses the deck with long, silent strides. He's already reached the dock when she dares to open her mouth and say she's sorry. He stops but says nothing. I'm sorry, she repeats, for Mom, for me, for everything. Martín has the right to say what he wants, to scream at her, Vania thinks. She wants him to scream and insult her like he never could her mother. But after a few seconds of silence, he starts to tremble lightly. She thinks he's on the verge of exploding with rage, and she's ready to take the explosion. Martín's trembling grows more intense until he can't take it anymore, and for the first time that day, he lets out a laugh, not a deaf bray like Hernán's, but a strong, clean laugh, which comforts Vania as if warm water were pouring onto her spirit. She laughs, too, but she doesn't know why.

It doesn't matter. It's my job, Martín explains. You have to know the client. Your mother has said the same thing her whole life. Deolinda and I laugh, but we just tell her yes, ma'am, yes, ma'am, and Martín lowers his head, imitating his own puppy dog eyes, so that your mother knows she's in charge and doesn't give us any more shit; he doesn't say it in quite those words, since that would show a lack of respect, but he thinks it. Vania would rather he say it. She'd like to hear Martín make fun of her mother with all of his words, but now she only sees the fisherman's smile and hears her own laugh, and the two of them standing on the dock keep laughing louder; their fit of laughter can't be contained, though Martín lifts his finger to his mouth to remind her that they have to laugh quietly; if they don't, then the lady will tell him she won't hire him again, who does he think he is, laughing so loud, and he'll say, Yes, ma'am, yes, ma'am, with his chin glued to his chest to hide his laughter. Vania is laughing so hard that she can't hide it; she can't control it; she steps backward and misses the dock; she's going to fall, but Martín sees her in time; he takes her by the arm and pulls her toward him. Be careful, he says, watch your step; she's practically landed in his arms and she doesn't feel like watching her step now; she only wants to close her eyes, tilt her head forward and brush her lips against the fisherman's hard, thick lips. And she does it. He pales. Mrs. Barandiarán's voice calls Vania from inside. She smiles. Finally, he smiles, too, but he releases her to get into the boat. Vania still has the urge to commit one more audacity: Come back at midnight, she whispers, through the back windows. He unties the ropes and starts the motor without taking his eyes off her. You're crazy, he answers and leaves without turning his back. Vania goes to her room, her heart ready to leap from her mouth and through her pores. He hasn't said no.

That afternoon is longer than the winter at the Barandiaráns' house. The others don't come home for lunch, and Vania has to endure lunch alone with her mother, who gossips the whole time about a bunch of ladies she's never met. Her mother always talks as if the whole world needed to hang on to every detail of her life. Deolinda doesn't have to listen, since she eats in the kitchen. Deolinda. After dessert, Vania tries to be useful, taking the plates to the kitchen; she finds a place at Deolinda's side and tries to start a conversation. The effort doesn't go very well. Deolinda just says something about the town where she was born, and Vania has no clue where it is. Still, Vania leaves the kitchen with the sense that she's discovered a new side of herself and that she's going to leave Pucusana after this weekend, not as a girl anymore, but as a woman, and a woman of the world.

The others come home later that afternoon. They took the boat down to Punta Hermosa and went to the beach and ate lunch there, but now they're tired and want to spend the rest of the afternoon lying on the deck. Vania is sorry that they didn't crash, but she's radiant, and nothing, no one can spoil her good mood. She counts every second remaining until midnight and suggests that the others go out to the disco that just opened two miles from Pucusana; they say it's awesome; go for it; I don't feel like going out tonight, but you guys should go. Hernán finds his little sister's enthusiasm strange, but it's not a bad idea, they'll think about it later. Vania waits the whole afternoon for it to be later. When night begins to fall she tries to talk the girls into going to the disco again. While she talks, she asks herself if Martín told his friends about their date tonight. She's sure he has, since he's a man; she's sure they've all given him advice and that they've laughed and made gestures she'd rather not see. That afternoon Vania caught Hernán on the deck telling Lucho about an obscene position that he wanted to try (or had tried?) with Karen. Vania didn't hear much; she walked away disgusted, but perhaps she wouldn't feel so disgusted if Martín wanted to . . . if her friends had told him . . . Vania is nervous. So while Karen and Verónica get ready, Vania interrogates them. What's up? Did you have fun with Lucho? And Hernán? They had fun, yes, they can't complain. And you, with your fisherman? Vania laughs and clarifies that he's not her fisherman; she only felt like shopping with him for a change of scenery. They laugh, too. It's a joke. They all laugh in complicity in a way they hadn't since last year. But now that they do, Vania no longer misses their laughter; now she's willing to invite them back next weekend, as long as they distract her brother and his current best friend. Now Vania laughs again, more heartily than ever.

Hernán finally decides to stay home; after all, they'll have just as much fun and they still have some weed. Vania, ever kind, says she's tired and is going to sleep. That's it, Vania, don't raise suspicions, calm before all. She has a full-length mirror in her bedroom, and she tries on her underwear in front of it. She has a pushup bra, but she doesn't know if it's appropriate. She tries on a purple one, too, which seems too childish, and a black one, which is more elegant but doesn't push her up; it's a piece of junk. Finally she settles on the first one with a little Brazilian thong. Her mother doesn't even know that she's bought these; of course she'd say she's too young to wear these things, but her mother is stupid, so it's easy to buy them. She puts Karen's leather miniskirt on over her thong; it doesn't matter; Karen won't find out, and Karen's not going to need it. A white blouse on top. When she looks at herself in the mirror, her eyes and lips already made up, she feels like she shines with a secret gleam and shudders. It's 11:30.

Downstairs, the party sounds like it's going strong. They're playing reggae and talking loudly. Vania puts on a bathrobe in case they see her. When she reaches the stairs, the voices betray that they've already had more than a few drinks, and it smells like cigarettes and pot. Jerks, Vania thinks, with Mom right there in her bedroom.

Dumb bitch, she replies, thinking of Mom, with everyone in the living room. She walks downstairs in trembling silence and turns toward the study, without the others seeing her. The stairs don't go directly to the living room but rather to the hallway that leads to the two back rooms they use when they have too many visitors; one of them serves as her father's study, on the rare occasions that he comes to Pucusana. Vania enters that room, closing the door slowly so no one hears her. She stays there with the lights out, letting the slowest seconds of her life tick by, even more slowly than the seconds of the afternoon, endlessly. At one point she hears Karen ask if this is the bathroom, and the door even opens a crack, but Lucho catches her in time, saving Vania by a hair. At 11:55, she opens the window and takes off her robe. A shiver runs down her spine.

At 12:15, she begins to ask herself whether Martín's going to come or what. The sea breeze chills the study, and she feels ridiculous, dressed up just for the window, just to be alone. For a moment she remembers Martín saying yes, ma'am, yes, ma'am, and maybe that's what he told her with his gaze, yes, Miss Vania, but don't scold me, just as he didn't drive faster before because he couldn't, but still he said yes; it's his job to say yes; she's his client. Nothing more. Vania wants to slam the window shut, to smash it against the window frame and put her robe on and go out to drink and smoke with the others and tell them, I've realized that I have to my spend time with you, since no one else pays attention to me. Never! Vania would rather swallow her tears than her pride. Happily, she doesn't have to do either, since the oar of the boat makes a sound below the window. Martín's there, standing, approaching in silence like her mother demands, lit only by the reflection of the moon on the sea.

When the boat stops, Vania takes the rope and ties it to the window hinge. Ironically, she holds her hand out to Martín, but he climbs out without her help. Once inside, they face each other. They haven't exchanged a word. They look uncomfortable. Finally, Vania feels him scrape her moon-white skin as he touches her arm and slides his finger up and down, running over her. She's paralyzed. Martín seems bigger than he did this morning. When he touches her lips, his hand seems to have descended from the sky. Vania feels like her chest is ready to explode, not because she's at that age, but because her heart pumps blood through her body as fast as Hernán drives his boat. She feels the urge to retreat, and he seems to notice, because he lets her go and takes a step back. Her voice a thread, she says no. Calmer, he approaches her again and touches her shoulder. His caress is like a ceremony of shy recognition. He goes up to her neck, and she lets a sigh escape. He gathers the courage to lower his hands just a little, running it over the upper part of her chest, down to the medal of the Holy Spirit that Vania's father gave her. She lifts her own hand smoothly and deposits his on top of her skittish breasts. His eyes glitter.

Outside, the music stops with a thud. Something has fallen. Martín grows nervous. What was that? Vania feels like they've suddenly awoken. My brother's outside, she answers. Martín steps back. They can't hear us, Vania says. The music resumes, and he draws close again to recreate the magic. Vania understands they need to hurry; every second is a risk, and she brings her mouth close to his. She knows that a good kiss has a bite, and she bites Martín's lip. He lets out an inaudible moan, and his hand descends down Vania's belly, toward the space between her legs. A chill makes her tremble to the last hair on her neck. Martín breathes with a cloying heaviness. Lucho's sick laughter trickles in from outside. Martín doesn't sound so nervous as upset. What do you want? Why did you bring me here?

Vania makes a gesture of annoyance. She shakes her head no; he takes her jaw between his hands. He doesn't squeeze too hard yet.

Vania doesn't know what to say. Something else falls outside with a dull thud, and laughing, they turn off the music again. Vania thinks a bottle has broken. She didn't want to go out in Hernán's boat tonight, that's all she can think to say to Martín; nothing else comes to mind; she didn't want to go to the disco. But her answers don't convince him. What? Are you just fucking with me? Huh? What do you want? What the hell do you want? And this time he doesn't just ask; he squeezes her jaw so tightly that his fingers leave a red mark. Come on, Hernán says, to the study! Let's go to the study! Or the guest room? They feel steps in the hallway. Even as her jaw is pressed between his fingers, Vania wants the whole house to sink into the sea, except the study.

But Martín doesn't think the same thing. His breathing, once rhythmic and heavy, accelerates. His movements, too. He pushes Vania to the floor. She wants to scream, but her voice won't reach her mouth, and besides, if someone came in, how would she explain how Martín got into the house? Martín gets on top of her, on her chest. He's heavy. Lost your voice? Huh? You don't talk anymore? Fine, then don't talk. Vania feels his hand squeeze her mouth shut and then his tongue on her neck, in her ears, while the music outside grows louder and louder. Suddenly he tears the leather miniskirt off her waist. And now Vania knows that she's afraid, afraid that her wishes will come true, afraid of not going out in Hernán's boat, afraid of not going to the disco. Martín's free hand runs over the pushup bra, looking for the clasp, while his legs begin to separate Vania's legs; she tries to escape, biting Martín's hand. He answers with a slap; Vania's head hits the floor, but she manages to pull the cord of the floor lamp which falls over the glass table with a shatter. Outside, the roar of the music doesn't stop.

Mrs. Barandiarán opens her eyes and thinks of a glass of water. She's dying of thirst, and Deolinda never remembers to set a pitcher on the nightstand. Hernancito's horrible music is playing so loud downstairs. Was that what sounded like a window breaking? The lady walks downstairs, wearing her avocado mask and her silk robe. She imagines she's a Venetian carnival figure. But what awaits her on the first floor is more than a carnival; it seems like the wreckage of a hurricane: beer bottles everywhere, even a broken flowerpot. Hernancito deserves to have someone tell him the truth now; her son has gone too far. But he's nowhere be found, neither he nor Karen. Lucho, on the other hand, is sleeping on the sofa with Verónica. Hernán? she asks. Vania? Is there anyone here? No, Vania isn't anywhere, but a dull moan calls out from the study, and something else seems to have fallen inside, hopefully not the TV. Hernancito, Mrs. Barandiarán thinks, he won't stop until he destroys the house. Resolute, she tries to enter the study, but the door is locked. Hernán? She knocks. Are you there?

Only silence answers, but she knows the door only locks from the inside. Hernán, she screams, if you're asleep, you'd better wake up right now. She doesn't even want to think that he's in the room with that girl Karen. What would she tell her mother? Son, we need to have a serious talk. Hernán? She almost feels relieved when she hears Vania scream, "It's me, Mom! I'm changing!" But she still insists that Vania open the door, and she knocks louder. Vania doesn't answer any more. Lucho and Verónica have woken up, and they come up behind her, curious. Even Hernán, who was in the other room, has gotten up, and he appears in the hallway at his mother's increasingly desperate knocking. Damn it, Vania! he screams. Get out of there right now! What's going on? Something falls in the water with a splash before Vania opens the door in her robe. Nothing, Mom, is all that she says. A lamp fell, but everything's fine in here.

PILLAGE
BY YOLANDA ARROYO PIZARRO (PUERTO RICO)

Her screams exceeded the volume that ordinary people were used to hearing, but nobody else was nearby. Everyone was rallying at the campaign closings of the usual politicians, and those who weren't observed the events from their TVs—and thus the echo merely bounced off the walls surrounding nothing, the empty space that wasn't alone in hearing but seemed to be alone in answering. Nothing. The nothing and her captors: they, too, received the sonorous impact of that huge, supernatural scream, but they ignored it as if they were indifferent to anguish, desperation, so much pain. Their impunity defiled the walls of the solitary alley.

The older of the two men held her from behind, by the neck, while the other clumsily tore at her clothes. She moved her head right and left as she kicked with all her strength and contorted her body like a rattlesnake. Sometimes she managed to bite the one who held her neck captive, only to get slapped harder or get her hair yanked in a way that always seemed like it would break her neck.

I began watching the spectacle by accident, frozen by the terror that struck me and confined by the knowledge that I was powerless.

Coincidence had brought me to that alley, right behind the huge trashcan—that now served as my hiding place—in search of empty boxes for the move I'd have to make in the following days. The opposition's victory was practically a fact, even though forty-eight hours remained until the vote. My position wasn't one of responsibility, in fact it was fairly insignificant, but I'd gotten it through a connection that didn't seem likely to be renewed. Without the connection, I couldn't continue performing my duties. No one else would hire me with my record, knowing my secret.

I mulled that over as I found some empty boxes, while the solitary corner separated me from the disturbance. The girl's howling had alerted me that something was wrong.

Hesitantly, I set the boxes aside to see better. I hadn't heard them approach, nor had they seen or heard me. They threw her to the ground and began to punch and kick her. I crouched to avoid being spotted, following some stupid survival instinct that rejected the idea that my superior physical strength would defeat those two much scrawnier men.

Sweating bullets, I covered myself with some of the cartons and bags from the trash in that cursed alley. I seized my necktie, as if to asphyxiate myself and by some magic disappear. I covered my mouth with one of my hands, I don't remember which, and clenched my jaw. Then I lifted my face, bathed in sweat. That was when I discovered it. It was an owl.

It observed the scene with big, open eyes, like I did. Curious, it turned its neck with rapid movements side to side; sometimes it seemed to turn its head around completely. It perched on a cornice, majestic, passing judgment over all that took place. It instilled terror and stirred up envy: envy because it could leave at any moment, on a whim, and not be missed. Yet it stayed. When the younger of the men grabbed the girl's hips, the bird opened its wings wide. It wasn't until the girl began to scream deafeningly and contort herself again, as if resisting her destiny, that the owl opened its beak and wailed.

The screech, like an insane hermit's, stopped the city, the loudspeakers, the ads, the placards in the infinite distance. The stars in the firmament succumbed to silence, to the lack of the moon. The two men, momentarily petrified, blindly looked for the origin of the hoarse whistle that didn't belong to the trapped throat. They discovered the crest of lustrous plumes on the king of nocturnal birds, sitting atop the roof of an abandoned building. In another dimension, a shaman invoked the deities to make the owl show its face. The bird did not appear in that other universe; he stayed with us in this one, here, in this hidden corner that twisted lives.

The feathered specimen was advanced in years, as was proved by his shriek, like an old lunatic's. Penetrating the darkness, crossing the sky between the sleepwalking clouds, the owl managed to materialize and fulfill its destiny of being an avenging angel waiting for her.

It let out another screech in the quiet eaves where a political banner hung, just at the moment when the little girl let out a powerful cry, a frenetic roar that gave no sign whatsoever of surrender without resistance. She joined her lament with more struggling, and her struggles were rewarded with more blows and dislocations.

The men changed places. That was when I noticed, still crouching, that the girl's face, now revealed, was no more than ten years old. Her eyes squeezed shut, resisting the beating; her bloody mouth was quilted with blows, her breasts were barely flowered but bruised, the space between her legs was destroyed.

I lowered my head and ran my hands through my hair. So many memories wandered through my mind, and much was revealed to me simply through the presence of that owl: the power of seeing behind masks; the quick, silent, movement of violence; the sharp vision of tears beneath the sheets; the link between the dark, invisible world and the power of the moon. The owl, with its dark reddish plumage, brown and speckled on its back, the yellow belly, sprinkled with stains and crossed by a few blurry, grayish stripes, knew to read my rancorous heart and the depth of my intentions.

Its short beak, curved and feathered at the base, opened again. This time its neck turned around completely; its talons were feathered to the point where the claws curved. Then it took off flying.

When I stopped watching the owl and returned my attention to the girl, the sinister figures had left, abandoning her. She laid naked on the ground, abused, injured, like a flower whose petals were forced off, whose petals had been crushed without a second thought.

Her breathing was shallow. Her heartbeats were vague, very light, according to what I could verify after I approached her. Most of her bones were broken, including her pubis; all of the orifices that my fingers touched were torn. I touched her breasts. Her skin languished, trembling, smeared with blood that was salty, sometimes sour, according to what my tongue discovered. Again, the nocturnal raptor accompanied the weak howl that the little girl let out, even more desolately this time, if possible, while I felt another shadow fall over her. The prognosis was predictable, a bird of ill omen. The owl's cry is always a sign of looming death.

Owls' feathers are velvety and soft; they make no sound when they hurtle through the black layers of the sky. The silence preceding the time an owl pounces is the silence of a bullet: you never notice until it hits you. Somewhere in the twilight, in the mercy of the land's darkness, I thought I heard something innocent break, and she emitted one last shriek before she expired.

I left the alley running after I washed my mouth and pelvis of fluids. The bird flew over my head, as if seeking a branch to rest on, as if wishing to perch. Then it dove.

SHIPWRECKED ON NAXOS BY ARIADNA VÁSQUEZ (DOMINICAN REPUBLIC)

I've never written, though I thought I wrote,
never loved, though I thought I loved,
never done anything but wait
outside the closed door.
—Marguerite Duras

I've been dreaming I have only one breast. But not a breast that knows the other is missing. No, nothing like that. It's just that I have one breast in the middle, like the Cyclops has only one eye.

I dream that I pause in front of a mirror, and a kind of little cone emerges from my blouse, diminutive, in the middle of where my two breasts should be. I take off my blouse, and then it appears, one strangely beautiful breast.

"What is your reaction to the fact that you have just one breast?"

"Reaction?"

"Yes . . . I mean, in the dream."

"I only have a reaction when I wake up. In the dream I feel nothing that relates to that word."

"What word?"

"Reaction."

"Do you feel strange? Do you want to have another breast?"

"No . . . I don't think so, I think I feel complete with that breast, I feel . . . as if I had a star born out of my chest, just one."

"A star?"

I want to talk about myself a little, just for today. Listen: I've lived in La Condesa for a year. It's a cheap room on a terrace. I pay 2,500 pesos a month. The rent includes laundry, gas, even cable. I don't have to pay for cable. Daniel let me know about the rent. He called me one morning, like he'd fallen from the sky, and he said: Do you really want to move? Yes, of course, I told him, and he gave the phone number to Dante and me. We called and the three of us went to see the room. Everything happened very fast. I could almost say Daniel decided for me. I'll talk about Dante later.

Sir Osbourne reads:

She stayed there, waiting on a salty rock in Naxos. Her arms have grown in length, and so she embraces her back, or vice versa. She clings to it and her eyes have deep circles underneath them, dark hollows from which another woman's gaze seems to emerge, a woman whom she will never be.

Her shoulder blades look like wings, and the thread is tangled in her hair, the cursed thread reminding her, telling her, do not weave, don't start weaving because waiting without concentrating on waiting is precisely what she should not do. She should wait just like that, anguished, shielded by her arms and legs, skin parched with exhaustion, eyes dead and saliva tattooed on the vertex of her lips. Watching, watching. Such is the waiting and you cannot weave, you cannot breathe deeply because in a breath a delicious instant dies in which he could come for her. Her fate no longer rests with the gods, though she has not ceased to believe in them.

"Why doesn't she leave the island? Why does she wait there, numbed?"

"Numbed?"

"As if nailed to her own body."

"I don't know. You tell me. It's your story."

Sir Osbourne is my landlord. That's what he calls himself, and he claims to be English. *I'm an Englishman*, he says in English, but I don't believe him. I think he just lived there for most of his life.

He's a very strange man. For example, he's never cared about my business. I sell cocaine and marijuana, sometimes ecstasy and hash. Only soft drugs. Sir Osbourne knows it, though I almost never deal at home. I don't like to. Besides, deep down, what I want is to be an artist. In the afternoons I make necklaces, bracelets, earrings, even purses. I take them to the girls who mind the little shops right here in La Condesa, and sometimes I sell them on the street. Not many purses sell; earrings do, and bracelets, but what earns the most money is coke. In any case, Sir Osbourne doesn't care whether I sell weed or bracelets, as long as I pay the rent and go downstairs once a week to talk with him.

I need to talk about Dante a little, just for today. Listen, because it's all I can say and I will say it counting backwards. I cannot tell this story any other way because it is mine. This is not a dream.

FOUR. I am outside the Camarones subway stop, smoking because I'm waiting for a customer. I had to go all the way to the San Juan Tlihuaja market because no one sells weed there now. I am tired, a little sad. My customer arrives and Dante is with him. It's the first time I see him and I want him, I want him for me. We don't talk. I see him and think: He is an artist.

We all go down and get on the subway. My customer talks about the weather, I watch Dante. My customer says something about blankets, sheets, moving. I watch Dante. I talk a little and we get out at the next station. We go up to the street and we walk a while longer until I pause and we sit down. I watch Dante. I hand my customer five joints and he puts them away. Dante goes off to buy cigarettes. I watch him and my customer tells me never to sell to Dante if he contacts me. Don't sell to him, I can only sell to him if they come together. I tell him to go to hell. He's not my dealer, he's a nobody. I watch Dante as he comes back and I want him for me.

Sir Osbourne declaims:

Woman, don't watch the window or the city. Don't watch anything.
Forget the three walls to the south: the labyrinth.
Shake from your eyes the giant walls that close off the path.
Don't seek the center, don't watch the monster; the minotaur.
Don't sense that it craves your Athenian.
Woman, don't watch the young warriors in the distance.
Don't ask what happened, who they are, where they are going.
Forget those walls that do not answer.
Woman, don't suppose that they have come from Athens to liberate her from her tribute.
Do not watch that armed man in the distance who discovers you.

Don't watch, watch nothing.
Woman, have no desire to unglue your arms and belly from your body to see him.
Don't tie yourself to his eyes, don't watch him.
Woman, don't offer your thread to that man, don't offer your sword, don't watch him.
Don't betray your people, your history, don't flee with the Athenian hero.
Woman, don't surrender to the first madness.
Don't escape Naxos, don't go with the hero, traitor, damned traitor!

"But why is she a traitor?"

"Because she loves."

Every Wednesday afternoon at 3:15 I must knock on Sir Osbourne's door on the first floor and sit in the living room for an hour to chat. At 4:15, a clock chimes. So I must leave. I always have to leave even though I don't want to, but I'm used to it now. It was part of the deal when I moved into my room.

Sir Osbourne doesn't require this of the other tenants in the building. Only me, because my name is Ariadne. Like that, with a *d* and an *e*, not Adriana or Ariana or Adrienne, but Ariadne, which is how I explained it when he asked for my name the day we came to see the room. I put a lot of emphasis on the ending, A-riaD-ne, because the fact is, it bothers me when people get my name wrong. He held still like a mummy, gazing into my eyes, he came close to my face and delicately touched the circles under my eyes. Then he said, looking neither at Dante nor Daniel: If you want the room, you have to come downstairs once a week to talk with me. He said: You are Ariadne. Do you know your story? No, I told him, what story? Will you take the room? he asked, and I looked at Daniel, waiting for his help, and he said, Yes, definitely. So everything was settled.

> *Sir Osbourne reads:*

> *Theoretical Postulates on the Three Mutations of Waiting, Based on the Greek Myth of Ariadne.*
> *The primary problem regarding the myth of Ariadne is that many vital parts have been eliminated with the passage of time and erased from the story, and thus marvelous fragments that hold the legend together are lost. We have three principal axes around which our theory is developed.*
> *First: The transformation of Ariadne's breasts into a single breast, which apparently relates directly to the first mutation of waiting and will be treated in later sections, as was explained in the introduction to this work.*

Sir Osbourne has a piercing in his tongue.

I dreamed that my mouth was salty. If I bit my mouth it bled salt, a lot of salt. My mouth was mysterious, as if it were the mouth of all the mouths of every face. In my dream I am sitting on a carpet covered with many treasures. I want to touch them, but for reasons that seem bewitched, I only touch my mouth. First I touch it and feel a light dusting of granules, and I don't understand what has happened. Then I squeeze my mouth with both hands; I want to snatch it off my face, I feel that it is my mouth, I feel a passion for squeezing it and suddenly it begins to gush salt, torrentially, a great deal of salt, and the carpet with the treasures begins to fill itself with salt, and I feel my home turns into a block, a block of salt.

"You don't despair from so much salt, I mean, in your dream?"

"No, no, I feel . . . I don't know, I feel light, crazy, like an hourglass filled with salt, I feel salty."

"Are you on an island in your dream?"

"An island?"

"Yes, with stones, boulders, salt."

"No, it's a carpet that stops being a carpet and turns into a mountain of salt."

"A mountain of salt?"

Everything's been very strange with Sir Osbourne, hallucinogenic. Each day that I come downstairs, we talk. Or rather, he reads. He tells me the story of Ariadne waiting on Naxos and he tells me that hers is my only story, her waiting is my only waiting, that woman is me.

I want to tell him about my life and sometimes I do. I tell him about my dreams while he puts on eye makeup, sitting almost directly in front of me in a Louis XV chair. Always with a little mirror in his hand. His gaze focuses on me only when I am the one who says something strange, then he repeats what I've said as if he were asking a question. But Sir Osbourne doesn't care about my stories. He believes I have no other story, and he's right, which is why I listen as he talks about me.

He talks and I pet his cats, which are everywhere. I haven't ever counted them, but he has a lot, a lot of cats. I can't really tell them apart, but everything smells like them. When I leave his apartment I smell like them, too. I feel like I'm half-enchanted cat, like Silenus leaving some myth. Sir Osbourne believes strongly in myths.

Listen, just for today. I want to talk about myself a little, I need to. I want to say THREE and begin: My cell phone rings. It's Dante. He wants ecstasy and hash, I want to get him into my life. I set up a meeting downtown the next day. He arrives with his hands in his pockets. His hair is coiled, super curly; he's tall, weak, restless, he has a jagged scar above his mouth. He is perfect, a human monster.

Two. Dante studies photography. I pay for his classes, I pay for everything because two years ago he left his parents' house to come live with me. Not here in La Condesa, we moved here just last year. He went with me to Clavería.

Dante is twenty-six years old. He doesn't have friends because he steals. He steals from everyone and spits on the subway floor, on the floor of the house, he spits in the pot where the ponytail palm grows. He lies, too. Sometimes he beats my breasts, my face, my left arm, my back. He gets angry when we don't have money, he gets angry when I don't get marijuana, when I laugh at his scar, when I don't kiss him at night. If I look at him without blinking he gets angry. Dante is an artist.

Sir Osbourne reads:

She could row with her arms, if she wished. She could turn her body into a boat and row until she arrived in Crete. But there would only be death for her in Crete. Better to wait; she opens her eyes with dementia and waits. Theseus . . . Theseus . . . Four centuries and Ariadne waits on the same rock, swaddled in her own arms. She begins to chisel a labyrinth into her breast. Her back bends in unfamiliar directions. Her arms keep growing and they cover her; they wind around her like a spool of thread. Her head bends to one side. Her hair grows wet with sand, but she still gazes ahead . . . Theseus . . . Theseus . . . Her torso pushes inward, toward the inopportune, her breasts shrink all the time, always, all the time, every

> *morning, her nipples tear apart. It is born, the myth is being born of which no one will ever speak. One breast, one single breast takes shape on her bosom. One single breast sprouts like a bubble in the middle of her chest and takes dominion over her ravaged body. All its milk, all its juices concentrate themselves, they turn into demons, they mingle. Theseus . . . Theseus . . . There lies every curse. She can't stop waiting, though she wants to stop waiting. It's not the thread, the thread no longer matters; betrayal doesn't matter nor does Dionysius's marriage nor Olympus. It is all too chilling, macabre. It's a story of spools of thread that are arms that join each other, that are breasts melting into a single breast. It is a history of waiting, of desire. There is no room for doubt.*

I think Sir Osbourne is a poet.

I only want to say ONE and try to count, try to say: There is no light. Everything is dark and he has just left. I get home and though it's dark, I know. I can tell he has left me. I write a list of things he stole from the room:

Guitar letters I Ching *Replicante* magazine my eyes eye drops all of the weed all of the cocaine all of the money his pillow yellow towel electric plug my eyes red candle scissors the OM.

I call Daniel, Daniel, come, and Daniel arrives and he embraces me. Then the power comes back in La Condesa. It's true, Dante is gone and he's left me hung up with my dealer, my customers, without my eyes. My life consists of counting from FOUR to ONE. All I see now is waiting for him.

> *Sir Osbourne reads:*

> *Secondly, salt. A version exists that every day comes closer to being proven, in which it is suggested that the Christian religion took the legend of Lot's wife, with a few variations, of course, from the belief that Ariadne's body, wracked by despair at Theseus's abandonment, united itself with the island of Naxos in the form of salt. This is the second mutation of waiting, which we will also take up in a later section.*

Sir Osbourne's house is a temple. The whole carpeted floor is covered with necklaces, ceramics, little closed boxes, plants, black and white photos, incense, thousands and thousands of candles which are never lit. Everything seems adhered to the carpet. It's very difficult to walk in there. You have to be extremely careful; Sir Osbourne doesn't like noise. His cats have never broken anything while I have been there.

Sir Osbourne is a nervous man; he gestures with his hands as if he were a mime. He only has nine teeth. I have never seen him eat breakfast, but he says that he takes at least three hours to prepare and eat his breakfast. Today he has not asked that I talk about him, but I talk anyway. I want to say that everything in his life is ritual.

Listen: I know nothing of that kind of waiting. I wait for Dante who does not arrive. I wait for my dealer. I'm drunk. I wait for my dealer, sitting on the stairs. On the terrace. At any moment, he'll arrive and he'll call me stupid and that's what I'll be at that moment. I'll have to pay the debt back but who cares. I'll have to start over, begin to see how I will bathe, dress, walk when I go out to the street, how, how will I do this? these pieces of things, eat, crack my knuckles, comb my hair, see . . . clean my eyes. That is the kind of waiting I'm talking about. Swallow three, four, five, eight crystals, to be able to get up and walk. This is not a sublime waiting like hers; I can't wait like that. This has nothing to do with solitude or rocks, or salt, or breasts. For me it is something in my skin, it's a burning, my veins burn, my mouth burns, throat on fire only stabs at saying words . . . I don't know what they say, hard sheet, words, everything wet, blanket, towel, the sad toilet, the ponytail palm, the ponytail palm, spit on the ponytail palm, spit, beat me or embrace me, tie up my fingers, tie them up so that they don't beckon me, fear of opening the door, the empty home, breathe the hot air, burnt, black, go out, drink tequila, tequila for breakfast, make him come back, make him come back and knock on the door embrace me.

Sir Osbourne reads:

The third part, which previous studies have not explored to the extent of this present compendium, is the possibility that a third mutation of waiting exists in the myth of Ariadne, as represented by the loss of speech on the protagonist's part, whose symbology is the falling of the tongue. A tongue which, in addition, seemed to have certain special qualities such as that of burning anything it touches. Regarding this, we should state that we do not have the concrete evidence required. However, we venture to suggest, on the basis of the three postulates of the mutation of waiting, that Ariadne was never rescued by Dionysius, just as he never carried her to Olympus to turn her into a goddess. Undoubtedly, Ariadne died of waiting, and it is this axiom that we will prove in this study.

Sir Osbourne has nine teeth. Nine teeth in his mouth and a crinkled earring in his tongue. Yesterday he did not open the door when I came. I think Sir Osbourne is nostalgic, as is his mouth. He is determined not to listen to what I say about myself, and regardless, I sit in his room on his carpet, I pet his cats and talk.

Sir Osbourne is angry because he doesn't like how I describe him. He is sad, too, because I insist on talking about my life. About Dante, about waiting. I have promised not to describe Sir Osbourne. I have promised not to talk about Dante. But Sir Osbourne will allow me to talk about my dreams, and about him as if he were not present.

I promise him. I promise to listen to that story about waiting on Naxos, I promise to wait for Theseus, call for Theseus, look toward a center where Theseus will appear. I promise to listen to my story and forget about myself.

I have dreamed I lost my tongue. The dream goes like this: I am on the floor and I feel threatened by many swords. I hold a spool of thread in my hands. I do not know what it is doing in my hands, I feel strange with it, I don't want it there. Suddenly I get up and begin to spin and spin, begin to wrap myself in the thread like a spider's prisoner. I spin and spin and I grow dizzy, I want to vomit, vomit everything, and I feel glad, immensely happy while I tangle myself and when I feel my whole body is entirely braided, my tongue falls out.

Nothing more. My tongue detaches from my mouth without pain, without blood, it just starts falling and as it falls, it drags and burns all the thread across my breasts and legs.

"And then?"

"Then it smells like burning thread and my tongue falls to the floor. I look at it and don't know what to do."

"Do you miss your tongue, that is to say, in the dream?"

"I don't know. I look at it. But I don't know if I miss it."

CHICKEN SOUP BY IGNACIO ALCURI (URUGUAY)

Antonio had waited a while for his order. As he picked at some breadsticks, a waiter with a bushy moustache approached.

"Can I offer you a glass of our best wine? Compliments of the house."

Antonio didn't recognize the brand, Satan's Locker, but he trusted the waiter's recommendation and accepted the offer. He drank the whole glass. It tasted a little bit strange. He decided not to order a second one.

The bread helped remove the bad taste from his mouth. Another waiter came over with the food, which had taken quite a while by now.

"Your chicken soup, our specialty."

"Exactly. That's why I came. Thank you."

Antonio spread the napkin across his lap and began to eat. The soup was much more delicious than he'd heard. A delicacy of the gods. He'd already eaten more than half the bowl when something caught his attention. The end of a hair was tangled on his spoon. His stomach turned a little. He lifted the hair to remove it from the bowl entirely, but the hair seemed endless. He tugged a few times until he came up with a hair that measured more than five feet in length. Indignant, he called the waiter.

"This is repugnant. Look at the hair I found in my soup. Absolute filth."

"I'm deeply sorry. Let me take your bowl, and I'll bring you more soup immediately."

"Why? Why change the liquid in the bowl just to bring me the same contaminated soup? Besides, this hair is too long. Something strange is going on here."

The other diners turned their attention toward the unsatisfied customer's raised voice. This encouraged him to continue his crusade for consumer rights.

"I demand to speak with the cook immediately!" he said, his chest swelling with pride.

"Okay, relax. There's no need to make a scene. Come with me to the kitchen."

Antonio and the waiter crossed the swinging doors. There they found the chef cutting a suspiciously large piece of meat.

"Hey, Willy, I've got a customer here with a complaint about the chicken soup."

"Seriously? You can't tell me it was bad . . ."

"Honestly, it's the best soup I've had in years," Antonio admitted. "But that doesn't justify the enormous hair floating in my bowl."

"I beg you to forgive me." The chef got upset. "It must have fallen out while I was cooking. To compensate you for this indiscretion, your dinner today is on us."

The chef's nerves raised Antonio's suspicion. That, and the fact that his head was shaved. Antonio pulled the hair from his pocket and let it dangle to the floor. It wasn't much shorter than the cook's full height.

"Do you think I'm stupid?" The situation was getting hairy. "I smell a rat. This hair can't be yours."

"No . . . of course . . . it must belong . . . to . . . the delivery guy from Moor Farm. Yes, that's it! He has really long hair. He must be a hippie or in a rock band. But he's very hygienic."

The sweat on Willy's forehead didn't lend his story credibility.

"You're hiding something."

"Me? Impossible."

The chef stepped aside, positioning himself in front of a large hanging bed sheet and extending his hands in a protective gesture.

Antonio couldn't resist. He pushed him and tore the sheet down. When it fell, it revealed a strange electronic structure. It resembled a doorframe, but full of cables and lights. And with a panel on the side.

"What is this?"

"Fine, I give up. I'll tell you everything. This is a time machine. We found it when we bought this house at auction. No one knows who the previous owner was. We use it for various purposes. It's the only thing that allows us to keep the business running in these times of crisis."

"This is beyond ridiculous! What does this have to do with the hair in my soup?"

"My brother Néstor and I are always using the machine to experiment with new flavors. A little while ago, he discovered that mammoth meat, well cooked, tastes like chicken, only much more flavorful. Soon it became our most popular dish. I suppose that in the rush to serve so much mammoth, one of the pieces didn't end up quite skinned."

"I don't know what kind of mental problem you have, but I refuse to keep listening to you."

Antonio headed for the door, but a sound made him stop. The monitor displayed "70 million years," and the portal emitted a great deal of smoke. A man dressed like a hunter appeared, carrying a velociraptor over his shoulder.

"Willy! You can put pork loin on the menu again. We've got enough for a couple weeks now," he said and made his exit.

"This is a violation of all the laws of quantum physics! Never mind the total lack of bromatological control. You'd make Stephen Hawking writhe, if he hadn't already been doing so for years."

"We didn't build the machine. We simply use it without any scruples or the least compunction about possible damage to the space-time continuum."

"Precisely. That machine should be in the hands of the government. And it will be. I'm going to report you to the authorities."

"Don't be an idiot. It's not going anywhere," the chef threatened.

"You're the idiot. I'm a kung-fu champion, so nothing and no one can stop me from heading to the Ministry of Industry and Energy."

"Maybe this super powerful poison will make you change your mind."

Willy took a bottle off the shelf; it was labeled with a skull and crossbones.

"If you think I'm going to drink that voluntarily, you're dumber than I thought."

"You're so narrow-minded." He smiled in a Machiavellian way. "I have a time machine at my disposal. Carlitos!"

The waiter with the bushy moustache entered through the swinging doors.

"Serve this gentleman a drink. Compliments of the house."

The chef carefully stuck a label that said "Satan's Locker" on the bottle of poison. He gave it to the waiter, who entered the time portal and dialed "15 minutes" on the monitor. A few seconds later, the waiter came back, carrying the now less full bottle. He made the "okay" signal with his fingers at the chef and left.

Antonio grew nervous.

"But . . . but . . . but, I . . ."

"The poison should be taking effect now. In a few seconds you'll be deader than Ray Bradbury's mother. My brother will use your corpse as bait to attract marine dinosaurs. Don't struggle, or your death will be more painful."

Antonio fell to the floor and started to foam at the mouth. In less than a minute he was dead.

"Néstor, you've got your bait now for the tripe stew!"

And Néstor came back to the kitchen, still dressed like a hunter, carrying a giant hook under his arm.

WOLF TO MAN
BY INÉS BORTAGARAY (URUGUAY)

Ludmila opened the door and exaggerated her annoyance, pressing her chin to her chest and spreading her arms in a pontifical gesture.

"Let me know the next time you'll be an hour late . . . How inconsiderate."

Muriel entered on her tiptoes, looking at the floor, making a show of her consideration through an absurd charade of concern about making a sound. Ludmila gave her a fierce look. Her eyes looked more fierce than blue. She really was angry.

"Excuse me." The girl used her most courteous voice as she entered. She knew when she used it, she got things more easily. The courteous "excuse me" was foolproof. All doors opened at once for her, as they would for a person who said "open sesame" and was one of the forty thieves or named Ali Baba.

"Well, come in. Visiting hours are almost over."

Ludmila inhaled and sucked in her abdomen, pressing her back to the wall, leaving space for Muriel. With her hand she signaled the only possible direction: a very short hallway, and at the end of it, the room, with two metallic beds, the little IV bag hanging from an iron hook. The air was gloomy; the little drip, drip fell with a rhythmic blink.

"I'm leaving. I've been dying for a cigarette," Ludmila said, smoothing her permed hair, with its tight, flattened curls. She had been a beautiful woman, with those proud cheeks, her height, her Slavic boastfulness. Muriel had inherited her features from her aunt, her wide face, her haughtiness. But everything seemed lessened in her, as if the gracefulness had washed out in the genealogical leap.

Ludmila slammed the door, and the anxiety in the air turned to pure silence. The girl listened closely, and she heard a raspy, arrhythmic breathing. She didn't want to be there. She didn't want to conduct this interview. The day was beginning to fade, and the fluorescent tubes weren't turned on yet. This place seemed like a crypt. There were mummies, and the air was cut into rays by the dying sun, with suspended particles of dust.

The first invalid was as tiny as an eight-year-old boy, and his eyes were half-closed. The girl noted his trembling and believed he was either dreaming or suffering. She didn't stop by his bed. The revolting man must have been 109 years old.

She looked at the second patient. He slept on his right side, facing the window. So much white hair, what shockingly abundant long hair. Just beyond him, the nightstand, and behind that the large window and the sky. That sky was a relief to her. It wouldn't be long until she left. She would return to the warm air and the noise of the street, after it was all over, in . . . half an hour? She snuck a glance at her plastic watch. Twenty-seven minutes until visiting hours would finally end.

She stood still. She didn't want to turn back, nor did she want to wake up the old man. She thought: If she had to choose a bed to convalesce in, she would always choose his, the one closest to escape. She remembered the stupid story that a priest had told her when she went to visit her grandmother three days before her death. A story he must have told every time he stepped into a hospital room, to be apropos, to instruct without ceasing everywhere, at all times.

Two invalids are convalescing side by side in a miserable sanitarium. The priest had said *sanitarium*. She learned that word then. *Sanitarium* made her think of *insane* and *aquarium*. One man is lying by the window. The other is not. The beneficiary tells the other everything he sees: the blue sky, people passing, autumn leaves swept by the wind, a rainbow, another blue sky, etc. The other one only complains about the bad luck that keeps him from the window and the world in motion. He envies his neighbor and goads him, accusing him of selfishness. One day the man by the window dies, and the one on the other bed finally can fulfill his dream of occupying the place next to the glass. He moves, thinking of new horizons. When the nurse finally tucks him in under the starched sheets and leaves him alone, he turns his head toward the window and concentrates on looking, seeking the glories he had only heard about before. There are no autumn leaves swept by the wind, no blue sky, no jubilation. All he sees is a grey wall rising to infinity. The end. The power of the imagination. Admonitory power. Resign yourself. Trust. Etc.

"You must be Muriel!" The booming voice startled her.

The man looked at her as he struggled to sit up. The big white shock of hair preceded him. Behind that, the ruddy face of a man from the country. The healthy color of fresh milk, the harvest, or a babbling brook, if these things were eighty-two years old.

"Come, dear, say hello to this old man."

The girl moved closer and pretended to give him a kiss, though really it was just a tender collision of cheeks.

"So you're the journalist?"

"The student."

"Very well, the journalist."

The girl smiled.

"Come, sit here." The old man motioned toward the leather armchair between the window and the bed.

The girl obeyed.

"And Ludmila?"

"She went out for a while," she said.

He raised his hand, making the "V" for "victory" sign with his fingers. The girl giggled, and both remained silent for a moment. He interrupted.

"So, journalist, tell me what you want this Old Wolf to tell you."

The girl thought that this *old wolf* was as much a joke as the recent celebratory gesture. She used her courteous voice and hurried the introduction.

"I'm in my second year of school. I'm studying communications, or maybe public relations. I really don't know yet. I have to choose my major next year. For the first quarter's assignment I have to do a political interview. Ludmila, my mother's cousin, told me that you corresponded with Castro, that you knew the president, and that you'd been in . . ."—the girl referred to a slip of paper with some small notes that looked to be made by a scattering of ants—". . . various guerrilla operations and a massive jailbreak."

"She told you correctly."

"And so I wanted to interview you."

"Could you hand me that pillow?" The man pointed to the foot of the bed.

The girl obeyed and placed the pillow by the headboard. He sat up a little more.

The door opened. A very fat nurse peered in from the hallway, looking at them with a certain mockery, a fighting stance.

"How are the grandpas?"

"And how's the most glorious nurse in the world?" the Old Wolf answered.

The nurse smiled, rolling her eyes.

"Look, Queen Gloria, look, this young lady is a writer, and she's going to write my memoirs."

"Don't believe anything he tells you," the nurse told the girl before leaving. "He's a real rascal."

The girl smiled insincerely, dug in her backpack, and took out a tiny tape recorder. She had to speed things up or she wouldn't get through the day's questionnaire, and coming back wasn't an option.

The old man seemed pleased with his immediate future. He cleared his throat and ran a hand through his mop of hair.

"First question. Ready, aim, fire. Cheer up, friend, life can get better."

"Is it true that you broke out of jail and that you know the president because you were companions in the Movement? Are you a seditionist?"

◆

Journalism and Investigation. 1A. Second semester.
A Subversive's Path
Assignment by Muriel Mendoza
Grade: Satisfactory. Average (6/12)

For this assignment I decided to interview Juvenal Soto, a revolutionary who participated in the great exploits of Uruguayan and Latin American history. My aunt takes care of him. She warned me that if I didn't hurry, I would lose the opportunity to meet a great man, an adventurer, someone who was a privileged witness to the second half of the twentieth century.

Below, a few excerpts from the story of his life.

"I can't begin these memoirs[1] without mentioning my father. All that I know and want, I have known and wanted thanks to him. José Artigas. I owe him my education and my sense of honor and devotion to this great homeland. I carry each and every sentence that he uttered in my memory, and when I find myself confused, I repeat his words to myself. They always help me find my way. Because he already said it: We cannot hope for anything that does not come from ourselves. Man is his own master. Just look at this man who was slandered and misunderstood, but who left us a legacy of wisdom, this man who carried a burning torch against the winds and tides to fight the oligarchy of his time, always in pursuit of his federal dream . . .

"Listen to me, Muriel. This wolf, this master of himself, has two bullets in his back, and yet he keeps walking tall. The wounds hurt. Of course they do. But what hurts more is to see hunger, horror, indignity. And I'm telling you, I'm not playing dumb, eh? I haven't always been this way; I won't pretend that I was born a revolutionary. I have a criminal record, and I'm not ashamed to have been an oligarch. If I told you that I was a good boy as a child, would you believe me? Catholic. Marist. From a Conservative family, White Party, white as a wild horse bone. Grandson of a Creole who accompanied Aparicio Saravia to the edge of the peneplains. He fought like a good soldier, and he died with his boots on. Say that I found reality difficult, that I saw inequality as violence. Say that I made a few good friends who lent me literature that plunged me into another world, that I read Rousseau, and I started to study Artigas . . . But to tell you the truth, the little book that changed my life was *The Call of the*

1. Memoirs? These aren't memoirs, Mendoza. Did the interviewee really think that your assignment consisted of writing his memoirs? I would like to believe that he spoke euphemistically. It would speak very poorly of your journalistic rigor if you hadn't cleared up this misunderstanding immediately.

Wild. Ah, London. Ah, that London. Why do you think I call myself Old Wolf? I'm not a simpleton, eh? It's not for the wolf who ruins the children's song, screaming that he's getting dressed, he's eating breakfast, and so on and so forth. No, no. It's because of London, and also Rousseau. It was he who first taught us: man is wolf to man.[2]

"I'm an Old Wolf because I was a young pup first. A little pup who understood his own nature and that to survive he needed to follow his primal instinct, and that perhaps this inexplicable ancestral instinct was also a threat. My nature is liberty. Liberty as supreme reason. The irreducible liberty of man. The new man. Have you read Rousseau, my dear? To renounce liberty is to renounce the essence of man, the rights of humanity, and even the responsibilities. Ah, I'm going to ask Ludmila to bring you a few little books to take when you come back tomorrow. Only if you can, of course, young lady.[3]

"As I was saying: I broke with the party and was seeking an alternative. The cause of the people never allows for delay, never. I found what I was looking for in the Movement, and with every operation, the movement gained strength. To cut the reins of power of the dominant class, to construct socialism out of revolutionary transformation, tremble, tyrants. Tyrants, *hijos de la chingada madre*, tremble!

---

2. It wasn't Jean-Jacques Rousseau who said this, but rather Thomas Hobbes. "Man is wolf to man" means this: In the state of nature, man fights a war of all against all. Even in the most total state of nature, man does not lose his rationality, and he tends to rise above the disorder. To be safe and to avoid innumerable dangers, subjects cede their rights to the State, which arises from that contract. The State, the Republic, the Leviathan permanently acquires men's rights in exchange for serenity. Soto's interpretation of these concepts is somewhat erratic, and one who claims to be master of himself and at the same time aligns himself with this school of thought, in which liberty is seen as deliberately deranged, only affirms this confusion.

3. It stands out powerfully that you have not eliminated these signs of orality. In future assignments, avoid these traces, as they very rarely matter to the end result of the written work.

"Listen, dear, don't be shocked if I let a few Mexicanisms slip out (and especially when it comes to insults, my weakness). Even though I'm Uruguayan, through and through, my adopted homeland was Mexico. When the darkness fell, it was there that I found a home, sustenance, and work. There I had my children (two sons, Emiliano and Anaïs, with my wife Celina, an exceptional being, and a daughter, Gabriela, who's better to keep at arm's length; another day I'll tell you about my first girlfriend, Amparo, poor thing). Look at how things are. The wolf grows old, and all his fruits are far away. Emiliano lives in Canada. We hardly communicate. He's a businessman, a snob in a sport coat. He's also a vegetarian and an environmentalist, one of those who rambles on about the plague of monoculture but buys a new TV and a car every year. Anaïs lives with his mother"—Soto makes the sign of the cross with his index fingers, as if casting a spell[4]—"in Michoacán. He studies lyric opera and works as a tour guide in Morelia. He has the eyes and determination of my mother, his grandmother.

"My dear, have you been to Morelia? Make sure you go. It's wonderful.

"I arrived in Mexico City in 1976. I only had the shirt on my back. I had been in prison for six years and three months, and I was quite grown up by then. Quite a bit older than the rest of my comrades. I'm not going to talk about that silence, much less the things I heard in jail. These are supposed to be my memoirs, not the ghost train.[5]

"I can tell you why I went there. In four little words: nothing less

4. It's advisable to use brackets to make this type of editorial note.

5. Again, before references in the context of a colloquial conversation, it's advisable to make any pertinent explanation in brackets. For example: [one of the attractions at Rodó Park, the celebrated amusement park with traditional rides—the roller coaster, the Ferris wheel, etc.]

than love. Nothing less than love, Miss Journalist. I was full of love, and I did all that I did for love.

"You look at me like I'm a soul in agony. Do I bore you? You want me to get to the good part, the action, the adventure, the jailbreak. Let's do it. What's done is done. I bit the bullet. Look at my decorations"—Soto cranes his neck out of his T-shirt to show me his scars.[6] "This one brushed my shoulder and didn't enter. These two did. One is still inside me. It's my talisman. I'd be crazy if I let them take it out.

"As I was saying: The plan was to take the city, storm the police station, the fire house, the telephone exchange, the banks. That was the goal of the action, though deep down it was an homage to Che, an invitation to fight for new ideals and change man, all through taking an entire city by ourselves. To show that we were capable of doing it. A whole city. Our dream laid out for everyone to see. We were swept away by this enthusiasm, and though the action only lasted for a few minutes, to us it was a great thing. It was my birthday, but I didn't tell anyone. We could concentrate only on one thing at a time, and I wanted to forget that the day was different, at least until the worst had passed, since there wasn't a place for miniature details, not when what was at stake was five hundred thousand times bigger than a mammoth.

"What do you want me to tell you? The operation failed by the thinnest of hairs. In a quarter of an hour our mission was more than accomplished. I played the role of a relative in the funeral procession that we staged to make our getaway. We got a hearse, laid wreaths of flowers on it, everything. What we couldn't do was cry or look mournful. We hit them hard, we thought. In Montevideo the group

---

6. Idem observation no. 4.

separated. Some of us were boarding a 199 when they intercepted us. That was when the shootout came, and then the horror."[7]

◆

The Old Wolf remained silent for a while. The girl didn't have the heart to ask him about the stolen money. And much less about his dead comrades.

The fat nurse stuck her head in, turned on the light, screamed that the visiting hours were over already, and pushed the dining cart into the room. Muriel hurriedly said goodbye. He asked if she would come back the next day, and she said yes.

As she headed toward the hospital exit, she failed to notice the stupefied pallor of the people she ran across. At the foot of the stairs, by the exit, she noted the pending topics: the jailbreak, his relationship with the president, with Castro. She underlined Castro.

Outside, it was night. She didn't return the next day.

Three days later, remembering her unfinished work, and facing the nearness of her deadline, she decided to visit him again. She told herself that this time she would get more facts about the man's supposed connection to Revolutionary Life In General. She needed some evidence. She arrived half an hour before visiting hours ended, insisting on her strategy of detachment. If she managed to be more incisive, that would be enough time.

The first old man blinked with his desperate tremor. The Old Wolf's bed was empty. Ludmila played solitaire, with all the cards spread out over the nightstand. She looked at Muriel, annoyed.

---

7. You lost the opportunity to stress the details of the confrontation and investigate the half million dollars that allegedly were stolen. A journalist must learn to ask questions with imagination and inventiveness when what he or she wants to know is thorny.

"Thanks a lot. The old man has been waiting forever for you. Ask him for the biography."

The girl opened a bag of meringues and offered her one. Ludmila's expression changed.

"I expected nothing less from you."

A sigh preceded him. He was exiting the bathroom. He was astoundingly tall; that man must have suffered growing pains. When he recognized the girl, he smiled and looked at Ludmila, defiant.

"See? Stupid hag. I told you she was coming back."

◆

"Let's see, journalist. I don't know where we left off, but I'm sure it was in the prolegomena. You're listening to a man who suffers from the undying hope that the world can be a better place. Do I sound old fashioned to you? Well, I am. I don't consider myself a saint. Absolutely not. Saints aren't my thing. But I have something very important, my greatest pride and the inheritance I'm going to leave my sons (or Anaïs, since the other, as I told you, doesn't want anything to do with me, he says I'm *inconsistent*), and what I have is ethics. *Ethics.*

"The history of this concept is fascinating. It first was connected to dwelling, to the place that one inhabits. *It is the thinking that affirms the dwelling of man*, I don't remember exactly which one of all those brains said it. My ethics are my house, the complicity between me and my soul.[8] My sons can feel proud to have a father who isn't, let's say, unpolluted, but who is honorable, yes, capable of living a life in accordance with his principles, and not many people can say that.

---

8. Fascinating. I invite you to find out who the author of this definition was.

"You must be thinking, this old man is full of himself. I'm telling you, I've known every kind in this life . . . Liars, savages dressed in sheep's clothing, sponges, opportunists. I'm telling you that the leftist or revolutionary name unfortunately leads to all kinds of snares. Shame is what some people ought to feel. It seems the name, revolutionary, buys them a morality, a prize, a crown. And today so many militants are rewarded only for having fought.[9] And then some go and show up in books, Tupamaros looking for utopia, Tupamaros today, tomorrow, forever, the Tupamaros' escape, the Tupamaros' ascension, Tupas down a secret passageway . . . I don't want any of this to-do in our book.[10] The truth is that I could have obtained some position, but I don't take charity, and convictions can't be bought or sold, since they're something you can't change.

"I have always been a fisherman, though I apostatized very young. (I had to do a tremendous amount of paperwork; they don't make it easy. I sent a letter to the Vatican explaining why I wanted to renounce the Catholic faith and everything, and I kept a copy. I'll show it to you later; it could be useful for our memoirs. It would be nice if a facsimile could appear in the book.[11]) But as I was saying, although I apostatized early, the song "Fisher of Men" identifies me like few others do, and the song comes straight out of the missal: 'In my boat / there are not gold or swords / only nets / and my work / You need my hands / my exhaustion / leave others to rest / love that wants / to keep loving.'

"I've worked at everything a little. What you might imagine. Everything. When I got to Mexico I worked as a dishwasher, I sold

9. Once again you wasted a good opportunity to ask whom or what he refers to when he talks about the militants who were rewarded.

10. Book?

11. Mendoza: you should have clarified the nature of this assignment firmly. It's unacceptable that you have not done so.

fried grasshoppers at a street market, I was a grave digger, I worked at a hostel on Lake Chapala, I swept, I ran a cactus nursery, I was a gardener and even a landscape architect. But what I liked best was fishing. I worked for large fisheries. One season I ended up in Manzanillo. That's when I met Celina.

"Look, when I met her she was heartbroken. Let's say that I consoled her. Poor thing. She was going to meet up with a boyfriend she had at the time. A total scoundrel. They were from Guadalajara and had left for the Pacific on different buses. They had agreed to meet at the entrance of the Hotel Puerta de Santiago on December 31 at six in the evening, sharp. She got there early, and the hour passed without the aforementioned scoundrel arriving. The New Year was approaching, and the poor thing realized she was stood up and alone (and not for the first time, it seemed). She got on a bus, all teary-eyed, and who do you think she sat next to? Eh? Who? Yes, yes. Right next to this millionaire of the heart. She looked so fragile and pretty, with those amber eyes. She was squeezing a handkerchief, and I remember that her knuckles were white, the way they get when you clench your fists and the bone shows through. I asked if I could help her with anything. She said no, but then the deluge came. She was in so much pain . . . I listened to her, saddened, but afterward my sorrow turned into rage. How could anyone have ruined this hope, her being who she was, her being a rosebud? I told her that my house had no great luxuries, but my neighbors—a very good family—had invited me for dinner at their house, and it would be more than a pleasure, it would be an honor to have her to join me. She doubted me; she scrutinized me. She wasn't interested in having a bad time, especially after such a disappointment. Yet it's clear that I had gained her confidence, because as it turned out, we toasted with the Valles several times that night, and when the hour arrived for the midnight embrace, when 1978 made its debut between the fireworks and all the raised tequilas, she looked at me, and I found the gleam of hope in her eyes . . . The hope that was born in us . . ."

◆

At the end of the second meeting, interrupted again by the nurse, the Old Wolf gave the girl the key to his house. She felt a little nervous, convinced at this point that getting the information she needed was going to be a long and difficult process if she followed the man's rhythm and digressions. He showed an enormous interest in lingering on the arboreal episodes of his sentimental education. There he showed an eagerness that vanished when the subject turned to his alleged revolutionary exploits. She insisted on Castro before she left the room. Smiling, he gave her the key to his house, and on the back of a napkin he doodled a map. Gloria grumbled, pushing the dining cart, and Muriel used her courteous voice to greet her unsuccessfully.

The house was two buses' distance from the center of Montevideo, near Melilla Corner, in a neighborhood with gardens of carnations and chrysanthemums. Ludmila lived fifty meters to the right. She had brought the old man food, washed his clothes, and swept his house for a decade, until he was hospitalized. The girl had never gone to visit her, because, to tell the truth, she had never been invited.

Ludmila's husband drank maté in the distance, sitting on a folding chair, surrounded by chickens. Muriel waved, but he saw nothing. He seemed intent on his silence, with the discreet attention of someone who needs to confirm that time passes slowly, like someone who auscultates the faint movements of a squashed cushion as it is freed and there, there, there, recovers its shape.

Three cats were guarding the door. The girl ignored them. She didn't get along well with cats. When she entered the house she held her breath, startled by an odor that washed over her. But it wasn't bad. It was only the smell of the river. All of the walls were covered. She saw a collection of antique weapons hanging on one wall, gathering dust. The Old Wolf could boast a few victories, thanks to some poker games. The biggest of all supposedly left him with this antique arsenal. There were a few Nahuatl tapestries, and, over the stove, a cracked Mayan calendar hung.

Muriel found the kitchen cupboard and opened the third drawer, first, in search of Castro's famous letters, and second in order of importance, the copy of the apostasy. Beneath a box of tools and another overflowing with tangled hooks, she found some papers tied with a red ribbon. A few silverfish skidded across them. She opened only three letters, and she didn't want to keep trying since she knew that she would tear them. Poor things. Those sheets of paper made her sad. They reminded her of a battered dragonfly, or of the Holy Shroud, the porous sheet that absorbed the form of Christ's face, according to the show about oddities that sometimes came on TV.

◆

Appendix 1: Castro's letters to Juvenal Soto[12]

◆

Now she came early, right at the beginning of visiting hours. She had a few things to say to the old man. He owed her clearer answers. A subversive's path needed foundations. When she saw the black cable edging the last stretch of the hallway leading into the room, the girl

---

12. It's unfortunate that these letters are completely illegible. They appear stained, and the writing is blurry. One can barely make out a year (1959) and the word "pinnacle," which appears various times. Likewise, the signature is indecipherable.

was alarmed. A diffuse white light shone out the open door. She thought of death. She heard the clamor of a small multitude, urged by the sound of a flash. The childlike old man, the trembling one, was gone. Ludmila, sitting on his bed, smiled with an honorable expression, her lips painted Ponceau red. A young man took a few pictures of her.

The black cable snaked through the room until it climbed up to a video camera positioned on a tripod at the foot of the old man's bed. He looked toward the window and didn't see her come in. Sitting in her chair was a man with pomaded hair and glasses in gold frames. His shirt sleeves were perfectly ironed. Muriel worried when she saw his pink, tidy nails. She heard him tell the Old Wolf, *Granma, my birthday,* and *nothing less than love.*

She didn't know whether to turn back or interrupt. She didn't need to do either. The man with the anachronistic pomaded hair raised his eyes and saw her. He seemed annoyed, but his annoyance couldn't be expressed; it was doomed to suffocate in a sacrifice to courtesy. With a gesture he signaled the intruder's presence to the Old Wolf. He turned to look at her and let out a laugh.

"Friends! Come, dear, come, let me introduce you to this man."

The girl said she didn't want to interrupt, and without giving the old man time to show his affection she excused herself, saying she had better come back later. She said it many times, in different ways.

"I'll come back. It would be better if I came back. I'll come later. After a little while, I'll come back."

She didn't. Once on the street, she checked to see if she had money and gathered a few coins. She entered an ice cream shop and asked for a cone with one scoop of strawberry and one scoop of lemon. The ice cream melted as she watched a few silver balloons tacked to the entrance sway over the sign that announced the new flavors of the month, waving over a couple who were desperately kissing a few meters away. She amused herself with the chocolate streaks on the cheeks, chin, and forehead of a little boy who observed her slyly in the mirror mounted on the wall. And then she noticed the reflection of her own neck, her washed-out eyes, her pursed lips, a certain spleen, a loss.

"Oh, well . . ." she said, taking a bite out of the cone, as if to say, *what can you do?* She smiled at the boy, knowing she, too, had an indolent, dirty face. Without waiting for an answer, she stood up to leave.

LOVE BELONGS TO ANOTHER PORT

BY SLAVKO ZUPCIC

(VENEZUELA)

Neither scapulas nor fibulas: I began to write this story nearly twenty years ago in La Entrada, a low-lying town beyond the mountains, just four kilometers from the Asylum of Barbula and eighteen kilometers from the crushed bones of St. Desiderius in the center of Valencia. It was a Sunday afternoon in June of 1986, and what I knew about my father, Zlatica Didič, was still very little, as well as what I knew about the rain of dead potatoes that befell Netretič the day of his birth.

I won't try to describe how Sundays were back then. I'll just say that I was sixteen, that the house where we lived was right next to a church dedicated to the Sacred Heart of Jesus, and that Sundays usually went by with me sitting in front of the TV in the living room. Though I heard the bells every fifteen minutes calling everybody to Mass at six, I simply hoped that the programmer at TV Caracas might think to replay even half of a chapter of *The Six Million Dollar Man*, or otherwise I might be so bold as to try to break one of the tubes hidden behind the screen.

Three years before that Sunday in June, I had given *Around the World in Eighty Days* to Salas Bustillos in exchange for a coverless version of *The Godfather* and a confession that he was the only man in his family who hadn't yet committed a murder. And it was only the day before when I discovered that William Faulkner, whom I'd tried to read through *Pylon* and *As I Lay Dying*, had signed my aunt's copies of his books. They were, they still are, two volumes from the green Aguilar collection dedicated to Nobel Laureates in literature, and my aunt had gotten William Faulkner to sign them after waiting at least five hours at the doors of the Valencia Cultural Center. While everyone else fought for one of the auditorium seats, believing, perhaps, that a Nobel Laureate would arrive by helicopter or escorted by bodyguards who wouldn't let any common citizen approach, my aunt waited for Faulkner at the bus stop by the Superior Funeral Home, and that's how she saw him step out of a bus with Salvador Prasel, a Yugoslavian writer who arrived in Valencia in 1951, the same year as my father, Zlatica Didič.

"Prasel was a minister, just like your father. Together they brought St. Desiderius's bones to Valencia, remember?"

With that, my aunt tried to close the conversation and resume the dinner blessing, the blessing that I had interrupted to show Leticia the book I bought that day at an auction downtown: a copy of one of Eugenio Montejo's first poetry collections, *Solitudes*, whose spaces had been filled with the minute and methodical script of a man who called himself Salvador Prasel and who sought to recover a photo album he had lost in strange circumstances.

"Minister of what?" Leticia asked.

"Of religious matters."

"Of Venezuela?" Leticia insisted, this time prodded by me, but then my mother began to talk about Carlos Gardel.

". . . rdel wore yellow shoes, and I just stood there, watching him, on Libertad Street, as if I had a premonition he would die on the next flight."

Everyone knew that talking in her presence about the man who had divorced her without prior notice was the one thing that could truly make her uncomfortable, and everyone understood that we should say no more on the subject: Aunt Aura, Uncle Pablo, Uncle Fernando, Leticia herself. Everyone except me, and the next day I turned off the TV. Without breaking a single tube, I made it disappear from my life. I carried the letters to my room, the letters that my father had abandoned the moment he left, along with his pipes, the 1978 World Almanac, an inflatable globe my aunt had given me with a plastic version of The Six Million Dollar Man when I passed second grade, the Larousse dictionary, a notebook, nearly blank, from the high school career I had recently finished, three graphite Mongol No. 2 pencils, the two volumes of William Faulkner's novels, and obviously, Salvador Prasel's photo album.

I moved everything to my room. I laid it out on my bed and the metal desk that Poija had given me two months before. I laughed at the thought that tonight Bill Niehous could walk past my house, surrounded by his kidnappers, and after writing four words in the manner of a title, "Croatian Circle of Venezuela," I began to feel like I was writing this story.

Three years later, the story was still a literary work-in-progress, but the annotations I had written were a mountain that kept growing, and one of my rituals at the end of every year was to discard unsuitable material and promise myself that in the new year I would finally finish the text that these notes were trying to incarnate and whose title suffered startling metamorphoses nearly every day.

The story was there, blurred and imprecise, in the annotations that I constantly wrote and zealously stored on the lowest shelf of the bookcase in my room. The story followed me; it obsessed me. Even under the pretext of a frustrated departure from Valencia to study dentistry in Caracas, I packed the story with its at least seven kilos of annotations.

On that occasion, the only people who came to say goodbye were the Chilean brothers I'd met in a writing workshop, to whom I'd once shown the first two paragraphs of "Little Love."

"And the story?" they asked in unison, almost accusingly.

"I'm taking it with me. I think I'll be able to finish it now. The working title is 'The Girls Who Work in Shops.'"

One of them smiled a little. The other acted like he hadn't heard me, and I, used to the incredulity in which even I participated, said nothing. Deep down I believed that to finish the story I only had to get away from my sister, who had torpedoed through her writing for nearly three years.

"What are you writing?" Her voice always reached me when she needed to wet her fingertips to turn the page.

"Something for my story."

"A chapter?"

"Yes, something like that."

"You know I want to write about him, too."

"Really?"

"I just don't think you know how to begin. Look: here, where you write 'my father the minister,' you should simply write his name."

"But he's my father and he was a minister."

"Fine, do what you want. That's why I'm going to write about him, too."

"And the letters? What'll you do with the letters?" My plan was that, with her answer, she would solve a problem I now considered unsolvable.

But she didn't answer. She never answered my questions at first, and another three years had to pass until one afternoon when I came home, destroyed and undermined by the Veterinary Department—my ability to change majors could only be compared to my ability to change the title of the text—the same scene repeated itself, and then with just three drops of spit she dissolved a blockage whose size had only grown since I tried to translate the letters with a Spanish-Croatian dictionary—not Croatian-Spanish—by Vojmir Vinja.

"Nothing. I'd give them to Salvador, Salvador Prasel, to translate."

That was the second time in my life I heard Salvador Prasel's name as a concrete reference and not just as the "Salva" who had come to La Guaira with my father. The next day I bought one of his books at the Cultural Bookstore, *Deepest Condolences*, a novel about the Second World War, whose back cover depicted him as a melancholy, gray-haired man, with Social Security glasses, a chubby face, and the metallic hooks of a dental prosthesis shining at the top of his fangs. After two days, I got Roberto Lovera to give me his phone number and the most relevant facts of his biography:

"220967. Sometimes he says he was born in Mostar. Other times, in Lubiana. Anyhow, the only thing that's certain is that his father was Serbian and his mother Croatian. He came to Venezuela in 1951, settled in Caracas, and made very good friends with Jose Ignacio Cabrujas and Salvador Garmendia. Then he worked in advertising for Colgate. He was platonically in love with a woman named Mary Monazin. Some people say she had a brothel. According to him, hers was a family home because all the girls . . ."

I stopped listening. I left my beer half-full and immediately walked out of El Caney as if I were in a condition to call Salvador Prasel that very day and tell him that I hadn't always been like this, but that I couldn't specify the moment, either, when my father's letters had started to come into focus only and turned my life into a gray cloud: absurd, trembling, remote, illegible.

A week later, when I called Salvador Prasel for the first time, he was recovering from angina pain that had kept him in the hospital and then at home for the last few months.

"What was your father's name? Where was he born? Does it matter that the letters have always sat in a trunk at your house, if you've only been able to smell and touch them? Do they belong to another attempt at a story? And if so, to what extent do their recipients exist, and are those two letters which appear so often, *s* and *p*, really my initials? Why are the copies of the letters he sent still in their envelopes, and one of them with a stamp? Did he happen to go to the post office and make copies of the letters that he sent and stick stamps on both? Doesn't it seem more likely that he never sent any of them, that he never dared to push open the mailbox, and that he went home after pasting on the stamps?"

If Salvador Prasel was trying to discourage me, his questions didn't have the desired effect. I remained on the line, and after I made an effort to respond, I asked for his help in translating the letters, and I asked him if "the sadly famous Z.D., traitor expelled from the Movement in 1948," who appeared on page forty-eight of *The Election of Air*, was his colleague the minister, or if it was my father, Zlatica Didič, which was to say the same thing.

He answered my request and pretended to have read the poems that I'd published a year before in *El Carabobeño.*

"Yes, it's true, I was also Ante Pavelić's minister." His voice sounded strange, as if each one of the words he uttered meant much more than it seemed. "We won't meet to work on the translation yet. Let me recover, and when you come over, bring me the album. One of the employees at the business must have stolen it from me. All those women were cousins," he concluded in perfect Spanish, very different from the Spanish my aunt said my father spoke and which I had never had the opportunity to hear.

Waiting for Salvador's recovery took much more time than we'd initially expected, and in one of our now frequent phone conversations, I dared to hint at the possibility of going to the Yugoslavian House, to what remained of the Yugoslavian House, to ask for a translator's help, but Salvador Prasel emphatically opposed this.

"No, not the Yugoslavian House. I'll recover soon, and then you can to come over whenever you want. In the meantime, buy Danilo Kiš's books and look for information about Saint Desiderius in a biography of Saint Gennaro."

I didn't stop calling him, in any case. At that time, a letter that my father supposedly sent Mary Monazin from Hamburg rested at my right side.

"How are you, Salvador? How have you been?"

Leticia, who now knew that I was in contact with with him, tried to raise the bar. She no longer threatened me with writing a story but now only challenged me with the prospect of someday embracing our father.

"Would you go see him? If he called and asked for you, would you dare to meet him? Would you dare to kiss the scar on his left cheek? Would you tell him about me?"

I didn't pay her much mind and kept calling Salvador Prasel. I even started to feel affection for him, and to put him in a good mood, I told him that my middle name was Corazón de Jesús, but I only learned what my middle name was the day I went to renew my identification card.

"Maybe you'd rather be called Carlos Armando, like von Shoetler. But never von Shoetler, like Carlos Armando."

Five months after I started calling Salvador Prasel, I abandoned writing "The Girls Who Work in Shops" and embarked on a new story that I thought of calling "News of a Communist Bride." I continued to carry the brown folder that contained my father's archived letters, perhaps because I'd gotten used to lamenting the impossibility of finding a good translator, or perhaps because they continued to be the best pretext to grow closer to Prasel, who at this point interested me much more than Zlatica Didič, especially after I'd spent so long thinking about the time he'd stepped out of the Bejuma bus with William Faulkner.

Another reason to explain the scant interest that my father's letters inspired in me then was the wrongful use the Chileans had made of the annotations I'd given them to read—stupidly, I hadn't merely shown them the annotations, but since the time seemed short, I had given then a carbon copy of my most polished notes when I left to study dentistry.

Maybe they were anxious since I hadn't finished writing it; maybe they were jealous of my frequent conversations with Salvador Prasel; or maybe they just wanted to surprise me. Humberto and René had sent one of these annotations to a mini-story contest, and for the only time in my life, "The Last Journey of St. Desiderius"—this time the change in title belonged to René Izurbeta—won with a unanimous vote.

If I were to try to establish a sequence of what happened, more or less exactly, I would have to say that a few weeks before the public reading of the verdict, I learned that René had duplicated part of my notes in the university's photocopiers. When I found out, I went to his office, and without needing to accuse him of plagiarism, I refused to accept his last proposition:

"You know what? I sent something to the mini-story contest at *PN.* If you win, we'll share the costs and benefits."

Four weeks later, when the journalist from *PN* called announcing the verdict, I didn't remember what René said. I only imagined what

Salvador Prasel would say when he read my story.

But Salvador didn't read those lines that had tortured me so much. He had fallen, going down the stairs at the mall: hip fracture, hip replacement, and at least four weeks without leaving the house and with no one to buy him the newspaper.

The person who did read these lines was Zlatica Didič. Sitting on his porch, he opened the newspaper as he did every day: first the sensational news on the last page of section D, then sports and entertainment in section B, international news and politics in section A, and finally, education, health, and culture in section C. It was on the last page of this section that he found my photo, and above it, the twelve letters of the name we both shared.

The fact that Zlatica Didič, Zlatica the father, read the story didn't mean anything in particular. The problem began when his friends and acquaintances read it, too, and called him to ask if he was the prize-winning writer and if he'd sent his first communion photo to the paper, or if it was simply a terrible mistake, the fact that they'd credited his name with the authorship of a story that mentioned William Faulkner, Salvador Prasel, and, of course, a very old Zlatica Didič who had come to La Guaira on a ramshackle ship, the *Castel Verde*, after passing Dr. Berti Riboli's medical exam.

Could it be that this Zlatica Didič, who walked through the air of a narrative heaven, who didn't see Salvador Prasel's tears and didn't even tremble at the threat of a bomb in the second mini-story, was the same Zlatica Didič who led the squadron near the oil well? Had he described himself this way? Magical, strong, and invincible, conjuring enemy power with his miraculous strength, telling Salvador Prasel about his recent meeting with Ante Pavelić, the orders that Pavelić had given him, the way that Pavelić had thanked him for his assistance?

"No, that's not me. I don't know who this could be. Maybe the son from my first marriage."

All the same, two days later, he called my house.

"Hello, I'm Zlatica Didič, and I just read a story of yours in *PN*."

"Hello, I'm Zlatica Didič, too, and until ten minutes ago I was watching *The Godfather* with the departmental film club."

What happened was that I had thought this was one of Ricardo's jokes, Ricardo, who had been known on more than one occasion to call the house of Uslar Pietri himself and ask if that was where they sold fertilizer for the oil fields. Or Leticia, though she'd now forgotten her old plan of writing the same story, who made her voice quiver, perhaps in imitation of the baritone DJ who narrated the adventures of Martin Valiant on Radio America, every time she saw me write an annotation in the notebooks that I'd bought at Majay's and that smelled like pizza, to parody a few lines published in *PN*:

"Did he wear the yellow shoes? The day of his death, did Gardel wear the yellow shoes that cost us so much?"

But I couldn't hear any of her teasing in the tremor of this voice. Never in our playing had it seemed so painful to talk, to vomit each word into the phone:

"I'm serious. I'm your father, Zlatica Didič, and . . ." The details that followed made it clear that this wasn't a joke, and after five minutes we'd agreed to meet.

"Wednesday the nineteenth, at six. Next to the monolith in the Plaza Bolivar."

How many years had passed since the first time I dialed the numbers on the gray telephone that would connect me with Salvador Prasel? Four and a half years, maybe five: sixty months in which, apart from his original album, I had only come to know his voice and his granddaughter's. His was a pulmonary voice, unsociable and severe, like his age. His granddaughter's was the exact opposite. It seemed like the voice of an eight- or nine-year-old girl, busy playing dolls and Atari, still without a boyfriend and with time to watch movies and ask her mother to take her to the pool. Every time we'd planned a meeting during those five years, he suffered a relapse of one of his illnesses and needed to be hospitalized. The last episode was a pelvic fracture, complicated, according to his last call, by symptoms of respiratory failure.

"It's called an embolism, a fat embolism, but in spite of it, I think we'll finally be able to see each other: Tuesday, at my house. Then you can tell me personally about Zlatica's call."

I was in Valencia, standing, like I almost always did, at my favorite pay phone. This was the fifth call I had made to the clinic where Salvador Prasel was admitted after the fracture, and the first in which I had gotten his granddaughter to pass the phone to him. He was in Caracas, in the same clinic where months before—I remember it well because my aunt had all his records—Alfredo Sadel had died.

In spite of the fact that the meeting with my father was planned for Wednesday, I promised to go to the meeting that Salvador Prasel had finally proposed, not caring that it meant I had to travel to Caracas. And so in just thirty-six hours I would get to the root of this mystery: the Valencia-Caracas bus Tuesday morning, a visit with Salvador Prasel and the translation of a few of the letters that would allow me to interrogate my father appropriately, a return to Valencia Tuesday night, meeting with my father Wednesday morning.

And so it had been planned how everything would happen and how my story would end in just one week. Before I left home, I called Prasel, and he told me he was well and waiting for my arrival.

I left Valencia at eight in the morning, and at 11:30, already on the Avenida Libertador, I started to look for building number 69. I made the trip on a tri-colored bus, one of those which—everybody knew—had very worn out brakes, which is why on a regular basis they crashed going down the Tazón slope. Five minutes walking to the metro, ten minutes in the metro itself, and then eight minutes walking again, thinking of what the old man might finally be like, how his lips, his immense ears, his eyes, the color of his eyes, and the wood of his cane would look.

I wanted to embrace him and ask about his health, true, but also ask him whether my father's version, according to my aunt, of their relationship was true and not just another example of our family's fantasy.

I walked slowly, looking at the addresses: 114, 106, 94, 78. Change of sidewalks: 103, 91, 87, from 85 to 73 in a single, immense building. Finally, at 11:45, I found myself in front of the building's empty lobby: I, Zlatica Corazón de Jesús, with the same letters I always carried with me in a manila envelope.

Thinking it best to rest and relax a little, I entertained myself staring at the plaque for one Dr. Pineda: psychiatrist and electroshock therapy. Then I went to a bakery and ordered an orange juice. At 11:55, trembling before the intercom, I pressed the second button in the fifth row, the charred button. Immediately his granddaughter's voice answered:

"Wait a moment," she said when I identified myself and asked for her grandfather.

I did it three hundred times. For at least five minutes I sat on the windowsill next to the door. To pass the time, I took one of the letters that my father sent or received from the manila envelope, and unable to do anything else, I brought it to my nose and smelled it.

Now desperate, the thought of leaving crossed my mind. I dismissed the idea immediately, put the letter away, and called again. After thirty seconds his granddaughter answered again, this time sounding distressed. In the background I could hear choked cries and a wooden chair falling, as if its legs were breaking.

It wasn't difficult to imagine her shaking, glued to the receiver behind the kitchen door, weighing it, caressing it. She was the one who told me that Salvador Prasel had died, that Salvador Prasel had just died. I removed my right hand from the charred button on the intercom and retreated without saying a word, without even murmuring an attempt at sympathy, but yes, cursing myself mentally, thinking that the "Finally, they're going to be translated" I had written in reference to my father's letters just two hours before in the newest of my graph paper notebooks was now less attainable than ever before.

"Zlatica, hurry," my mother began to complain.

"I'm sure he's writing something for his novella," Leticia said, thinking that I wasn't listening. "I was reading his new notes yesterday, and he's changed the name again already."

"Now what's it called?"

"Air Hygiene."

"He should just call it 'Hygiene.' Or 'The Last Journey to St. Desiderius.'"

When I finally emerged from my room, I had neither Salvador Prasel's books nor William Faulkner's novel in my hands. Only the prayer to St. Desiderius that I had pulled out from my right Adidas before putting it on. I squeezed it in my left hand, but no one noticed.

My aunt, my sister, and I walked toward the back seat of the LTD that waited for us by the fence, and immediately it pulled out, its wheels kicking the dust off the old highway toward Naguanagua.

Contrary to what I had expected, the guy acting as chauffeur preferred not to drive on the highway, and instead he followed the bus route I took every day, but at almost two hundred kilometers an hour. First the Bar Alaska on the right, then the old seminary, then Ana

Enriqueta Terán's house on the left. The alpine stretch with the house that belonged to the Arcays, who went to Mass every Sunday but never said hello to the other Arcays who also went to Mass, though I didn't know where they lived. The monkey's snack bar, the burro's stop, and the impossible house of Maria Estela, who for a year made me leave home every day at noon to try to brush against her body in the aisle of the bus that united us, the only thing that united us.

Finally, after Naguanagua's commercial district, the stretch in front of the barracks, still green, came the Salesian Agronomy School and then the Avenida Bolivar, which in just four minutes led us to the parking lot closest to the monolith, beside which, my soul believed, my father would already be waiting for me.

But he wasn't there; he hadn't arrived yet; and Leticia and I walked around the monolith. I remembered that a year before I had written a story that imagined a similar meeting which was preceded by the apparition of a child, angel, or ghost on a skateboard. The father in the story had arrived two minutes later, and in the last line of the story, he confessed that the angel on the skateboard was his brother.

Leticia complained about the sun.

"He's unrepentent," she said, and together we kept looking in the hell that surrounded us for the colors that would announce our father, and in the case of a close sighting, the scar on his left temple that our aunt had told us so much about and which we'd learned to contemplate in photos since we were small.

"He must have been in one of Suleiman the Magnificent's wars. Our father carried a sultan's sword in his right hand, and when he tripped over a rock, he fell and hit his head on its handle made of white gold and precious stones."

"Wouldn't it have been World War II?"

"It could have been, but remember that his passport says he has no scars."

Five minutes later, our eyes stumbled over the scar from the photographs that he had forgotten on the console when he left, carelessly, or maybe voluntarily, as if he were trying to erase any possible link with the past. We had studied every millimeter of that scar, every elevation, every decline, the tiniest intention of transforming itself into a keloid. The scar greeted us, first in Serbo-Croatian, then in a Spanish that insisted on sounding like the Italian Victor spoke when he appeared in our second grade classroom for the first time.

The scar and I exchanged names.

"Zlatica Didič."

"Zlatica Didič." It seemed like all the men in the world were named Zlatica Didič. After spelling my name for so long, trying to make even one well-educated ear understand it, begging someone would appear in my lifetime whose name was at least similar, here, exactly one meter from the front of the monolith's base, a scar appeared before me that wasn't merely named Zlatica but also, when you asked its last name, repeated, just like I did, the five letters that my mother would have liked to clear from my ID.

We walked toward one of the side benches, and it was there that the scar showed it had a handkerchief and with the handkerchief it constructed a throne for Leticia.

"I told you we should have met at the Intercontinental Hotel."

"You were right, but I wanted to be a little closer to St. Desiderius."

"Saint who?"

"St. Desiderius. According to Salvador Prasel, you and he brought St. Desiderius's bones to Valencia."

"I don't know any saint by that name. Besides, I don't know who Salvador Prasel is."

I refused to answer his questions and tried to change the subject. After thirty or forty minutes had passed, we had nothing left to talk about, and the three of us started to look at our watches. I mentioned St. Desiderius again to see how he would react.

"What a strange name. It's a saint's?"

Something in the atmosphere warned me that this would be our last meeting, and when the driver appeared, as if to indicate our time was now up, my father and the two of us said goodbye with an embrace.

"How did you get that scar?" was the last thing I asked him.

"A stab from a companion on the journey on the *Castel Verde*," he said before definitively saying goodbye, leaving as his only trace the fulfilled promise of a pack of letters, diaries, and documents, no longer written in Serbo-Croatian, but rather in a mix of English, French, and Spanish, that arrived at my house after five days and with which I set out to rewrite my story, or better yet, to begin a novel.

BIOGRAPHICAL NOTES

Diego Trelles Paz (Lima, Peru, 1977) studied film and journalism at the University of Lima and received a doctorate in Latin American literature from the University of Texas–Austin. He has published the short story collection *Hudson el redentor* (*Hudson the Redeemer*, 2001) and the novel *El círculo de los escritores asesinos* (*The Circle of Assassin Writers*, 2005), which was translated into Italian. He contributed to the homage *Roberto Bolaño: Una literatura infinita* (*Roberto Bolaño: Infinite Literature*, 2005) and wrote the prologue for *El arca. Bestiario y Ficciones* (*The Ark: Bestiary and Fictions*, 2008). He is currently a professor of Latin American literature and cinema at Binghamton University, New York.

Oliverio Coelho (Argentina, 1977) is the author of the novels *Tierra de vigilia* (*Land of Watchfulness*, 2000); *Los invertebrables* (*The Invertebrates*, 2003); *Borneo* (2004); *Promesas naturales* (*Natural Promises*, 2006); *Ida* (*Departure*, 2008); *Un hombre llamado Lobo* (*A Man Named Wolf*, 2011); and the short story collection *Parte doméstico* (*Domestic Part*, 2009). He has held writing residencies in Mexico, New York, and South Korea, the latter stay resulting in *Ji-Do* (2009), an anthology of contemporary Korean fiction. He contributes articles and reviews to the cultural supplements of the newspapers *La Nación*, *El País*, *Clarín*, and *Perfil* and currently writes about publishing for the magazine *Inrockuptibles.* He was named by *Granta* as one of the best young Spanish-language novelists.

Federico Falco (Argentina, 1977) is the author of the story collections *222 patitos* (*222 Ducklings*, 2004), *00* (2004), and *La hora de los monos* (*The Hour of the Monkeys*, 2010), as well as the poetry collection *Made in China* (2008) and the novella *Cielos de Córdoba* (*Skies of Córdoba*, 2011). He holds a degree in Communication Science and received his M.F.A. in Creative Writing at NYU. *Granta* named him one of the best young Spanish-language novelists.

Samanta Schweblin (Argentina, 1978) is the author of the short story collections *El núcleo del disturbio* (*The Nucleus of Disturbance*, 2002), which won the Haroldo Conti National Prize, and *Pájaros en la boca* (*Birds in the Mouth*, 2008), which won the Casa de las Américas Prize. She has held residencies sponsored by FONCA (Mexico), Civitella Ranieri (Umbria, Italy), and the Berlin Artists' Residency through the German Academic Exchange Service. Her stories have been included in many anthologies in Argentina, Cuba, France, Peru, Serbia, Spain, Sweden, and the United States and have been translated and published in more than twenty countries. *Granta* included her in its list of the best Spanish-language novelists.

Giovanna Rivero (Bolivia, 1972) won the National Literature Prize of Santa Cruz in 1996 for her short story collection *Las Bestias* (*The Beasts*) and won the Franz Tamayo National Story Prize for her story "Dueños de la arena" ("Owners of the Sand"). She participated in the International Writing Program at the University of Iowa and received a doctorate in Latin American Literature at the University of Florida. She has published the short story collections *Contraluna* (*Against the Moon*, 2005), *Sangre Dulce* (*Sweet Blood, 2006*), and *Niñas y detectives* (*Girls and Detectives*, 2009), as well as the novels *Las camaleonas* (*The Chameleons*, 2001) and *Tukzon, historias colaterales* (*Tukzon, Collateral Stories*, 2008).

Santiago Nazarian (Brazil, 1977) won the Conrado Wessel Literature Prize for his novel *Olivio* (2003). He also wrote the novels *A morte sem nome* (*The Death With No Name*, 2004), *Feriado de mim mesmo* (*On Vacation from Myself*, 2005); *Mastigando humanos* (*Chewing on Humans*, 2006); *O Prédio, o Tédio e o Menino Cego* (*The Building, Boredom, and the Blind Boy*, 2009); as well as the short story collection *Pornofantasma* (*Pornoghost*, 2011) and many stories published in Brazil, Europe, and Latin America. He was named one of the most important Latin American writers under thirty-nine years old at the Hay Festival in 2007. He is also a translator and screenwriter.

Antonio Ungar (Colombia, 1974) has held various jobs in Bogotá, the Orinoco jungles, Mexico City, Manchester, and Barcelona. He is the author of the short story collections *Trece circos comunes* (*Thirteen Common Circuses*, 1999) and *De ciertos animals tristes* (*Of Certain Sad Animals*, 2000). His novels *Zanahorias voladores* (*Flying Carrots*, 2004) and *Las orejas del lobo* (*The Ears of the Wolf*, 2006) have been translated into French. His stories have appeared in various anthologies, as well as in magazines in Portugal, Italy, Germany, France, and the United States. His novel *Tres ataúdes blancos (Three White Coffins*, 2010) won the XXVIII Herralde Novel Prize. He currently lives in Jaffa.

Juan Gabriel Vásquez (Colombia, 1973) is the author of the short story collection *Los amantes de Todos los Santos* (*The Lovers of All the Saints*, 2008) as well as the novels *Los informantes* (*The Informers*, 2004), *Historia secreta de Costaguana* (*The Secret History of Costaguana*, 2007) and *El ruido de las cosas al caer* (*The Sound of Things Falling*), winner of the 2011 Alfaguara Prize. He has also published a collection of literary essays, *El arte de la distorsión* (*The Art of Distortion*) which included an essay that won the Simón Bolívar Journalism Award in 2007, as well as a short biography of Joseph Conrad titled *El hombre de ninguna parte* (*The Man from Nowhere*, 2007). His novels have been published in England, France, the Netherlands, Italy, Germany, Poland, the United States, and Israel. He has translated works by John Hersey, Victor Hugo, John Dos Passos, and E. M. Forster, among others. His books have been published in fourteen languages and in approximately thirty countries. He has lived in Barcelona since 1999.

Ena Lucía Portela (Cuba, 1972) is the author of the novels *El pájaro: pincel y tinta china* (*The Bird: Brush and India Ink*, 1999), *La sombra del caminante* (*The Traveler's Shadow*, 2006); and *Cien botellas en una pared* (*One Hundred Bottles*, 2002), which won the Jaen Prize in Spain and the Prix Deux Océans-Grinzane Cavour in France and has been translated into French, Portuguese, Dutch, Polish, Italian, Greek, Turkish, and English. She also published the novel *Djuna y Daniel* (*Djuna and Daniel*, 2008) and the short story collection *Alguna enfermedad muy grave* (*A Very Grave Illness*, 2006). Her story "El viejo, el asesino, y yo" ("The Old Man, the Murderer, and I") won the Juan Rulfo Prize from Radio France International in 1999. In May 2007 she was selected by the Hay Festival as one of the thirty-nine most important Latin American writers under thirty-nine years old.

Andrea Jeftanovic (Chile, 1970) is a sociologist and earned a doctorate in Latin American Literature from the University of California, Berkeley. She is the author of the novels *Escenario de guerra* (*Theater of War*, 2000) and *Geografía de la lengua* (*Geography of the Tongue*, 2007), as well as collection of interviews and testimonies titled *Conversaciones con Isidora Aguirre* (*Conversations with Isidora Aguirre*, 2009), and the short story collection *No aceptes caramelos de extraños* (*Don't Take Candy from Strangers*, 2011) and is the co-author of the book *Crónicas de oreja de vaca* (*Tales from the Cow's Ear*, 2011). Her stories and articles have been included in many national and international compilations, and she contributed to the essay collection *Hablan los hijos. Discursos y estéticas en la perspectiva infantil* (*Children Speak: Discourse and Aesthetics from a Child's Perspective*, 2011). Among other honors, she has won the National Arts and Culture Council Prize for the best published work and an honorable mention in the Gabriela Mistral Literary Games Prize. She currently teaches at the University of Santiago in Chile.

Lina Meruane (Chile, 1970) is the author of the short story collection *Las Infantas* (*The Princesses*, 1998) as well as the novels *Póstuma* (*Posthumous*, 2000); *Cercada* (*Enclosure*, 2000); *Fruta Podrida* (*Rotten Fruit*, 2007), and *Sangre en el ojo* (*Blood in the Eye*, 2012). Her play *Un lugar donde caerse muerta* (*Not a Leg to Stand On*) was published in a bilingual edition in the United States in 2012. Her work has been translated into German, French, Hungarian, and English. The story in this volume, "Hojas de afeitar" ("Razor Blades"), obtained second place in the Third Erotic Stories Competition in the magazine Caras (2006). She has been awarded funding from the Arts Development Fund, the Guggenheim Foundation, and the National Endowment for the Arts. In 2011 she won the Anna Seghers Literary Prize in Berlin. She currently teaches literature and creative writing at NYU.

Alejandro Zambra (Chile, 1975) has published two collections of poetry, *Bahía inútil* (*Useless Bay*, 1998) and *Mudanza* (*Change*, 2003), as well as the novels *Bonsai* (2006), which won the Critical Prize and the National Book Council Prize in Chile; *La vida privada de los árboles* (*The Private Lives of Trees*, 2007), which was published in English by Open Letter; and *Formas de volver a casa* (*Ways of Coming Home*, 2011). *Granta* included him in its Best of Young Spanish Langauge Novelists issue.

Ronald Flores (Guatemala, 1973) has published the short story collections *El cuarto jinete* (*The Fourth Horseman*, 2000) and *Errar la noche* (*To Wander the Night*). He is also author of several nonfiction works, *Maíz y palabra* (*Corn and Word*, 1999); *El vuelo cautivo* (*The Captive Flight*, 2004); *La sonrisa irónica* (*The Ironic Smile*, 2005); and *Signos de fuego* (*Signs of Fire*, 2007), as well as several novels: *Último silencio* (*Final Silence*, 2001) which was translated into English; *The Señores of Xiblablá* (2003); *Stripthesis* (2004); *Conjeturas del engaño* (*Conjectures of Deceit*, 2004); *Un paseo en primavera* (*A Walk in Springtime*, 2007); *El informante nativo* (*The Native Informant*); and *La rebelión de los Zendales* (*The Zendales' Rebellion*).

Tryno Maldonado (Mexico, 1977) is the author of the short story collection *Temas y variaciones* (*Themes and Variations*, 2002) and the novels *Viena roja* (*Red Vienna*, 2005) *Temporada de caza para el león negro* (*Hunting Season for the Black Lion*, 2009), a finalist for the XXVI Herralde Novel Prize, and *Teoría de las catastrophes* (*A Theory of Catastrophes*, 2012). He coordinated and edited the anthology *Grandes hits, vol. 1. Nueva generación de narradores mexicanos* (*Greatest Hits, Vol. 1: The New Generation of Mexican Narrators*, 2008). He lives in Oaxaca, where he has been an editor for *Editorial Almadía* and *sur + ediciones*.

Antonio Ortuño (Mexico, 1976) is the author of *El buscador de cabezas* (*Head Hunter*, 2006), *Recursos humanos* (*Human Resources*, 2007), a finalist for the XXV Herralde Novel Prize, and *Ánima* (*Soul*, 2011), as well as the short story collections *El jardín japonés* (*The Japanese Garden*, 2006) and *La señora rojo* (*Mrs. Red*, 2010). He is a regular contributor to publications such as *Letras Libres* and *La Tempestad*, among others. *Granta* included him in its Best of Young Spanish Language Novelists issue.

María del Carmen Pérez Cuadra (Nicaragua, 1971) has published the short story collection *Sin luz artificial* (*Without Artificial Light*, 1994), which won the Rafaela Contreras Central American Competition for Women's Literature in 2004. In 2003, her poetry collection, *Diálogo entre naturaleza muerta y naturaleza viva más algunas respuestas pornoeroticidas* (*Dialogue Between Dead Nature and Living Nature Plus a Few Pornoeroticized Replies*) won an honorable mention in the Mariana Sansón National Competition for Poetry Written by Women, as did her poetry collection *Monstrúo entre las piernas y otras escrituras antropomorfas* (*Monster Between the Legs and Other Anthropomorphic Writings*) in 2005. Her stories have also been included in anthologies such as *Schiffe aus Feuer. 36 Geschichten aus Lateinamerika* (*Ships of Fire: 36 Stories from Latin* America) and in *El océano en un pez* (*The Ocean in a Fish.*)

Carlos Wynter Melo (Panama, 1971) is the author of the books *El escapista* (*The Escapist*, 1999); *Desnudo y otros cuentos* (*Naked and Other Stories*, 2001); *El escapista y demás fugas* (*The Escapist and Other Flights*, 2003), *Invisible* (*Invisible*, 2005); *El niño que tocó la Luna* (*The Boy Who Touched the Moon*, 2006); *El escapista y otras reapariciones* (*The Escapist and Other Reappearances*, 2007); *Cuentos con salsa* (*Stories with Salsa*, 2009); and *Mis mensajes en botellas* *electrónicas* (*My Messages in Electronic Bottles*, 2011). In 1998 he won the José María Sánchez National Story Prize. In 2007 he was selected by the Hay Festival as one of the thirty-nine most important Latin American writers under thirty-nine years old. His work has been translated into English, German, Portuguese, and Hungarian. He writes regularly on his blog: www.carloswynter.com.

Daniel Alarcón (Peru, 1977) is the author of *Lost City Radio* (2007), which won the PEN USA novel award, as well as the collections *War by Candlelight* (2005) and *El rey siempre está por encima del pueblo* (*The King Is Always Above the People*, 2009). He is the founder of Radio Ambulante. His most recent book is *Ciudad de payasos* (*City of Clowns*, 2010), a graphic novel co-authored with the illustrator Sheila Alvarado. He lives in California.

Santiago Roncagliolo (Peru, 1975) has published the novel *Pudor* (*Shame*, 2004), which was made into a movie, and *Abril rojo* (*Red April*, 2006), which won the Alfaguara Prize and the Independent Prize for Foreign Fiction for its English translation. He has also published the short story collection *Crecer es un oficio triste* (*Growing Up Is a Sorry Job*, 2003). He has written several true stories about Latin Americans, such as *"La cuarta espada"* ("The Fourth Sword") and *"El amante uruguayo"* ("The Uruguayan Lover"). His work has been translated into seventeen languages. The Hay Festival and *Granta* both named him among the best Latin American writers of his generation.

Yolanda Arroyo Pizarro (Puerto Rico, 1970) is the author of the short story collections *Avalancha* (*Avalanche*, 2011), *Historias para morderte los labios* (*Stories to Make You Bite Your Lips*, 2010), a finalist for the PEN Club Prize, and *Ojos de Luna*, (*Moon Eyes*, 2007);

which won the National Literature Prize in 2008. She also has written two books of poetry, *Medialengua* (*Half Tongue*, 2010), and *Perseidas* (*Perseids*, 2011). In addition, she has published the novels *Los documentados* (*The Documented*, 2005), which won the PEN Club Prize in 2006, and *Caparazones* (*Shells*, 2010). In 2007 she was selected by the Hay Festival as one of the thirty-nine most important Latin American writers under thirty-nine years old. In 2011 she received a Latino Residency Fellowship from the National Hispanic Cultural Center.

Ariadna Vásquez (Dominican Republic, 1977) is the author of the poetry collections *Una casa azul* (*A Blue House*, 2005) and *La palabra sin habla* (*Word without Speech*, 2007), as well as the novel *Por el desnivel de la acera* (*By the Slant of the Sidewalk*, 2005). A selection of her poems was published in the book *Safo: Las más recientes poetas dominicanas* (*Sappho: New Dominican Woman Poets*, 2004). She won two honorable mentions in the Dominican Republic Casa de Teatro International Story Competition in 2001 and 2003. Her work was also included in the anthology *Onde, Farfalla e aroma di caffe: Storie de donne dominicane* (*Waves, Butterflies, and the Scent of Coffee: Stories of Dominican Women*), published in Italy in 2005.

Ignacio Alcuri (Uruguay, 1980) is the author of *Sobredosis pop* (*Pop Overdose*, 2003); *Combo 2* (2004); *Problema mío* (*My Problem*, 2006); *Huraño enriquecido* (*Enriched Shyness*, 2008); and *Temporada de pathos* (*Season of Pathos*, 2010). He participated in the anthologies *El arca* (*The Ark*, 2007) and *Esto no es una antología* (*This Is Not an Anthology*, 2008). He was a writer for the radio shows *Justicia Infinita* (*Infinite Justice*) and *Vulgaria* as well as the television show *Los Informantes* (*The Informers*) and was a columnist for *Neo* magazine and *El País de los Domingos*. He currently forms part of the press team for *Montevideo Portal*, is a presenter and writer for the TV program *Reporte Descomunal* (*Enormous Report*), and a member of the humor section of *la diaria*. Since 2007 he been a member of the stand-up comedy group *De Pie*. His website is www.multiverseros.com.

Inés Bortagaray (Uruguay, 1975) is the author of the short story collection, *Ahora tendré que matarte* (*Now I'll Have to Kill You*, 2001) and the novella, *Prontos, listos, ya* (*Ready, Set, Go*, 2008). Her articles and stories have appeared in the volumes *Pequeñas resistencias 3* (*Small Resistences 3*), *Esto no es una antología* (*This Is Not an Anthology*) and *22 mujeres* (*22 Women*). Her work has also been published in national and international publications such as *Zoetrope: All-Story*. She co-wrote the screenplays for *Una novia errante (A Wandering Bride*, 2006), *La vida útil* (*The Useful Life*, 2010), and *Mujer conejo* (*Rabbit Woman*, 2011).

Slavko Zupcic (Venezuela, 1970) works as an occupational physician and psychiatrist. Among his published books are *Dragi Sol* (1989); *584104: pizzas pizzas pizzas* (1995); *Barbie* (1995); *Tres novelas* (*Three Novels*, 2006); and *Médicos, taxistas, escritores* (*Doctors, Taxi Drivers, Writers*, 2011). He was a finalist for the XIX Herralde Novel Prize and was selected as one of the thirty-nine most important Latin American writers under thirty-nine years old. He posts weekly on his blog, *Cuartientos*.

Diego Trelles Paz (Lima, Peru, 1977) studied film and journalism at the University of Lima and received a doctorate in Latin American literature from the University of Texas–Austin. He has published the short story collection *Hudson el redentor* (*Hudson the Redeemer*, 2001) and the novel *El círculo de los escritores asesinos* (*The Circle of Assassin Writers*, 2005), which was translated into Italian. He contributed to the homage *Roberto Bolaño: Una literatura infinita* (*Roberto Bolaño: Infinite Literature*, 2005) and wrote the prologue for *El arca. Bestiario y Ficciones* (*The Ark: Bestiary and Fictions*, 2008). He is currently a professor of Latin American literature and cinema at Binghamton University, New York.

Janet Hendrickson's translations have been published in *Words Without Borders*, *n+1*, *Zoetrope: All-Story*, *Mandorla*, and *Virginia Quarterly Review*.

Open Letter—the University of Rochester's nonprofit, literary translation press—is one of only a handful of publishing houses dedicated to increasing access to world literature for English readers. Publishing ten titles in translation each year, Open Letter searches for works that are extraordinary and influential, works that we hope will become the classics of tomorrow.

Making world literature available in English is crucial to opening our cultural borders, and its availability plays a vital role in maintaining a healthy and vibrant book culture. Open Letter strives to cultivate an audience for these works by helping readers discover imaginative, stunning works of fiction and by creating a constellation of international writing that is engaging, stimulating, and enduring.

Current and forthcoming titles from Open Letter include works from Bulgaria, Catalonia, China, Germany, Iceland, Poland, and many other countries.

www.openletterbooks.org